Dance with DEATH

THE FOUR FAMILIES | BOOK TWO

BRYNN FORD

More from the Author
www.brynnford.com
brynnfordauthor@gmail.com

CONTENT WARNING

This book contains explicit sexual content, violence, and mature themes including scenes where consent is not sought or given. The author in no way condones such heinous acts, but rather seeks to immerse the reader in the true horror of the characters' experience. This book also contains suicidal themes. This is your trigger warning—reader discretion is advised.

SERIES NOTE

"Dance with Death" is book two of three in the Four Families trilogy. It is not a standalone and the books must be read in order. Book one—"Counts of Eight"—is available now. The author plans to release book three by early 2021. The cliffhanger ending may leave you gasping and desperate for the finale in book three. Best of luck to you, daring readers.

BOOKS BY BRYNN FORD

THE FOUR FAMILIES TRILOGY
Counts of Eight
Dance with Death
Pas de Trois

THE BLACK TIES DUET
Blue
Switch

For dark romance writers everywhere,
your boldness inspires mine.

Thank you being unapologetically daring.

PROLOGUE
NIKOLAI

2 ½ Years Ago

CRIMSON CIRCLES THE drain beneath my feet. With my head bowed beneath the flow of water, I scrub the dried blood from my matted hair. I hadn't planned to get my hands dirty on this latest business trip, but it had proven necessary.

I had to disband an entire factory after one of our commodities escaped. The local authorities had zeroed in on our site in Budapest after the young blonde money-maker somehow got away from the men I paid to steal her, keep her, and train her.

She went to a local hospital and the police were called in to take her statement on what she had told them was a kidnapping.

It was.

But if she'd known better, she would've kept her mouth shut. Needless to say, the girl has...disappeared, as has the police report she filed.

All of my Budapest commodities are gone.

Decommissioned, so to speak.

I've potentially lost hundreds of thousands that could've been made from these female assets. They were the reason I had blood on my hands. But they weren't all a loss. I was able to recirculate half the girls through my family's other factories in Prague and Minsk.

My stress is at an all-time high. This is not how I expected my trip to turn out. I'm not exactly looking forward to explaining to the board why the Mikhailovs no longer have a factory in Budapest. Furthermore, it will give my father a reason to blame me for any losses we incur next quarter, regardless of the fact that his needless interferences were the reason our sales tanked last quarter. All of this on top of the fact that I've returned home to deal with a surly talent slave who continues to deny me her submission.

I toss my hair back as I lift my head from beneath the flow of the waterfall showerhead. I blink the water away from my eyes and movement from within my private en suite bathroom catches my attention. I turn my head and stare through the steam-fogged glass enclosure.

I can see that it's my *rabynya*, and I can feel her there as well. Her fear of me is still palpable and it makes me hard, but it also frustrates me. She's a fighter, and though she's become reluctantly obedient, I haven't yet earned her full submission.

But then, why is she here?

I watch her standing there in the doorway that links my bedroom and bathroom, and she watches me, too. I finish cleansing myself, scrubbing away the blood that dried on my skin during my long journey back from Budapest. Blood she'll never know had been present at all.

As I rinse the last of the soap from my skin, she takes a step, moving from where she wavered in the doorway to firmly plant herself in my bathroom.

I dip my head beneath the water to hide my smirk. I turn off the water a few moments later and pop open the shower door, reaching out to pull a white towel from the bar on the wall. I scrub it over my hair briefly before wrapping it around my waist. I step out, dampness coating my skin, knowing the shine will highlight the lines of my muscles to aid in luring her in.

I walk to her, stopping just in front of where she stands. I look down at her bowed head, wondering if this is the moment she's chosen to show her submission, to give me her loyalty.

I wait.

She lets out a sigh and then takes off her shirt. She's bare beneath. I fight the urge to smack her perky little mound and twist her nipple until she screams for me to stop, but I force myself to stay still.

She takes off her cotton shorts next, the ones that mold to her beautiful, rounded ass and creep upward when she dances in them. I should be surprised when her panties come down, when I suddenly find her naked in front of me, but I'm not.

I knew this day would come.

I let her linger this way, in her own purgatory where she came to me needy and waits for me—bare and vulnerable—to give her what she wants.

"Tell me what you want, *rabynya*."

I already know what she wants.

Attention.

Affection.

Comfort.

Touch that brings her pleasure instead of pain.

She's sad that I took her dance partner from her. But Jamal just wasn't quite right for her—or for me—so I'd had to take him away. She's lonely, completely unaware that a new partner will be given to her in just a couple of months. I'm happy to let her think that I am the only place she will ever be able to turn for comfort.

She *should* turn to her master to fulfill that need.

I have every intent to take advantage of her fragile state.

Boldly, she lifts her head and slowly meets my eyes. There's fear there behind the sapphire blue—fear and desperation and longing.

"I want you, *moy khozyain.*"

I grip her waist with both hands and turn her, backing her up to the marble countertop. She swallows, her eyes locked on mine as I stare and press myself against her. I loom above her, my breath steady but heavy, exhaling my internal flames over her, reminding her that I was born from hellfire.

A reminder that she's come to the devil asking to be burned.

Her features have softened from her normal cold as ice stare. Her eyelids seem heavier as they droop to hang a sultry frame over her blue irises. Her eyebrows are relaxed from the way they usually slant toward her nose, wrinkling her forehead sternly. Her lips are parted and rosy in color, and I feel her shallow breaths puffing against my throat.

"You want me," I say slowly, pressing my half-hard cock against her. "You want me…to do what?"

This question is her test.

Will she back down, afraid to speak her truth?

Will she prove herself to be a rebellious slave and demand rather than ask?

Or will she tell me what she thinks she needs and sweetly ask her master to oblige her?

I tilt my head, watching her carefully as she decides how to respond. I run my finger through a single strand of her dark brown hair, dragging it all the way down to the end. She presses her eyes shut as her breath catches in her throat.

"I want you to…to make me feel like I'm not alone. To share pleasure with me. Will you please, *moy khozyain?*"

She opens her eyes and I capture her chin in my hand. I gently tilt her head upward so she's forced to look at me.

I'm happy with her response because she's acknowledged her subservience. She must ask without expectation, knowing that her master will decide the answer. Eventually, I will have her trained to know better than to ask me for anything, but I'm feeling generous.

Perhaps because my violent rage has so recently been released upon the now decommissioned commodities from the Budapest factory.

I bend over her slowly, seductively, inch by inch, lowering my lips until they touch hers. It's hardly a brush of my lips on hers, but it melts her. She slinks and I let go of her chin, letting my hands drift down her chest. As my fingertips drag over the peaks of her nipples, they harden instantly. She whimpers and I smile.

"Do you feel lonely, Anya?"

She swallows. "*Da, khozyain.*"

"Do you want to feel cared for?"

"*Da, khozyain.*"

My hand falls between her legs and I cup my hand over her cunt. "Do you want me to make you come?"

Her whole body sinks against my grip. "*Da, khozyain.*"

I take off the towel, letting it drift to the floor as I bare my hard cock. She gasps, surely expecting me to bend her over and fuck her hard, as I normally do. But instead, I lower to my knees, seeing the opportunity in this.

I drag my fingers along her folds, teasing and testing as I watch her face. She's dripping wet with need for me. While I intend to enjoy watching my slave finally submit her will to me, I also intend to learn. I study as I touch her, cataloging every twitch of her features, every gasp, every whimper, every moan.

But something interesting happens in my study—I lose myself in her pleasure. As time ticks on, as my fingers work faster, harder, testing the pressure and speed she needs to make her come, I find myself in awe of the look on her beautiful face.

Could she be more?

She comes on my fingers, hard and sated, with a drawn out "*oh*" falling from between parted lips.

She *is* more.

She always was.

But I'm the devil and she's not ready to reign in hell with me—she may not ever be. But this…this is promising.

She came to me.

She gave herself to me.

She took a grave risk in coming to me this way. Her experiences with me would have told her that I might beat her, burn her, drown her, fuck her, hurt her in any manner of my choosing. That gamble may have been just enough reason for me to provide her with an insurance policy. If she can give herself to me now, perhaps she will be worthy of me in the future.

Only time will tell.

CHAPTER 1

Anya

Present

ONE. TWO. THREE. *Four. Five. Six. Seven. Eight.*
One. Two. Three. Four. Five. Six—

Nikolai's gun slams against my temple, knocking me sideways onto the floor. A ringing sound explodes behind my ears and my vision blackens at the edges before clearing.

I start to push off the floor with my palms, but the hard heel of Nikolai's dress shoe slams down heavy on the outside of my left ankle, holding me in place.

He twists his foot, grinding into my flesh. I'm dumbstruck and silent in the moments before my brain registers pain. I'm confused at first, but as he lifts his foot and slams it back down again on the same spot, jamming the hard ridge of my ankle bone painfully into the marble floor, I know exactly what he's doing.

Over and over, he stomps.

Each stomp is more forceful and intentional than the last. He grunts with each slam, his teeth bared and anger flashing blackness in his eyes. His slicked back hair becomes undone— along with his self-control—and ash-brown strands fall across his forehead with each movement. The darkest rage I've ever seen contorts his face, and I see him as none other than the devil before me. It's as if my pain has sent me straight down to the depths of hell to be punished as he pleases in his kingdom of nightmares.

Each hit jolts pain through my entire body like I've never felt before.

His foot slams.

My ankle bruises.

The pain shoots sharp and fast up through my leg, into my hip, screaming warnings at my mind to get away.

But I can't.

My muscles stiffen, guarding against the attack, but there's nothing I can do to avoid the electric current of crippling ache that shoots through my leg with each hit.

Over and over again.

And then there's a crack.

I open my mouth to scream, but no sound comes out. Everything is dulled by the consuming pain, even the sound of my own torment.

My ears ring for what feels like an eternity of silent aching and then, without any warning, the volume of reality is suddenly unmuted and cranked up as high as it will go.

I scream.

I break into sobs.

Something's torn or broken or completely fucking shattered inside me. All I can think about is the pain for long, searing moments.

Nikolai stops.

He stills.

He crouches on his haunches beside me, reaching out to wipe tears from my face.

"Don't touch me!" I shake my head, jerking away from his touch.

He pinches my chin sharply between his fingers and

thumb. "Perhaps now you understand the pain I felt finding you naked with him in the bed *I* gave you," he seethes.

My face responds with a twisted grimace of disgust as I meet his eyes. If I didn't know him as well as I do, I might say his gray eyes look glassy, covered in a sheen of angry tears. I look a little longer, stare a little deeper, hoping to see something there, *anything*—something more than the washed-out gray that masks who he truly is.

"Rotten whore," he spits before pushing to stand and my gaze falls away from his toward the floor. "You can have what's left of her, Ezra. I don't suppose she will dance anytime soon. She's useless to me now."

Ezra suddenly appears at my side, and I realize only then that Kostya was there, holding him back. As Nikolai walks away, Ezra kneels beside me and I roll onto my back in heaving sobs.

He reaches beneath my shoulder blades, lifting me gently, curling me toward him and hiding my naked breasts from the world around me. A true gentleman even amidst the horror; I love him all the more that he provides me whatever little comfort and protection he can when so much power has been stripped from us both.

A swift motion catches my eye and I turn my head to look just as Vigo Vittori rushes toward us. My breath charges wildly in and out of my lungs, nearly forcing me into hyperventilation.

Vigo is coming closer, walking fast. When he comes upon me, his leg sweeps back and I hardly have a moment to figure out what he's doing.

"No!" Ezra shouts, and tries to shift me away, but it's too late.

Vigo kicks, driving his toe into the side of my injured ankle. A whole new lightning bolt of pain shoots up through my leg and my head rolls sideways on Ezra's lap as I try to curl away.

"Whoops," Vigo says flippantly as I grunt and whimper through another explosion of pain.

He steps over my writhing body to get to Nikolai. I watch over Ezra's shoulder as I pant out breaths filled with pain. Vigo claps Nikolai on the back as he runs a trembling hand through his disheveled hair.

What right does Nikolai think he has to be shaking over this when I'm the one writhing in pain?

"Come, let's discuss business," Vigo says, glancing back at me with vicious intent. "I think I can make you a fair offer for your talentless slave. I could use another broken doll. Tell me how much your broken Russian doll is worth to you."

Ezra once asked me what could be worse than death.

I thought it was this life, but I think I'm about to discover an even more terrifying existence.

I'm about to be sold to the Vittoris.

CHAPTER 2
EZRA

ANGUISH IS A word I didn't know the meaning of until this very moment.

Torment.

Suffering.

Those words meant nothing to me before now.

The tears of my blue-eyed girl spill onto my bare thigh as I cradle her, curling her against my body. I'm shaking, truthfully trembling from head to toe.

And I feel completely useless.

"Fuck you, Nikolai!" I scream at his back. "You're a coward, a weak excuse for a man."

I regret opening my mouth before the words come out, but my mind is on a different plane of existence and I'm not thinking clearly.

He whips around to face me and there's a beat that pauses us both in a rage-fueled stare. His eyes are glistening with smoky gray fire and his features are clouded with violence.

I've never been afraid of this man.

Not until now.

I keep my eyes on him as he rushes forward, his hair falling in ruffled pieces across his creased forehead. I flinch as he pulls his arm back, fist raised, his lips snarling and baring his teeth.

He's coming after me *now.*

I roll Anya onto her back on the cold marble floor to get her out of the way as I rise up to my knees, ready to defend myself. But I'm so jarred by what's just happened, so off-centered by it, that my reaction is slow and pointless.

His fist collides with my cheek, his knuckles bumping into the side of my nose as he follows the throw of his punch all the way through. He hits me so hard that my head throws to the side, catching me off-balance. I put my hands out to catch my fall to the floor and my palms land with a smack against the marble.

I shake my head, throwing off the reverberation of the hit, and I push up to my knees again.

Nikolai doesn't say a word to me.

He doesn't spare another glance.

He doesn't grant another opportunity for insult.

He walks away with Vigo Vittori, heading up the grand staircase with sharp, quick strides. I take a steadying breath, watching, waiting, until he turns and disappears from our sight at the top of the stairs. Silence gives way to noise and stillness returns to movement.

As I turn to help Anya, I find she's already pushing up to a sitting position, powerfully using adrenaline to fuel her independence. Black streaks from her tears stain her face, remnants of the make-up she wore last night.

I reach for her face, holding her head still so I can search her eyes, but she's already sheathed her blues in ice. As I brush the tears on her cheeks with my thumbs, I practically jump out of my skin at the unexpected touch of gentle fingertips on my shoulder.

A woman crouches beside me. I notice Anya's eyes widen

as I turn to look at the person who appeared suddenly at my side. Renata Vittori balances gracefully on her haunches in her high heels, wearing a perfectly tailored pant suit.

The side of her mouth curls up and her tongue clicks. "Heartbreaking how quickly he's destroyed you both. A shame really, your performance was stunning. I was looking forward to next year's entertainment. I suppose all things come to an end, though, don't they?"

"Leave us alone," Anya growls.

I'm surprised by her demeanor, though I understand it. She speaks through clenched teeth, jaw tight, rage and hurt painting a dark shadow over her beautiful features.

My hands fall from her face as Renata forces her way in, lifting Anya's chin with two fingers. "If my brother purchases you, you won't feel quite so confident in your tone with our family. If you thought Nikolai had a firm hand with you…" she trails off, jerking her hand away, causing Anya's head to bob.

Renata uses my shoulder to push herself back to her feet and she strolls away, heels clicking on the marble. She glances over her shoulder at me and the corner of her mouth curls up, giving me a look I can't decipher. But it's a look that makes my stomach hurt.

Anya starts to shift onto all fours and I rush to her on my knees, putting my hands on either side of her waist, whether to stop her or to steady her, I don't even know.

"Get me out of here," she huffs through a heavy breath. "Get me out of here, Ezra."

I nod though she isn't looking at me. "Where?"

"To my room, take me back to my room."

"Okay," I agree, and rise to my feet.

Anya doesn't wait for me to help her; she's slowly crawling forward, wincing as her injured ankle slides over hard, cold ground. She's as stubborn as ever in her independence.

"Stop," I tell her as I bend down to grip her sides. "Come here."

I pluck her from the floor with ease. Her tiny frame, my strength, and the fury inside me make it considerably easy to lift her. I turn her against me as I hold her and she latches her hands around my neck. She's huffing out breaths of pain, as though she's laboring through it. I don't even want to try to imagine the hurt she feels right now. One glance at her quickly bruising and swollen ankle tells me it's not right. I can't say for sure whether it's broken, but it's definitely not fucking right.

Kostya follows as I step onto the staircase. "She goes to her room, you go to yours," he says.

I ignore him and keep moving, shaking my head in disbelief that he thinks I'm just gonna drop her off and leave her. He's gonna have to fight me if he wants to separate me from her.

I take Anya up the grand staircase, feeling the eyes of guests upon us.

Is someone going to stop us?

Try to hurt us more?

Take her away from me?

I don't know anything about the four families except for the fact that they are all monumental pieces of shit.

I don't tear my eyes from my girl as I take her upstairs and the knife in my heart twists to see her this way. It's not the first time, but fuck, I'm so sick of seeing her like this that it's making me fucking insane.

"I've got you," I tell her, but I don't know if I really do this time or if I ever really did before.

She can't respond, and I'm not even sure she hears me. She's just trying to get from one second of pain to the next.

I move faster as fresh liquid pools in the corners of her eyes. I make it down the hallway and rush her into her bedroom, moving toward the bed.

"No," she stops me, "put me on the chair."

I take her to the armchair in front of the window, lowering her slowly to sit. She keeps her injured leg outstretched in front of her and props it on the ottoman, placing her uninjured right leg down on the floor. Her hands fall naturally toward her wound, landing just above her ankle.

"There's tape and…and adhesive wrap," she says, pointing to her dresser, "in the top right drawer."

I pull it open and find what I need right away. Her drawers are meticulously organized. Her underwear is folded neatly beside her well-worn ballet pointe shoes and the supplies she uses to care for her dance-battered feet. I bring her what she asked for and Kostya's hand lands on my shoulder.

I shrug it back, shaking him off. "No. I will fucking break your nose if you try to take me from her right now."

His eyes narrow on me, then dart to her. "Five minutes," he concedes and steps back.

I'm shocked by the concession, grateful for it, but I don't have the time or concern to mull it over. I drop to my knees beside Anya. She's picked up the roll of half-inch-wide white tape and is picking at the edge, trying to free the end of it from the roll. Her agitation grows as she *picks* and *picks* with trembling fingers.

Pick.

Pick.

Pick.

"Fuck!" She throws the tape onto the ottoman. It bounces off, tumbling to the floor and rolling away. Her fingers dig into her hair and she yells again, "Fuck!"

My shoulders tense, my entire body gone rigid at the way she unravels.

It's wrong.

This is all wrong.

I force myself to keep my cool, but I feel like I might unravel with her. I lean and grab the roll of tape, forcing my hands to stay steady, not to tremble and mirror her actions, but to be strong and give her the steadiness she so desperately needs.

It's all I can give her.

I pull the end of the tape free and keep my voice calm. "Where do you want this?"

She exhales long and slow. "I need to immobilize. I don't know if it's broken."

She pants as if getting those words out were an exhausting feat. Looking down at her rapidly swelling foot, I understand why.

"Okay," I tell her. "It's okay, Anya, I've got you. Just tell me what to do and I'll do it."

With every second that passes, an invisible syringe of uncertainty injects an ounce more fear into my veins, rushing through me painfully, bringing fiery rage into my chest.

I push down the anger and fear.

I have to.

I can't lose it when she needs me the most.

She points to a spot on her leg, a couple of inches above her ankle bone. "Wrap it all the way around my leg here, tight, but not too tight."

I nod and unwind the tape, ripping off a piece that's large enough to wrap around her slender leg. I stick the end on the side of her leg and put my thumb over it, holding it in place as I give a tug to make it taut. I wrap it around—the piece is long enough to go around almost twice—and rub my fingers over it to make sure it's secure.

"Take another piece," she says, then pauses, blowing out a shaky breath through her lips. "Put the end here." She points to the piece I've just wrapped around her. "Straight down, over the ankle bone, under my foot, back up the other side. *Tight*, Ezra."

I do as she tells me, but before I wrap beneath her foot, she sucks in a deep breath and pulls her toes backward. Her face contorts as her foot trembles and she releases it, letting it fall forward again to a relaxed position. Fresh tears push their way from her eyes and she grits her teeth.

"Oh, God," she sobs. "Fuck. You have to push my foot back, Ezra. Hold it while you tape it."

Shit.

Seeing her this way, knowing the pain she's feeling, literally rips me in half. I can honestly feel it tearing down the middle of my stomach. My own tears threaten to spill, but as hard as it is, I pull everything back inside me and hold it in.

I've gotta keep my shit together for her.

I wrap my hand slowly and tenderly around the side of her foot, barely touching, watching her eyes for change with each millimeter of movement as my skin brushes along hers.

"Just do it," she grunts out her insistence to get this done and over with. Her voice is a growl, primal and animalistic.

I don't warn her, I just do it. I pull her foot back until her toes are pointing at the ceiling, forming a right angle with her leg. She lets out a shriek and groans, panting through the agony again.

Loving instinct nags in my gut to let go of her foot, to step away, to stop causing her this torture. But I fight it and pull the tape around her foot tight, securing it like a stirrup all the way around to the other side.

"Quick," she huffs. "Two more pieces around to hold it up. Cover it all tight with the wrap."

I work fast, adding more tape just as before to stirrup her

foot in place. I take the athletic bandage wrap and cover the tape, coiling it around her ankle and over her foot.

We both huff out a breath when it's done.

"Do you think it's broken?" I ask.

"I don't know. I can move it. It hurts. It just hurts so much, Ezra."

I bend, pressing a kiss to the edge of the bandage on her leg. "What can we do for that? Will he send a doctor? Does he have medication here?"

She falls back in her chair, her head tilting to the ceiling as she rests it on the back. "He's the one who did this to me. Do you honestly think he would send me a doctor? He didn't when he broke my nose."

"He broke your—" I stop myself, hearing the tone of my voice rising in tension.

Stay calm for her.

I shouldn't be surprised to know he's broken other parts of her body before. I've seen how effectively he's destroyed her.

"We need to get you in bed, get your foot propped up to help with the swelling."

Her chest heaves in slow, concentrated, heavy breaths.

She's still for moments.

But then her breathing suddenly skips and stutters as sobs fight their way out of her lungs. She lifts her head and falls forward, reaching for me, and I'm right there to meet her. Her hands grab my shoulders and she's trying to pull me into her arms, but I'm wary, right next to her ankle, and I don't want to hurt her or have her hurt herself.

I shift as I get to my feet and scoop my arms beneath her legs, lifting her from the chair, moving her toward the bed. When she practically screams her panic into my skin, right over my heart, it vibrates inside me from head to toe. It shocks my very being and jolts me into tears right along with her.

I lay her down softly on the bed and reach over to grab extra pillows. I start to pile them beneath her foot—one, then another—trying to get as much lift as possible to help reduce the swelling.

I bend over her to kiss her cheek, her forehead, her lips. I don't give a shit about what Kostya sees, though I suppose I should. He might tell Nikolai I had my lips on hers again. But when she's hurting, when she needs me the way she does, I can't bring myself to give a fuck. He's already hurt her. He's already—

Fuck.

He's talking to Vigo about my blue-eyed girl.

A fresh wave of nauseous unease washes over me as I press another kiss to her shoulder. I straighten, intent on getting a shirt or something for her to wear so she's not lying there topless, but apparently, my time has expired.

Kostya's hands land on my shoulders and yank me backward. I stumble away from the bed before rolling my shoulders and throwing my right arm with a fist intent on decking him as I spin. He ducks the punch and comes after me. The fucker is quick, grabbing my wrist and twisting my arm behind my back. He wrestles my other arm around behind me and holds my wrists together with both his hands, grinding my bones together.

"Your room. Now," Kostya demands, spinning me and pushing me toward the door.

"At least let me get her some clothes—" I whip my head around to look at Anya, but he wrenches me again.

"Just go!" she shouts before her voice is swallowed by a sob. "Just go, Ezra. Don't make it worse."

I want to be with my girl.

I *need* to be with my girl.

But I can't.

I'm being forcefully taken from her when she needs me the most.

I plant my feet, trying one last time to resist and get back to her, but our eyes meet and her voice is quiet and steady, though it's forced. "Please. Don't make it worse."

If our love had a theme song.

Don't Make it Worse.

CHAPTER 3

Anya

ONE. TWO. THREE. *Four. Five. Six. Seven. Eight.*

One. Two. Three—

"Fuck!" I scream out at my ceiling for the millionth time over the course of the day.

The swelling is getting worse. The exposed part of my foot where my toes peek out bulges painfully against the tape and wrap Ezra had applied for me hours ago. I can see it's changing colors. A dull shade of gray-blue peeks out from beneath the edge of the bandage.

I huff out breath after breath, hoping that some of the pain will subside with each exhale, but it doesn't—it only gets worse. I try to let my mind drift to something else, *anything* else, but I can't. It just hurts so much and I can't even count my way through it.

I'm going to get up, I tell myself. *I need to get up and move.*

With a grunt, I swing my legs over the side of the bed. I yelp as I slowly lower my left ankle to the floor. I dare to let my toes touch, just a tap to the carpet to test how it feels.

Even the simple softness of the carpet shoots a bolt of lightning through my foot. But I know I need to try. I have to try to stand and find out whether it's broken. I inhale deeply and push through my good foot to stand, settling all my weight on my right side. Carefully, I roll my injured foot flat to the floor.

Toes first.

Then the ball of my foot.

The arch.

The heel.

I'm tensing every other muscle in my body in fearful anticipation of pain until my foot rests on the carpet. I suck in another breath and gradually shift my weight from right to left.

Inch by inch.

Pound by pound.

Before I can stand fully with my weight balanced equally on both sides, I'm cursing and lifting my foot back off the floor. It hurts too much and I just can't bear it.

Will this heal?

Will I ever dance again, or has he ruined me for good?

Tears burn as they form a layer over my eyes and threaten to spill down my cheeks. But then I steel myself, straighten my spine, tap into my last reserve of strength, and force myself to take one single, goddamn step.

"Shit…" I tremble, trying to hold back an oncoming sob. "I can do this. I can do this."

I hobble once, but I'm forced to step through the ball of my injured foot. I can't flatten it on the floor and put weight on it at the same time. But I can do this. I can limp on my toes. I can get to my dresser. I can finally put on some clothes.

But then what?

I stagger, uneven step after uneven step, until I reach my dresser. I opt for a black, silk chemise nightgown—pants are far too complicated for me at the moment—and put it on quickly.

My stomach growls, hungry for the lunch I missed, but there's no way I can make it down the grand staircase to the kitchen. Even if I could, I have to consider how Nikolai might react if he sees me.

The image of Vigo swinging his foot back and ramming it into my ankle pops back into my head. It's an image that punches painfully in my gut. It makes me want to fall to the floor and crumble in fear. He wants to buy me and Nikolai walked away with him.

Would Nikolai really sell me?

He'd always told me that I would be useless to him without my talent, and he'd just taken my talent away.

Oh, God.

What if I never dance again?

The most unsettling thing of all is the fact that he hasn't come to check on me yet. He hasn't come to kick me while I'm down. He hasn't come to soothe me while gaslighting me into believing this was all my fault. He hasn't come and I've never been more terrified.

Everything is happening so fast. Last night, I thought I had at least another year with Ezra. Though it would have been another year of captivity under Nikolai's control, it would have been another year of survival, nonetheless. I could have loved and been loved for the first time in years.

I gasp as I realize that being loved was what led to this. Ezra had made a mistake falling for me. It was a tragedy that I'd fallen for him, too. Now we are both going to pay the price, though I don't know how high that price will be yet.

I make a slow trip to the bathroom and somehow manage to wash my face and brush my teeth. I force myself into utter denial of the reality of being sold to another and how that might change my life. My mind only presents me with a detached concern that Vigo may not grant me time to care for my personal needs in the way I'd grown accustomed to.

If I'm sold to him, will I have my own bathroom?

Will I have my own room?

Will I be stuffed into a box and shoved beneath his bed, only to be let out for his entertainment and abuse?

A cold prickle runs up my spine, causing me to shudder in fear of that possible reality. Then I let that prickle ripple away from my body and put that energy into caring for myself while I still can.

I just can't face the idea of being sold. Denial may save my sanity. I allow my thoughts to separate from my reality and float through a pretend existence where my pain is only felt if I think about it; where the coming events of my day are going to be normal, business as usual. But every few seconds, my foot moves or my weight shifts, and the pain shoots through me all over again. As each jolt of pain ebbs, it pushes me down, the gravity of my emotion warning that I might soon be a sobbing mess, flat on the ground beneath me.

I use the toilet, but as I hop and turn to wash my hands, I hear the door to my bedroom fling open and it startles me.

Is it Nikolai?

Vigo?

I'm frozen as I hear movement just outside the bathroom door. It's cracked open, but all I can see from where I'm standing is the shadowed outline of a man. They move forward and the shadow grows larger.

I jump as the bathroom door swings wide without warning and I nearly topple, swaying off-balance. I grip the edge of the countertop to steady myself and realize quickly that it's Kostya.

He doesn't move. He just stands there, still and brooding in the doorway.

Has he come to take me to Nikolai?

I wait.

But he doesn't command me. He doesn't grab my arm and pull me away. He doesn't do anything at all.

A few breathless moments pass before he reaches into his pocket. He steps toward me, and though I want to step back, I can't. I'll fall if I try.

He slams his palm down on the corner of the countertop and leans forward. "Hide them. Only one a day."

He tilts his head down in a nod and as quickly as he appeared, he's gone. It takes me moments to relax enough to let out the breath I'd been holding. I look down at the countertop to see three small, round, white pills in the spot where his hand landed.

My heart leaps. I reach for them immediately, plucking them from the marbled surface, and hold them in my palm. I turn my hand over to look at them and I hesitate. I don't know what these are. My first thought is that they must be for pain, but I can't fathom why Kostya would give me something for that on his own.

Nikolai was so furious with me. He *wanted* to cause me pain. I can't imagine him asking Kostya to give them to me.

What if this is a trick?

What if these little white pills are meant to drug me, hurt me, drive me into the depths of insanity?

But…what if they'll make the pain go away?

My body forcefully rejects any thoughts of denying myself the possibility of relief. Though the rational and stoic part of me tells me I should flush them down the toilet and muscle through the pain, I know I just don't have it in me to endure this any longer—no matter the risk of taking an unknown drug.

Without allowing myself another moment to think, I toss one of the white pills into my mouth and turn on the faucet. I cup my hand under the flow to catch some water and tip it into my mouth.

I swallow.

I close my eyes.

I pray for relief.

Where am I supposed to hide these?

I start my slow, strained hobble back into my room, crossing to the bed. I bend to open the drawer on the nightstand. I open the forever closed copy of Vladimir Nabokov's *"Lolita,"* a book that has sat in that nightstand in all of its mockery since the day Nikolai first brought me to Mikhailov Manor. I place the pills on the pages within and close the book. I shut the drawer and let myself fall backward on the bed, scooting carefully and lifting my ankle to rest on the stack of pillows Ezra had arranged for me before.

As my eyes fall shut, my memory flashes with a lightning bolt of green, the brilliant color of Ezra's eyes. I put my hand over my heart, feeling the *thump, thump, thump,* as I wonder what he's thinking about and if he's okay.

What will Nikolai do with him when I'm gone?

When, not if.

I start to cry, my emotions finally catching up to the physical pain, bringing about a whole new kind of ache.

Heartbreak.

Heartbreak for me, for Ezra, for us and what we had, what we could have been, what our lives would be if we'd never been stolen but had found each other all the same.

I gave him my heart and he gave me his, but it was all for nothing. We weren't allowed our own possessions when *we* were the possessions. We had both let down our guard, gave into love, and in that love, we lost control.

But God, it had felt so good to lose control with him.

I turn my head, looking toward the center of my bed, and

my mind tugs at memories of our love making last night. It was stupid and reckless to do it here, and now we're paying that debt. Though I should regret it with every jolt of pain in my ankle, I find that I don't regret it at all. Ezra had given me the best night of my life and my bedsheets still hold the smell of him. It's a sweet peaches and cream sort of scent mixed with the raw masculinity of his natural musk—like summer and sunshine.

I close my eyes and breathe in the scent of him on my pillow, forcing my mind to wander through those memories of our night together. It isn't long before I start to feel the effects of a foreign chemical running through my system, making the memories twist, shift, and morph into strange waking dreams.

I guess another thirty minutes or so pass before the pills truly start to take over. I spend that time internally screaming, hating myself, hating Nikolai, even at times hating Ezra for his very existence and the fact that he wasn't here with me to ease this pain with pleasure.

Then, the pain begins to fade, not disappearing entirely, but dulling into the background. An invisible ring of calmness swirls around my brain, looping around my senses and corralling them together into a faraway cage inside my mind. Feeling is there—pain and emotion, love and anger—it's all there, but it's distant, secluded.

I feel something resembling peace.

I shut my eyes again and begin to count until I finally fade away into a dreamless, painless sleep.

One. Two. Three. Four. Five. Six. Seven. Eight.

One. Two. Three. Four. Five—

CHAPTER 4
EZRA

"OPEN YOUR EYES, *mal'chik.*"

Something *thwacks* against my cheek and my head rolls on my shoulders. Another *thwack* and my eyes snap open.

I lift my head with a gradual wobble, coming out of an awkward sleep where I'm sitting upright. As my head rises, memory creeps in from the corners of my mind. I recall that I was in my room before, pacing and panicking about Anya being left alone. I remember Nikolai coming in with Kostya. I remember yelling, throwing a few punches, then going down hard after a blow to my head and a stun gun into my side.

Now I'm in a room I don't recognize.

The space is large and open—it's probably about half the size of our dance studio—with a high ceiling. There's a picture window across the room from me that spans the entire width of the space. The crisscrossing muntin divide it into smaller square panes, slicing across the sunlight which shines in from low on the horizon. Sheer, ivory-colored curtains hang open on either side of the vast window, framing the light in the way they stretch from floor-to-ceiling.

The room is neat, its openness broken only by a few pieces of furniture. Off to my left is an oversized, wooden desk—

there's a stack of papers resting on top and an expensive-looking executive chair behind it. There's a seating arrangement in front of me with a couple of cushioned armchairs, angled toward each other, across from a brown leather couch. In the far corner of the room, near the window, sits another matching armchair.

And then there's me.

I attempt to lift my hand to run through my hair, but it's trapped. I look down to see that my arms are tied behind a tan, cushioned chair and I've been positioned with my back to the corner of the room, in line with the door. I'm situated in such a way that I can see everything happening in the room. There's something unsettling about that and it rolls nausea through my stomach.

I pull on my arms, but they're tied tightly at the wrists behind me. Coarse rope is coiled and wrapped around them, irritating my skin. My shoulders ache from this position with my arms wrenched behind me. I try to move my legs, but my ankles are bound to the chair legs. I tug against my restraints, but they don't budge. I only earn myself more rope burn in the process.

My muscles feel tired when I move and my head aches. The way they knocked me out succeeded in wearing me down enough that I hardly have it in me to fight to get free.

Nikolai moves in front of me, looming above, looking down upon me with his arms dangling at his sides and his fists clenched in annoyance. I tilt my chin to look up at him and his gray eyes catch mine.

"I've brought you here for one reason and one reason only," he says. "You deserve to be punished for your indiscretion with Anya. Now you're going to witness the consequence of her actions."

"Where are we? Where's Anya?"

"We're in my home office."

"*Where's Anya?*" I nearly shout at him.

"You'll see her in a moment," he tells me.

A shadow of movement behind Nikolai catches my attention. I blink, making sure I'm seeing clearly as Vigo Vittori dissolves from a grayed-out blur into clarity. He moves to sit on the armchair in the far corner. He crosses his ankle over his knee and leans back, laying his arms casually on the rests— calm and cocky as fuck—as if he's here to enjoy the festivities.

My neck muscles tug instinctively, bunching with tension as I drag my eyes away to look up at Nikolai.

The way Nikolai's face contorts in a strange mixture of rage, hurt, and heartache, I know something's not right.

When has anything ever been right here?

My heart skips a beat, then begins to pound roughly, bringing me from still resignation to caged-animal status with only a few pumps. I jerk, throwing my entire body forward against my binds, but it's useless.

Nikolai doesn't flinch.

My binds don't loosen.

All I've managed to do is force the coarse fibers of rope to rub into my raw skin just a little bit deeper. The door clicks open and my head whips toward it.

I hope it's Anya.

God, I hope it's not Anya.

Kostya appears first, holding the door open as he grips Anya's elbow, supporting my injured, limping, blue-eyed girl as she hobbles forward into the room. She flinches with every other step. She limps on the ball of her foot across the traditional ivory and green rug that covers the hardwood floor. There's a dull *thud* on the carpet each time she sets down the cane she uses to support her weight—the very cane she beat my ass with the first night I was brought to Mikhailov Manor.

The roaring thump of my racing heart stops. The tender organ falls into my gut with a crash that makes me sick. Anya does her best to stand straight, to keep her shoulders back and her chin held high in her usual powerful way, but the internal struggle is written all over her beautiful face.

My stomach rolls and heaves.

I feel sick seeing her this way, her ankle battered and her soul power-squeezed in a vice.

Kostya shuts the door behind her, and she moves on her own to the center of the room. She turns her head to look at me and she tells me a thousand words with her brilliant cobalt eyes.

I'm sorry.

I love you.

I have no regrets.

But…move on from me.

Stay strong and move on from me.

Her eyes say it so profoundly, it's impossible to ignore.

Forget about me and move on.

It makes me gasp. She's given up hope. It's as clear as the spotless windowpanes in front of us that she's given up hope.

My chest heaves with heavy breaths as she looks away from me. She stares straight ahead, facing the center of the wooden desk as Nikolai moves to sit behind it. Settling into the oversized chair, he resembles a king sitting on his throne, the master and ruler of everyone in this room.

"I do not know where to begin with you, *rabynya*," he says with an edge to his tone. "I do not know which words are best to describe what your actions have made me feel."

Bravely, my girl responds out of turn, "I'm never at a loss of words to describe the way *your* actions make me feel, *khozyain.*"

Perhaps I've rubbed off on her a bit. It makes me proud, though it also scares the shit out of me.

Nikolai slams his fist down on the desk and we all jump, startled by the sound and force of it.

Except for Vigo.

He doesn't startle; no, instead he *laughs*, and my spine runs cold.

"I should have listened to my father," Nikolai says through gritted teeth, spitting heat and fury at Anya. "He told me you would turn out like this. He warned me what would happen if I let a slave have as much freedom as I've granted you."

Anya tilts her head. "Freedom?"

Nikolai stands, whipping around the desk, and he strikes like lightning. He wraps one large hand around her throat and lifts. I half-hope she'll raise her cane and beat the shit out of him, but in her surprise, she drops it, her hands coming up to cover his.

"Get your hands off her!" I scream and writhe.

He lifts with force until she rises to her toes on her one good foot while the other foot hardly touches the floor at all. She's nursing it carefully, even when she's being attacked.

"I gave you a home," he scolds as she claws at his hand. "I gave you food, shelter. I bought you clothing that other women would be jealous to have in their closets. I gave you space. I gave you a place to dance. I cared for you, and all I got in return was a slap in my face for letting you spend time alone with your *pet*."

Anya's eyes widen as she swallows, fighting against his chokehold. But then, she forces her lids to droop, narrowing her gaze at him pointedly. Somehow, she's found her strength to finally fight back against him, but for the life of me, I can't understand why she's fighting him now of all times.

Because she's given up hope for a future.

She chokes out the words, "Ezra is my lover, not my pet."

I sigh, letting out a harsh breath. For the first time I feel the irritation she always had with me. All the times I fought back with my words, all the times I just couldn't keep my mouth shut, and she'd give me that look. I feel her side of it now.

But I also feel impressed.

Proud.

Happy that even when she's facing an uncertain and violent future, she would use that word and call me her lover. But then I feel sick, sad, on the verge of heaving in shallow sobs of heartache for what's happening to her...to us.

Nothing good can come from this situation.

Nikolai releases her with a snarl and she falls heavy to her feet. She loses balance, tilting awkwardly toward her injury, and crumples to the floor, catching herself sideways on her palms.

"I no longer wish to look at you," he says, turning his back on her and circling around the desk to sit regally in his chair. He opens a drawer and pulls out a pen. "I gave you everything you needed to be happy, and you've done nothing but disappoint me. I know now that you were never worthy of being mine. You have been a lesson for me, *rabynya*. An expensive and time-consuming lesson. Women are best left to being whores and sluts, a hole to fuck and nothing more."

He flips a page from the stack on his desk and scribbles on one of the papers. He flips a few more and scribbles again. "You're no different. You're just another slut who will spread her legs the first opportunity she's given. I'm selling you to Vigo. Consider it your lifelong punishment for betraying me so brutally."

He's fucking selling her to Vigo Vittori.

Instead of thrashing and screaming, I'm stunned into silence. I'm so disturbed by this news that I can't move.

I can't breathe.

I can't think.

I blink, once taking me to darkness and again bringing me back to reality. I blink back into existence and my gaze falls on Anya. Her sapphire blues are right there to meet me.

She's still on the floor.

She hasn't risen.

Her face hasn't changed.

If anything, she looks accepting, as though she expected this news all along. I think we both had, but the reality feels as though a chisel has been slammed into a long crevice in my soul, finally splitting me, forcing me to break apart and rip right down the middle.

She holds me in her eyes as tears form in hers, making shimmering pools of blue. That's the moment it hits me—I might never see my blue-eyed girl again. Adrenaline rockets through my veins, jolting me back to my livid, violent, fully aware self.

"Don't you fucking *dare!*" I flail, throwing myself viciously against my bindings. "Don't you *dare* fucking sell her to that monster! I swear to God, I'll kill you! I'll kill all of you, you fucking monsters!"

Nikolai pushes to his feet, laying the pen down on top of the stack of paper. He tilts his head toward Vigo and side-steps out from behind the desk. Vigo stands from the armchair in the corner, taking his time to button his black suit jacket, brushing his hands down to smooth the fabric before crossing to the desk. He takes Nikolai's place behind it and lifts the pen.

"No!" I scream. "Don't you fucking sign that, you piece of shit! Sign that, and you sign your own goddamn death certificate. I'll murder you and your entire fucking family!"

"There's a long line of people who would like to end my family," Vigo says casually, not even bothering to look up at me. "You'll have to get in line."

He scribbles on one page.

Then another.

He lays the pen down and reaches out to shake Nikolai's hand. Their palms meet with a clap that bursts like lightning in my mind.

The deal is done.

"I think I've taken up enough of your time, Nikolai. I'll be taking my new belonging home now."

Home.

Fuck, where is he taking her?

How will I find her?

What the fuck do I do?

"Don't do this." I stare Nikolai down, begging unashamedly. "Don't do this to her. You know what will happen to her if you let him take her. Don't do this. I know you don't hate her as much as you say you do."

"Shut your mouth, *mal'chik*, or I'll shut it for you," he growls, but he can't maintain eye contact with me.

He knows what he's doing, what he's done.

Fuck, it's done.

Anya has shifted to all fours on the floor and her head hangs in defeat. Vigo crosses to her, crouches down to his haunches in front of her, and lifts her chin with his fingers.

"Tell me who you are now, *schiava*."

I don't know any Italian, but it doesn't take a genius to figure out what he's calling her.

Slave.

Just the same as Nikolai.

Anya's voice is a whisper, but it doesn't waver. "I am slave to the Vittori family. I am your belonging."

Nikolai slams the drawer shut on his desk after returning the pen, a reverberation of wood smashing against wood. For a moment, his eyes are hazy, conflicted, and his shoulders slump,

42

unnaturally heavy. Then he straightens, lifting his chin with a snap, and storms to the door.

"You may go," he tells Kostya as he passes. "Leave Ezra here. I'll return for him when I feel like it. Anya is Vigo's concern now."

He flings the door open and breezes past. Kostya follows him out and the door slams shut behind them.

"No need to be sad, my Russian doll." Vigo tilts his head as he strokes Anya's hair. "We will have fun together. Just you wait and see. Go and say goodbye to your pet before we leave. I'm afraid you won't be seeing him again for quite some time."

Her back rises with a sharp inhale but otherwise, she remains still.

"Go on, my doll." He pushes to his feet and circles around behind her, a predator eyeing his prey. "Crawl to him…unless you want to learn what happens when you make me wait."

Anya moves forward, carefully dragging her injured foot as she crawls to me across the carpet. When she reaches me, there's a pause, an eerie stillness of uncertainty. Then, Vigo puts his shoe on the back of her swollen ankle. I don't know how she managed to squeeze her unusually wide foot into her sneaker or pull on the tight jeans she's wearing. Her eyes widen as she registers a fresh round of pain.

He presses down slowly and I'm chomping at the bit. "Get your fucking foot off her," I growl.

He grins. "Your infatuation with each other is quite perfect, you know." He removes his foot and crouches beside the both of us. "I will always have leverage with you because you both went and fell in love. Give me your sadness, hmm? Have one last moment together, a treasured, tragic goodbye that will torture both your minds late into the night." His smirk is devious and he stands suddenly. "Up, *schiava*. Climb onto his lap and don't keep me fucking waiting."

Anya's head drops for a beat, but she lifts it again just as quickly. She slowly places her hands on my knees, one and then the other. Sliding her slender fingers forward for purchase, she pushes hard through my thighs to carefully bring herself to stand.

Somehow, she manages to spread her legs and straddle me, settling on my thighs. She always did have impeccable balance, but it seems so much more impressive when she's forced to do this with only one walkable foot.

Air rushes in and out of my lungs. My brain is overloaded with the sensory stimulation of Anya on my lap and with Vigo by my side. It's a swirl of good feelings and awful feelings and eerie, creepy vibes from the pervert demanding to witness our final goodbye.

"Very good," Vigo says beside us, stepping closer, nearly touching my side. "Now, have your tragic goodbye."

Anya shakes. She tries so bravely to hide it, and though Vigo might not see it, I can feel it. She swallows hard as her eyes meet mine. The blue softens as her icy armor melts away and my heart finally fails. It can't find a steady rhythm. It speeds up and slows down and stops and starts.

It's erratic for her.

I don't give a shit about giving Vigo his tragic moment to hold over us. I don't care what he witnesses. I just need her to know before she's gone. I know she feels the same when she drops her forehead to mine, drawing my energy and attention to focus solely on her. She cups my cheeks in her delicate hands.

"I love you," I tell her. "I love you more than my freedom. I'm not giving up, Anya, I won't."

She sighs. "I love you, Ezra. That's why I need you to let me go. Just focus on yourself, okay? Survive."

She tilts her head to press a soft, precious kiss to my lips. Her gentleness is still and chaste. But after a few moments, I part my lips, begging her for more. She gives, letting us fall into a sultry kiss.

Is this the last kiss?

I hold nothing back, pouring all my love, my heart, my soul into my kiss, taking the time to taste every inch of her mouth. I memorize the way she tastes, the way her body feels molded to mine, the glorious heat between her legs in the way her desire is inexplicably linked to mine. I sob once into her mouth as I feel her tears slip along both of our cheeks. I taste the salt of them as they slip down over our lips, bleeding into our kiss.

It's one of those perfect moments.

Tragic, yes.

But perfect, all the same.

Until Vigo insists on reminding us how our lives have been destroyed beyond reason.

He grabs Anya's hand and lifts it away from me. The motion breaks our kiss and we both turn to look as he places her small hand on his tented trousers.

Sick motherfucker.

My passion for her explodes in a supernova of rage against him. I lose control of myself and thrash again, but I only end up hurting Anya in that uncontrollable surge. She slips backward down my legs and clamps one hand down hard on my shoulder to hold herself up. It was an instinctual clench of her grip to grab hold of something rather than falling backward to the floor—only her other hand had already been removed from me and had instinctually grasped Vigo's groin.

Her hand grips his erection momentarily and then she rips it away, tilting her body away from him with a gasp.

He only smiles.

"Patience," he says, snatching a fistful of her hair and yanking her off me without any effort. "You will have plenty of time to interact with that, my pretty little girl."

He drags her toward the center of the room by her hair. She scrambles to stay on her feet, only she's forced to use her injured ankle to do that given the swiftness with which he pulls.

The pain on her face screams loudly in my soul.

Vigo releases her in front of the leather couch. She's lost her balance entirely with the way he tosses her around and she immediately falls to sit.

I've seen her scared before. I've seen the look on her face when she thought she was going to die by Nikolai's hand. But this fear that grips her is something else entirely. It's the uncertainty of what's next that scares her, and fuck, it terrifies me, too.

Vigo bends, reaching down to grab the cane she walked in with earlier. He holds it out for her and she takes it from him slowly, eyeing him warily as she does.

"Use it now to walk if you must. Come," he commands, walking to the door.

"Anya," I call after her as she rises, fighting through pain with tears pouring from her eyes.

The look she gives me is something indescribable.

She looks…lost.

Broken.

Hopeless.

Yet still *devoted*.

Taking in a long, steadying breath, she asks, "Mine?"

"Yours," I reply.

It was never a question that I would always belong to my blue-eyed girl.

CHAPTER 5

Anya

WHEN I FIRST came to Mikhailov Manor over three years ago, I brought with me a single suitcase. I'd left New York with Nikolai willingly, not knowing that I was meant to be his slave. He revealed himself as the benefactor who had funded my talent development over the years, and he offered me a training opportunity in Moscow that I simply couldn't pass up.

He told me to pack everything I would need for a two-week excursion into a single suitcase and leave with him right away. I should have known better when he told me I couldn't contact my family, couldn't tell my roommate or my friends.

He made it all seem so urgent. I was barely twenty-one at the time. I was naïve. I thought I was invincible. I convinced myself that this man—with his handsome face and charming smile—couldn't possibly mean to do me harm. He'd been my secret benefactor after all—an attractive older man who wanted to give me his attention.

So, I did what he asked, packed my suitcase, and left.

Sitting in the backseat of the black sedan in front of Mikhailov Manor, I watch as Kostya brings that same silver hard-shell suitcase to the car. The trunk pops open and I spin in my seat to look, though all I can see is the raised trunk lid blocking my view. I hear a thud, as I assume the suitcase is tossed inside, and then the trunk is slammed shut.

I meet Kostya's eyes for a quick beat and he tilts his head toward me in farewell. I pat unconsciously over the pocket of the jeans I had somehow managed to pull on. I have two more of the white pills Kostya had given me tucked away there.

My gut tells me to save them, to hide them somewhere safe as soon as I arrive at the Vittoris' home. My gut tells me more pain is to come, which will be harder to endure than the pain swimming around my ankle.

I didn't see Nikolai again after he stormed out of his office. He hadn't even said goodbye to me. It shouldn't matter, but in some twisted, warped way, it hurts my heart. The things he said to me when he signed the papers and sold me to Vigo had hurt.

Acknowledging that hurt reels nausea through my belly. His words shouldn't matter to me. He hates me now, just as he always had.

At least, I thought he always had.

Somehow, what he said to me in his office makes me question everything I thought I knew about him. He called me a slut and a whore, but he had also said that he cared for me. He thought he gave me everything I needed to be happy.

Happy?

But it doesn't matter anymore.

My life with Nikolai is over.

My life with *Ezra* is over.

No. Stop.

Don't think about it.

I gulp down my heartache as I straighten my spine, sitting up taller in my seat. I turn my head to look out the tinted window to my left, away from the manor, watching as the wide, white flakes of snow steadily fall to the ground.

Ezra melted the ice of my soul. His love warmed me, thawed me from winter to spring. He gave me hope where there was none, and I'm grateful for that. It was nice to live in that lie for what we had, but I know it's over now.

If we're lucky, the best we could hope for is a brief sighting of one another at the next quarterly meeting in three months. But I don't know that either of us will survive that long.

Tears climb from deep within me, threatening to crash onto a shore of pain from the tidal wave of grief that swells. If I let these tears fall, if I let myself think about my love with even an ounce of hope, I will drown in this heartache. Falling in love dropped me into this sea of hurt and *I will drown in it.*

I can't let that happen.

I have worse trials to face as Vigo's new slave.

I let the slow snowfall inspire me, freezing a thin layer of ice over this grief-filled sea. It's cold and the ice hurts me in other ways, but it provides a surface to stand upon, allowing me to walk above my grief as it churns and waves in a torrent of despair-ridden water below. Walking on this thin ice is a torturous way to survive, but it keeps me from drowning. The ice will thicken over time. The more Vigo hurts me, the more layers of protection I will add.

I have to.

It's the only way to protect myself.

The car door to my right opens and I turn my head to watch as Vigo slides into the backseat beside me, slamming the door shut behind him.

I turn away and wipe the welling tears from my eyes with the back of my hand. I do it quickly, hoping he won't notice, but I know he probably will. I can feel his attention on me, hot and oppressive.

The last of the guests from the four families—aside from

Vigo—and their slaves and drivers left yesterday. Kostya slides into the driver's seat and takes us to the helipad to meet the pilot.

Vigo's eyes are on me as Kostya pulls away, starting down the long drive from the manor steps toward the gate in the distance. I spin in my seat to look behind me as we drive away and my heart stops.

Ezra's been set free from his bindings and I see him at the entrance, screaming at Nikolai. He sees our car and he rushes down the steps and out onto the driveway, running toward us.

No.

Go back inside. I shake my head, wishing he could hear my internal thoughts.

His rash actions always make everything worse.

Yet, in the same way, they make everything better.

I watch the man I love chase after me, though we both know he'll never reach me. It's one final moment, one final *I love you* to wrap around my heart before the ice freezes it solidly in place.

I watch as Ezra drops to his knees in defeat, knowing the impossibility of the situation. Then I force myself to turn around, press my eyes shut to harden myself, and turn back into the cold, hard bitch I was before Ezra appeared in my life as a slave.

Within that cold hardness lies contempt, returning quickly and rising a ball of indignation in my chest. I look over at Vigo to show him my disdain. Our eyes connect, but all I see is a dangerous sort of humor where my heartache, to him, is entertainment.

He lifts his arm and stretches it to lay across the back of the seat behind me, leaning in close. "Tell me, what was it about Ezra that made you fall so hard?"

I cross my arms over my chest and turn to look out the

window, watching as we pass through the gate at the end of the drive and turn onto a dirt road that cuts through the thick forest.

"I don't want to talk about him."

He chuckles. "Of course not. It breaks your sad, fragile heart, doesn't it?"

I glare at him, but he seems disinterested in my reaction.

He pulls his arm back and reaches behind him to grab his cell phone from his back pocket. I look away when disinterest falls naturally into total disregard, and I hope he's done talking to me. Thankfully, he seems to be, tapping away on his phone screen.

Vigo reminds me of Nikolai in many ways. Both of them are handsome, quite unfortunately disarming in their good looks. Vigo is only a year younger than Nikolai, though he looks nearly a decade more youthful. Nikolai has always let his anger age him, but I know Vigo doesn't carry the stress of his vileness the same way.

Vigo finds humor in his torment.

His eyes hide his madness, which is all the more unfortunate for the victims who capture his attention. They could bewitch prey into believing they were safe with him. The soft, honey-brown color of his irises are unique in the way they give him a light, warm, youthful appearance. His thick, black hair falls in precisely styled, imperfect curls, framing his face in ebony waves. He's lean and tall—taller than both Nikolai and Ezra. There's a certain kind of power he holds in his height alone, being able to look down upon every monster and master he comes into contact with.

He's smooth, sophisticated, handsome, depraved, and dangerous. But all my time spent with Nikolai has prepared me for whatever is to come from this horrendous beast.

I can survive this.

I can survive *him*.

But do I want to?

We follow a winding, dirty path for thirty minutes through the swiftly darkening forest. I know this because there's a digital clock on the dashboard that allows me to count the minutes as time passes in tense, horrible silence.

From the narrow, dusty car path, surrounded by dense foliage, the forest opens without warning onto a clearing. The car crawls forward into the large circle of open space, angling off to the left as it moves forward toward the black tarmac at its core. A helipad exists in the center and resting upon it is a helicopter. This is the only way to escape the Mikhailovs' land. The helicopter doesn't stay here—it only comes when Nikolai calls for it.

The car creeps to a stop, and as the engine cuts off, the propellers of the helicopter whir into life, beginning a slow spiral above the craft. Vigo and Kostya slip out of the car without a word to me. I scoot across the seats to the other side of the car and peer out the window, letting my eyes transfix on the propeller blades as they move.

My one and only method of escape is coming to life in front of me. But instead of taking me away to safety, it will take me into a captivity that's likely worse than I dare to imagine.

The trunk is slammed shut before I even realize it was opened, the sound of it startles me. Kostya drags my suitcase toward the helicopter as Vigo approaches the sedan, flinging the door open beside me. I flinch as he thrusts his hand inside, beckoning me.

"Come," he orders.

I shrink away from his outstretched hand. There's an independent woman in me that I suppose Ezra brought back to the surface—she scoffs at the gentlemanly offer to assist me from the vehicle. I want to balk at the offer, but then I realize that

I do actually require assistance. I nearly start crying, realizing how Nikolai has disabled me, hopefully only temporarily.

I sigh, taking his hand in resignation, and I carefully shuffle out of the car. I'm thankful for my dancer's balance as I'm forced to stand on one foot, the gravel surface proving to be an uneven and uncomfortably lumpy landing. He doesn't offer me the cane he'd taken from Nikolai's office before we left.

Did Kostya put it in the helicopter with my suitcase?

I'm forced to hop a couple of steps toward the back of the car so Vigo can slam the door shut behind me. Then he drops my hand and regards me with a lift of his thick, black brow. The corner of his mouth twists upward and there's humor in his eyes as he turns and walks off toward the helicopter. He comes to stand beside it after fifteen or so paces, his strides long and quick. He turns toward me, still balancing precariously beside the car.

"Come," he shouts to me, summoning me forward with a wave of his hand.

My eyes follow the path his feet traveled. Fifteen paces for his long legs would be twenty for me under normal circumstances. But I was trading strides for uneven limps and hops, half of them along bumpy gravel before shifting to black asphalt. My eyes trace the path I need to walk and find Vigo at the end. He's smiling gleefully at the torment he's about to witness. He wants to watch me struggle; he wants to view my pain, my disgrace.

I won't let him have the satisfaction of watching the pain brush across the features of my face. I steel myself, inhale deeply, and force myself to take a normal step, with both feet on the ground. My ankle screams, aggressive agony tearing through my limb. It takes everything that I have to hide the fact that I'm screaming on the inside. I'm determined to walk to him without the humiliating limp, determined to hide my weakness, but my internal scream slips out to an audible whimper with only the second step.

I lift my injured foot from the ground as I huff out a few breaths, blowing out the urge to cry and sucking in strength to get there.

Just get there.

There's no other way for me to do it but to limp on the ball of my foot.

I see the satisfied smirk adorning Vigo's face as I concede to my injury. It pleases him to see me succumb to my shame, the ballerina broken so effectively that she can't even walk.

Oh, God.

Will I heal? Will I be able to dance again?

Kostya walks past me as I move forward, and he catches my eyes before tapping the backs of his fingers twice beneath his chin.

Chin up.

I'm surprised for that brief connection with him, and I'm thankful for it. I never really trusted Kostya, but I recognize the kindness in that gesture—not to mention the pills he gave me. Perhaps I misjudged him from the beginning.

His gesture reminds me that I'm strong, proud, and determined. I lift my chin to show Vigo that truth as I continue onward. I force a subtle smile to my face, a look of determination meant only to anger him, because I want to wipe that look of amusement off his face myself.

The blades of the aircraft pick up speed as I come within reaching distance of Vigo. They whip the wind and dirt from the ground beneath me. He turns away and climbs on board, offering me no assistance, but I wouldn't take it anyway.

I reach deep within to pluck out my stubbornly

independent streak, giving myself the fortitude required to finish this part of my journey. I force myself to move, to push, to ignore my pain for the moments it takes me to step up and drag myself inside the fuselage.

Panting, I fall into the seat beside him, and he smiles at me, perfectly pleased with himself for being such an arrogant prick.

I feel some relief once I'm finally sitting, thankful that I have the weight off my foot. At least the seat is comfortable. The interior of this helicopter is extravagant, practically screaming that it belongs to one of the four families with its leather seats, elegant overhead lighting, hardwood-inspired flooring, and extra leg room.

I push down on the arm rests to straighten myself in the seat. Vigo reaches across me, his hand darting across my legs. I jerk backward at the brush of his fingers along my thighs, scooting my bottom back as far as I can. He shoves his hand down between my hip and the armrest, rooting around until he finds the latch for the seat buckle. He pulls it out, drawing the strap across from the other side of me, and secures me in my seat.

His hand drops and lingers on my thigh and I don't take my eyes off it. I can feel his breath, hot and sticky, against my neck as he leans in close. His fingers slip up the inside of my thigh and I act on instinct, even though I should know better. I smack his hand and push it away, throwing his unwanted touch from my body with a snap—something I *never* would've done with Nikolai.

And then, I flinch because I realize what I've done.

I brace for his anger, for new pain to come raining down on me.

But it doesn't come.

Not as the fuselage door is shut behind me.

Not as the co-pilot climbs aboard.

Not as the helicopter lifts from the ground.

Instead, I'm met with the same sinister, knowing smile that's haunted me since I was used by Vigo before, when Nikolai gave me to him as payment for the information he wanted about his family's death.

I shudder at the look.

He reaches for me again, but this time he drags his knuckles down the side of my cheek. Again, I act on instinct, ignoring everything I've learned about being a proper slave. My gut tells me to fight Vigo, not to submit, and it goes against everything Nikolai has groomed me to become. I flip my arm around to toss him off, but he snatches my wrist in his hand, again with a smile.

He pries my fisted fingers open with his other hand and sucks my index finger deep into his mouth. I swallow as my body sinks away from him, my face scrunching in disgust. He pulls my finger out slowly, his teeth grazing across my skin. His silent, unwavering eye contact is unsettling.

He releases my wrist and turns away, settling back in his seat. He ignores me again in favor of his phone. When I'm certain his attention is locked on his screen, I rub my hand on my jeans, urgently wiping his saliva from my finger as I finally release the breath I'd been holding.

Soon after, we lift into the sky and I look out the window at the grounds below. The dense forest stretches on for miles around Mikhailov Manor.

The first time Nikolai took me off the grounds by helicopter was to attend my first quarterly meeting. That was several weeks after my one and only escape attempt where I'd gotten myself lost in the woods and came face to face with a gray wolf. Nikolai had come after me and found me just in time.

That one attempt had been all I needed to know that escaping wasn't possible. But when he flew me away that first time weeks later and I looked down at the forest below—just as I am now—I fell into a crippling panic. It took the view from above to cement the fact that I was completely and utterly at his will—at the will of the four families.

It reminds me that I never stood a chance of breaking free.

Ezra doesn't stand a chance of breaking free.

I press my palm to the window as we pass over the shadowed outline of Mikhailov Manor, trading it for dark and desolate wilderness.

I'm forced to watch as we leave my love behind.

My possibility, my hope, every good thing Ezra brought to my life is gone.

Done.

Over.

And I don't know if my heart will ever beat the same way again.

CHAPTER 6

Anya

WE SPEND THIRTY minutes on-board the helicopter before we land on a private airstrip. It belongs to the four families—owned and operated, just the same as the airstrips in Italy, Ireland, and Louisiana—and I can make an educated guess that it's off-grid from the authorities. We transfer from the helicopter to a private plane owned by the Vittoris and in no time at all, we're taking off into the night.

This next part of the journey will be long. I recall from my previous trips with Nikolai to the quarterly meetings hosted by the Vittoris that the plane ride was four or five hours nonstop.

Those hours with Nikolai in close quarters had always been trying. Thankfully, he'd spent most of that time on his laptop or phone, preparing his sales facts and figures for the meeting ahead. When he wasn't doing that, of course, he was enjoying the free use of my body for his pleasure.

As the plane levels out at its cruising altitude, Vigo pockets his phone and turns on me with that twisted smile. My heart hammers for the uncertainty of how this time will be spent alone with Vigo, remembering how Nikolai could so brutally use and abuse me, and wondering how much worse it will be with this monster.

My hands tremble as my mind flashes back to when Vigo used me once before.

Suddenly, I'm very aware of the pills in my pocket and even more aware of how my ankle throbs and burns. Travel hasn't been kind to the swelling, and I feel the pain of it more and more as minutes pass. But that pang in my gut that tells me to wait to take another pill, to bide my time, to get through for now because I'll need them more later, returns with unsettling force.

"Get up," Vigo commands. "Come to me."

I should behave as I've always done for Nikolai.

I should get up and go to him without question, and I should do it immediately.

But he was right before. Ezra has brought my fight back to life and I can't seem to let myself do as I'm told. Ezra had nearly managed to bring me back to the woman I was before captivity, and I knew how dangerous that was now.

Yet, in a visceral way, it somehow feels like a betrayal to do as I'm told now. If I were a better slave, I would say it feels like a betrayal to the master I've known for over three years, but that's not true.

Obeying feels like a betrayal to Ezra and to the light and fight he brought back into my life.

Stupidly, I ignore the command and tightly press my eyes shut. I send a private message to Ezra in my mind that he is *mine* and I can nearly hear him echo back his own promise.

Yours.

Vigo speaks with an eerily calm tone and I open my eyes to see a sickening smirk on his face. "I think you underestimate my disregard for your well-being, *schiava*. I will happily jump up and down upon your broken foot." He repeats his command, "Get up. Come to me."

I stare at him. "No."

Oh, my God.

Why did I just say that?

Why am I being so stupid?

My love for Ezra has made me so fucking stupid.

His smirk ticks but doesn't falter as he unbuckles his seat belt and rises to stand. We're alone in the cabin, sitting across from one another in an arrangement of four, oversized, cream-colored leather seats. He could do anything he wanted without interruption from another. The awareness of that prickles beneath my skin as he steps toward me.

"Get. *Up.*"

I lift my chin to look up at him and instantly, I feel small… small and insignificant as he towers above me. The way he looks at me shakes me to my core. Without even making a conscious decision, my hands fall to my belt and unbuckle it, and I rise to stand.

He opens his arms. "Come here."

I take one wobbly step toward him and the distance is closed. Chest to chest, I'm forced to let him wrap his arms around me. His feet shuffle him closer, pressing up against my body.

"Arms," he says, his chin resting on the top of my head.

With great shame, I snake my arms around his waist.

"There's a good girl. *La mia piccola bambola Russa.*"

I grit my teeth in frustration and fear as he speaks to me in Italian with a quick tongue. It terrifies me not to know what he's saying.

"I don't understand Italian," I tell him, trying to soften the hard edge that keeps finding its way to my voice.

"You will learn some," he says. "You are *my little Russian doll. La mia piccola bambola Russa.*"

Oh, God.

I don't want to end up like one of his dolls. I've heard

Nikolai speak of Vigo's habits before, his tendency to collect and keep women caged and at his mercy. I've seen first-hand how uncared for they are—malnourished, tired, unhealthy, fearful. Of course, I knew I would become one the moment I was sold, but the understanding of what that would truly mean hadn't registered until now.

"Good girls do as they are told. S*ì?*"

I press my eyes shut and force out the reply he wants from me. "Yes."

"*Sì, Papà,*" he corrects me.

My gut clenches as nausea rolls through my belly.

I don't need him to translate that.

I'd always known Vigo preferred younger girls. I knew he was depraved. But if this captivity was going to be a "*yes, Daddy*" situation, then I was fully unprepared for the sickness that might be waiting for me in his keep.

Somehow, I manage to repeat the words out of necessity, though my voice cracks, along with any defiant resolve I thought I had against obeying him like a good little slave.

"*Sì, Papà.*"

His hands crawl up my back and his fingers spread my hair apart into two thick sections from the back of my neck. He brings the long ends over both of my shoulders, half on one side and half on the other, until it dangles in front of each of my breasts. As he steps back to look at me, his hands come forward over my shoulders. He grips each section of hair in his hands, fisting the parted lengths in his grip next to my ears. His hands form makeshift ponytail holders, clutching my long hair in two pigtails.

He grins that demonic grin of his. "You are older than my other dolls, but you still look young like this. You'll be perfect."

"Perfect for what?" I ask quietly as I stand still in front of him.

He clicks his tongue, tilting his head. "*Papà* did not give you permission to ask questions, *bambola Russa*. Get down on your knees and apologize."

Vigo turns and moves away. A few short steps take him to a couch, situated sideways along the outer wall of the cabin, just behind the cluster of four seats we sat in before. He lowers to sit on the matching cream-colored couch and leans back. Vigo spreads his arms wide and lays them dominantly across the backrest. He spreads his legs apart and beckons me with a tilt of his head.

"On your knees. Crawl to *Papà*."

Papà.

If he says that word one more time, I might vomit all over his leather seats.

I obey because I have no other choice, though that feeling of betrayal still haunts me. I bend carefully, shifting all my weight to my right foot as I lower to the floor. I attempt to be graceful about it, but really, I'm only letting myself fall, catching myself on hands and knees.

There is nothing graceful about me with this horrid injury, and I feel tears spring to my eyes at the thought of it. I was once one of the most graceful ballerinas in the world—it kills me to think that this injury won't be treated, it won't heal correctly, and as a result, I may never dance again.

It's a possibility I can't fathom so I force that thought away, back to the dark corner in my mind.

Even with my weight off it, I feel a whole new kind of hurt as the floor pushes against the top of my ankle, forcing extension of my tendons and stretching them painfully. Thankfully, it's not far to travel, crawling to him as he asked. It's a few short drags of my swollen ankle across the floor before my head is in-between his knees.

I look up at him and wait.

"You know what I want you to do." He reaches down and unlatches the buckle of his belt, but he returns his arms to the back rest before finishing. "Do the rest. Take care of your *papà*."

I swallow the bile that threatens to force its way up my throat. I shuffle forward on my knees and I have to put my hands on his legs to steady my wobbling, queasy body.

I reach forward to finish what he started—to unbuckle his belt, unhook his button, pull down his zipper. Vigo bites his lip as he regards me with his head cocked to the side and a satisfied smirk.

"Show me how well Nikolai has trained you. Take out my cock and suck."

My eyes remain open though it feels like they're closing as my mind drifts inward. It's incredible how easily I can slip back into servitude for survival's sake, doing what's commanded of me in order to endure for another day.

Nikolai *had* trained me well, truthfully, and so I knew how to get through this. It's nothing more than a job, a task I have to complete.

I'm sorry, Ezra.

I have to obey to survive.

Still, Vigo's aura manages to make it all the more repulsive. There's something wrong with him, something unnatural about him that screams madness. Somehow, I think giving him a blowjob on his private jet will only register as a one on his sickness scale to ten.

I do what I have to do.

I pull down the elastic band of his underwear and free his gradually hardening cock. His girth doesn't outmatch Nikolai, but his length does, enough that he could easily choke me with his erection.

But comparing two monsters is pointless. Neither of them are Ezra. Neither of them could ever compare to the way Ezra could fulfill all my wants and needs. I gave him my heart and soul completely, and he gave me his. Regardless of the fact that this sexual act is forced beyond my control, it feels like infidelity, disloyalty.

The shame of that is heavy on my mind, though I try to drift away like I'd always done with Nikolai. I inhale courage and freeze my soul with an icy barrier to grant myself fortitude. I lean forward and suck the tip of him into my mouth.

Vigo groans and his large hand lands on the back of my head. "*Sì*, that's a good girl." He presses down. "All the way."

He gives me no time to adjust to his intrusion as he pushes my head down hard. I cough and gag around his length, my stomach heaving as he sinks into the back of my throat. My eyes widen and I feel them begin to water. He holds me in place though I try to lift my head away. I huff in breaths through my nose and he simply won't let up.

His hips lift from the seat to pulse his cock inside my mouth, impossibly deeper, as his fingers dig into my scalp, burrowing in painfully hard. I force my eyes to close, trying not to vomit, focusing on the shallow breaths through my nose.

But then he takes that away from me, too.

His fingers come down to tightly pinch my nostrils shut.

My eyes snap back open as I gag and splutter and truthfully fight for air.

"*Sì, la mia piccola bambola Russa*," he moans. "Take it."

My heart races as adrenaline kicks in, panicking me into fighting him. But it's no use, his grip on my scalp is tight and his cock in my mouth is oppressive. He's not letting me get away. The sooner I accept that, the better.

I *know* that.

And I could have just given in and gotten through it before now.

But now, *now*, Ezra's green eyes flash across my spotty vision and suddenly, I'm angry.

I'm angry and frustrated and furious because I let myself lose control. I let myself fall in love with him. I let myself hope again and that was the most dangerous thing of all.

No.

Having hope wasn't the most dangerous thing.

It's the aftermath of hoping, the loss of it, that endangers what is left of me now.

Still, the lightning flash of Ezra through my mind inspires the bit of fight he'd somehow managed to conjure up in me before I was sold. I unsheathe my teeth and clamp down on Vigo's cock. This startles him, and he thrusts upward hard, stabbing at the back of my throat. I haven't bit him hard, just a nip to catch him off guard.

He digs his nails into my scalp, gripping my hair and pulling me back forcefully. I gasp for a breath as my lips slide free from his invasion. Saliva drips sloppily from my mouth as he separates me from his cock. He pulls his hand back and slaps me, his knuckles punching into my skin as he strikes me with the back of his hand.

I tumble to the side, landing on the floor as I yelp from the unexpected hit and the new burst of pain. My vision blinks out, then fades back in with dots of light around the edges.

I scramble to get up, managing to get on my hands and knees, facing away from him, but he's already standing, ready to come after me. His foot lands hard on the back of my swollen ankle and I scream.

The pain shoots a crippling ache through my leg, making me freeze, my body going rigid to tense against the hurt.

He's on me like a lion leaps for a running gazelle. His arms latch around my waist and he flips me over in a flash, slamming me to the floor. I land heavy on my back and the little air I've managed to catch escapes with a whoosh.

Vigo's hands find my knees and spreads them wide as he scoots up between them, kneeling. He reaches for the button on my jeans, pulls the zipper, and tugs my pants down with a hard jerk. My body drags toward him as he wiggles and peels the denim away, taking no care for the way my ankle flops as he gives a final tug and I scream from another jolt of pain.

He pushes his pants down, and without so much as a beat for me to cope with what's about to happen, he grabs my hips and drags me toward him, my legs open around him. He slaps my sex with the back of his hand, forcing me to whimper in disgust with the painful slam of his hard knuckles.

No.

No.

No!

I pick up my legs, preparing to kick, but he places his hands on my hips and digs his thumbs into the hollow spots between bones on either side.

As I start to cry, I shout, "No!"

I'm unable to fight as he tilts my hips, lifting my bottom from the floor. I can't fight as he pulls me closer. I can't fight as he angles his tip.

Then he slams into my pussy, hard, raw, dry.

I don't even try to hold back the tears now. They pour from me freely as Vigo painfully fucks me.

"Good girls don't hurt their *papà*. Good girls take cock with gratitude. Thank me."

Fuck you.

I fucking hate you.

I hope you die and suffer an eternity in hell.

I don't want to prolong my agony.

I turn my head to the side and say, "Thank you," between sobs and feel like a coward for doing it.

Vigo fucks me until he's done with me and leaves me a crying mess on the floor. He covers himself, straightens his suit, returns to his seat, and pulls out his phone as if nothing had happened.

He's done with me.

For now.

I stare blankly at the cabin's bathroom door beside me.

I feel hopeless, helpless, already dead.

My tears only come harder and faster when I think of Ezra. I can't help but think of him. My life with Nikolai had been a complacent wreck of servitude, but it had been predictable.

My heart feels shame now because I'm angry with Ezra. The raw ache of being fucked dry was something I'd been able to endure before. But then Ezra showed me love, showed me pleasure, showed me wanted touch and affection, and in doing that, he ruined me.

He loved me and he ruined me.

All at once, I feel as though I love him and hate him. I love him for everything he gave me, and I hate him for giving me anything.

Ezra gave me love.

Ezra gave me hope.

Ezra lifted me higher than I knew I could go.

And because he did, I have farther to fall in disgrace.

CHAPTER 7

Anya

WE'VE ARRIVED IN Palermo, but this is not our final destination. We've landed on another private airstrip where we transfer from the jet to one of the Vittoris' helicopters. Now that we've arrived in Italy, we'll be trading land for water, flying across the Tyrrhenian Sea. The Vittoris have their own island, somewhere off the coast of the mainland, though I doubt it could be found on any map.

The four families work together to keep their secrets, using their wealth, their reach, their political power, and social influence to protect them.

Our helicopter charges ahead into the darkness, crossing over the deep black sea which looks still, almost peaceful in the night.

But it doesn't fool me.

That black ocean below is ready to swallow a person whole if they should fall into its serene trap. It was much the same as Vigo. He always seemed so...unaffected, so calm, appearing still and quiet. He was, by all accounts, a subtle man...until his internal storm broke the surface into crashing waves and twirling violence.

Another twenty minutes have passed by the time our

helicopter lands and I'm exhausted.

I watch out my window as we close in on the Vittoris' private island. It's a tragically beautiful place. There isn't a sandy beach around the edges, but rather mountainous drop-offs where the seawater has rubbed away at the edges of land over time, creating steep cliffs.

As panic begins to spread across my mind, I imagine the rocky edges eroding away with great speed, the brutal ocean splashing across and scrubbing away the filth of the four families, reclaiming the island and swallowing it whole.

But truthfully, the sight of their rocky shores is magnificent—magnificent and overwhelmingly disturbing. Escape from their shores is impossible without an aircraft, but it doesn't matter.

I'd given up on escaping a long time ago.

Our helicopter lands at the edge of one of the cliffs—we can hear the waves violently crashing against the mountainous side, even above the roar of the helicopter rotor whipping the propeller blades overhead. The breeze they create is chilling in the winter air.

It's not far to the car and I manage to hobble to it mostly without issue. As I settle into my seat and look out through the window over the cliff's edge, I briefly wonder if I should have hurled myself over it. I shiver, not just from the cold, but from the thought and how easily it had come to my mind.

Am I capable of doing such a thing?

Am I capable of ending my own life?

A driver takes us away from the helipad at the cliff's edge, following a gravel road that curves around and down toward a hidden path. The dirt-covered road is obscured from above by some of the most fascinating pine trees I've ever seen. Nikolai told me once they were maritime pines. Their trunks reach tall toward the sky, no branches hung low, only splitting off at the very top where they sprout into plush, green pine needle clusters that look like soft grass overhead.

I watch the trees pass by on our silent drive to our final destination. The car stops ten minutes after we've left the helipad, and my mind circles around panic-inducing thoughts.

Where will he keep me?

How will he hurt me?

Who will I be when he's broken me completely?

Ahead, illuminated by the headlights, is a grand, metal gate. It's framed by two large, stone columns on either side. A letter V is engraved on a circular plate at its center. Moments later, the gate slowly reels open, the V splitting right down the middle.

As we drive through, I turn in my seat to watch it close behind us, noting that a black metal fence extends out beyond the two stone columns on either side. The fencing goes as far as I can see before disappearing into the darkness.

We travel the dirt path, which continues beyond the gate for another thirty seconds or so. Then, the rumbling of the wheels over gravel switches to a smooth and pleasant silence as we shift onto a concrete paved driveway. Turning to face forward, I watch the headlights lead as we follow the path.

Gradually, the Vittoris' massive home is revealed. We trade concrete for cobblestone as the car turns and passes between two more large stone columns. There are lantern-style lights affixed to the tops, signaling the entrance to their piece of the underworld.

Beyond the lantern-lit columns, the grounds open onto a vast cobblestone square. In the center rests an ornate fountain with three-tiered bowls which rise from the middle. There is no water running through it now, perhaps because it's the middle of the night, but the stillness of it seems somehow disquieting.

The driver circles the car around the fountain and parks just in front of the main entrance to the mansion. He practically leaps from his seat, exiting the vehicle swiftly to open the door for Vigo. Vigo gets out without a word and I remain still. I have no desire to move.

I'm not ready for this.

I'm not ready for whatever is to come.

Vigo doesn't care what I am or am not ready for.

The driver arrives at my door and pulls it open. I get out slowly, carefully, begrudgingly, taking care to keep the weight off my injured ankle as I rise to my feet. As I settle my balance, the driver pops open the trunk. He pulls out my silver hard-shell suitcase and places it on the beige and brown cobblestone as Vigo stands beside him, typing furiously on his cell phone. He stops then, putting the phone inside his pocket.

He looks up at me, then to his driver, taking in a breath as if he's just come back to reality after being lost in cyberspace. I would be perfectly happy to have him ignore me in favor of his phone—anything that keeps his attention off me.

He tilts his head toward my suitcase with a furrowed brow. "You can toss that," he tells his driver. "She's a slave. She doesn't have any belongings."

Does his driver speak English? He must.

Vigo wants me to understand that I am nothing, that I *have* nothing here. Otherwise, I imagine he would have given that command in his native tongue.

My chest sinks as a heartbroken sigh rushes out of me. I don't know what's in that suitcase or if there is actually anything in it at all. But it's *my* suitcase and *my* belongings. More than anything, this makes me feel worthless.

My pictures of Lidia...Are they in there?

My ballet shoes?

My clothes?

My goddamn pillowcase that smells like Ezra?

Goddammit!

At least with Nikolai I still had pieces of myself. Vigo has taken away my humanity before we've even crossed the threshold of his garish home.

I open my mouth to let words of objection tumble out, but I clamp it shut immediately. It's pointless to argue with a master who cares nothing for me—the heartache and pain it would cause is avoidable and so, I choose to avoid it.

"*Si, signore,*" the driver says and tosses what's left of my possessions back into the trunk.

Vigo moves around him, coming in close to me. I manage to avoid stepping back as he invades my space. He straightens, bringing himself to his full towering height, and looks down upon me.

"A few things you need to know before we go inside. Members of my family are addressed with respect. You don't cross their path or mine. When you're not in your cage, I expect you to stop and bow your head when you see a Vittori, and wait for them to pass or direct you further." He tilts his head, reaching out to pluck a strand of hair from my shoulder, and twists it playfully around his finger. "Not that you'll be out of your cage when you're not with me. But what you're doing right now is disrespectful. Bow your head to me."

I shut my eyes as I lower my head in defeat.

"Good. Now try to keep up. I'm tired and I need to get you settled in your new accommodations before I can rest. Come. Follow me."

He turns and stalks off with long strides, and dammit, he's quick. I limp along after him with no hope of catching up. He enters his home through a wooden door set back in an alcove.

It's two steps up onto the landing; two steps that I struggle to hop over beneath the brick-layered archway that beckons us to the front door.

Somehow, I manage my way inside to see Vigo impatiently waiting to close the door behind us. The moment I enter, I'm met with an unsettling feeling, a feeling that nags in my stomach that I don't belong here, and that I need to leave immediately.

Only, I have no choice.

I have no option to leave.

The uneasy feeling is going to be a permanent part of my life now.

Part of that feeling is the sound.

There *is* sound here—voices, faraway music, the noise of multiple people living together under the same dwelling. Mikhailov Manor had been filled with such overwhelming silence that I'd nearly forgotten the noise of living. And that's all the more disturbing because this is sound made from the lives of monsters.

I look around as Vigo yells out something in Italian, and a female voice responds somewhere in the distance. It looks different without the members of the four families gathered here for the talent reception and quarterly meeting—I'm able to see the details of my new prison.

The entrance is wide open. The receptions I've attended in the past have been held right here over the square-tiled flooring. Entryway tables beside me stand tall and narrow, accentuated by ornately framed mirrors above them. The russet-colored frames match tiny square tiles on the floor, which punctuate the corners of the larger taupe tiles, making a pattern of large and small squares.

A few steps past the entryway door is an alcove that opens to the left, a transition into rich, hardwood floors designating where the piano room begins. A black, grand piano sits on the far side near a large window with a small seating area in front. I can recall listening to one of the Vittori talent slaves play piano here before.

There's a staircase to the right which curves around the wide, rounded entry space, leading up to a balcony landing at the top. Past that single balcony is an archway, though I can't see beyond it from the ground floor. There's an ostentatious gold and crystal chandelier that hangs from the center of the space, blocking my view.

I stare at the steps and their curved, metal railing, wary, wondering if I'll have to find a way to drag myself up to the second floor.

God, I'm just so exhausted.

"Come," Vigo says and walks straight ahead.

I follow him as he strides across the wide, circular space. Straight ahead is an open archway that leads into the kitchen. There's a gigantic island immediately in front of us, the long edge spreading out to my right, easily spanning eight or nine feet. This kitchen is stark white and sterile, in direct contrast to the warm, mahogany and cinnamon tones in the entry.

It's far too clean and it reeks of bleach.

The smell triggers me, reminds me of the smell in Ezra's room after Jonathan was taken, after I'd seen Kostya bring out his old bedsheets with their splashes of red. My pulse accelerates and I gasp in a shaky breath.

Vigo turns right before reaching the island and walks along the side of it closest to us, moving straight toward a dead end beside the refrigerator.

Except, it's not a dead end.

He presses on the drywall and it pops open, swinging on a hinge—a hidden doorway. I nearly stumble backward in surprise, but I catch the edge of the island to steady myself.

Behind the camouflaged entry is a metal door with a keypad. Vigo pauses so he can cast a smug glance at me over his shoulder.

"Your new home is behind this door. Would you like to see?"

No.

Fuck no.

Though I'm shaking my head with wide, frightened eyes, I know the only acceptable answer a slave should give, so I quietly say, "Yes."

"Try again."

I swallow and force my pride down my throat, my voice coming out as a horrified whisper. "*Si, Papà.*"

"Good little doll."

He enters a code onto the keypad and the metal door clicks open.

I can hear my pulse pounding in my ears.

A stab of instinct punches in my gut, telling me that my new existence will be unimaginably worse than I feared.

CHAPTER 8

Anya

THERE'S A PART of me that wants to fall to my knees, grovel, and beg for Vigo not to take me behind that metal door. I want to plead with him, tell him I've been trained well, that I've been a good slave for Nikolai, and that I'll be compliant, obedient—I'll be better than I was on the plane.

God, what has my life become?

Nikolai has been slowly sucking the life out of me for years, edging me into submission until I gave in completely. Yes, I had fucked up falling for Ezra, bringing him into my bed, betraying Nikolai's trust, but I'd been a model captive before my indiscretion. I had paid my dues. I'd earned graces in his home, been trusted to do what I was told, was given freedom to go about my business when Nikolai was working.

Some sort of righteous indignation rises suddenly in my chest, an oddly placed feeling of superiority that I was a slave who should be treated better than Vigo's usual standards.

But it's stupid to feel this way.

A slave is a slave. I belong to Vigo now—he's the master of my fate. Still, it's hard to shake that feeling and it upsets me more when I realize where it comes from.

Ezra.

He had built me up, made me feel proud, cherished, loved, *worthy.* Ezra has efficiently and viciously ruined me with his love. I *hate* how he's ruined me.

But fuck, how I miss him, want him, love him with every ounce of pain his turbulent presence has brought into my otherwise predictable slavery.

Mine?

Could he still be mine if he no longer exists in my world?

Vigo holds out his arm, drawing me from my chaotic swirl of emotions, and beckons me forward. I move slowly, knowing there's no use in fighting it, though I still wish I could.

I reach Vigo and peer beyond him. There's a dark staircase beyond the door and looking down it makes my heart stop beating.

"Down," he commands. "Go."

I'm terrified to find out what's at the bottom of that staircase. The walls against either side of the steps are painted solid black. I can see a light shining from the landing at the bottom, but all that's visible is a light-gray concrete floor. My heart starts beating again with a jumpstart that makes my pulse thrum, pounding behind my ears, beating out the message that there is danger here.

Run.

Run far and fast.

I will my beating heart to slow because I can't run from this. I press a hand over my chest and close my eyes, inhaling a steadying breath so I can focus on one step at a time in this nightmare.

But then Vigo kicks at the heel of my uninjured foot and I snap my eyes open, quickly reaching out to grasp the doorframe with both hands. With most of my weight on my good foot, his incessant tapping at my heel threatens my balance.

"Time is tick, tick, ticking away. Go now," he says, timing the way his toes tap against my heel with his *ticks*.

I make myself do what I have to do.

Slowly, I descend, leaning all my weight against the rail as I hop down the steps. It's embarrassing to be so inelegant in my movement. My pride is in my grace, and I've lost all of it with this one dreadful injury.

Hop after hop, step after step, I arrive in the basement. I no longer need to put all my intent and focus on making it down the stairs and so, it shifts to taking in my surroundings.

I see, but I wish I could unsee.

"I'll be right down. Forgot something," Vigo calls from the top of the steps.

No.

No, no, no.

I want to go back.

Take me back to Nikolai!

This cold room at the bottom of the stairs is no larger than the bedroom I was given at Mikhailov Manor. To my left is a concrete wall that matches the concrete floor.

But to my right... To my right...

I hear Vigo's footfalls on the steps behind me and I whirl around, crashing into his chest as he lands on the bottom step.

"I'm a good slave. You know I am. You don't have to lock me in down here. I won't attempt an escape. I promise you. I *promise*."

He smiles down at me sinfully with his hands behind his back. "Oh, I know you are a good slave. But this is where I keep my dolls. This is your new home, *la mia bambola Russa*."

I swallow hard as he steps forward, forcing me to step back, his chest pressing against me heavy and insistent. He moves steadily and I move with him, though I don't want to.

Beside me is a floor-to-ceiling wall of plexiglass, divided

into three separate compartments, each only just wide enough to fit a twin-sized mattress.

And in each of the three boxes are women.

One in each box.

They look starved, tired, lonely, seething. I'm sure there are a plethora of other terms which could be used to describe them, but I simply can't name them all. They each sit slumped in their corners, shaking, fearful, eyes trained on Vigo as they cast surreptitious glances beneath their lashes with their bowed heads.

A bright light shines overhead in each of the transparent cubicles, illuminating their crude living quarters. A blanket and pillow, stained and dirty, on top of a thin mattress on the floor. A small metal toilet in the corner. Holes drilled into the plexiglass at head height for air and to speak through. Metal dog bowls sit on the cold, hard concrete flooring.

Vigo moves until my back slams into the far wall, the last of the three boxes beside me. I jump at the pressure of Vigo's aura as it pulses blood lust after me.

"Please," I beg, bowing my head, ashamed, contrite, desperate.

"I think you've been spoiled," he says to me. "I think you have a bit of a chip on your shoulder. You think you're cold and dead inside and that nothing can hurt you. Well, I will be glad to be the one to educate you. I can always find a way to hurt you more. There is a bit of a problem with your accommodation, though."

"P-problem...?" I stutter.

What's happening to me?

I don't stutter.

I'm confident.

I'm concise.

I *was*, but perhaps here, I am not.

He tilts his head toward the third cage. "The problem is there's already a doll living in your house."

The girl inside senses her presence has been noted. She slowly stands from where she sat in the corner but she doesn't step forward.

"Each of my dolls gets their own private space. But I suppose my math was a bit off when I purchased you. You see, I now have four dolls, you included, but only three doll houses. Of course, there is only one reasonable way to fix this problem…"

My inhale is shaky.

He presses against me, pinning me to the wall with his body, though his hands remain behind his back.

What's behind his back?

"Well? Aren't you going to ask about my brilliant solution?"

Unwillingly, I ask, "W-what's your solution?"

His face brightens with a demented sort of smile and it twists nausea through my stomach. He steps back and moves toward the third cage. The woman inside moves away, pressing her back against the far wall. Her hair is pulled into two, long, tangled pigtails, as though it's been some time since it's been brushed. She wears a simple cotton dress—reminiscent of child's clothing—with a plain A-line shape that ends at the knees.

She's visibly trembling as Vigo approaches. I watch as he enters a number into another keypad. The door pops and opens just a crack. Vigo is careful not to show me what he's hiding, keeping his back turned away from me. I expect to see the girl attempt an escape as Vigo steps back, making a clear exit for her.

But she doesn't.

She shakes her head viciously, eyes wide and wild, shivering in fear of him.

What has he done to her?

My God.

What will he do to me?

"Get in," Vigo commands me.

"Please...*please*..." I beg him.

"Begging is disrespectful. It's weak and pathetic. Are you weak and pathetic, my little Russian doll?"

I take in a quick breath and pause before speaking, making sure my voice comes out steady and calm. "No."

"Then, get in."

My mind screams at me to run, to fight, to cower, but I manage to move my body forward despite the screaming sirens in my brain. My eyes well up with fearful tears as I step across the threshold from the open space into the transparent box.

The other woman and I both jump at the sound of metal clanging against the concrete floor. Vigo has tossed in a kitchen knife. My eyebrows bend in confusion, but then the hinged plexiglass shuts and I whirl around, slamming my palms against it.

"Anya, pick up the knife and kill her." Vigo grins. "Do it quick...before she decides to kill you with it first."

He steps back and crosses his arms over his chest. His head tilts to the side. His honey-brown eyes burn into something resembling hellfire.

When I hear the blade slide against concrete, I whip around to see the woman holding the knife. She backs into the corner again like a feral animal, though she holds it at her side, pointing the tip outward toward me.

Oh, God.

My breath catches and stutters in my chest. My heart races at lightning speed. My sudden distress signals my body to pump adrenaline, hard and fast, through my veins.

My life is in immediate danger and I have to protect myself. I don't even feel the pain in my ankle as I rush backward, stepping onto the thin mattress so that I can press my back to the opposite corner.

Why didn't I pick up the knife?

Oh, God.

She's going to kill me!

My mind prepares for a fight, but then the woman starts to cry. Streams of tears fall like waterfalls down her pale, sunken cheeks.

I don't know what she's thinking, if she's about to attack me or crumble into a sobbing mess. Her anguish tempts my own, and though it nearly makes me want to give up, give in, let her rush me with her blade and end what's left of my life, I know that I can't. That fight that Ezra brought back to life within me rears back and roars through my heart.

Yours. I can hear his voice inside my mind and it refuses to be ignored.

I stand defensively, ready to fight her for the knife and kill her if it's what I have to do.

But I will wait for her to make the first move.

And she *does* make the first move.

Only it's not the move I expect.

She looks at me, her dark eyes catching mine. She speaks in perfect English and her accent is undeniably American which, of course, reminds me of Ezra.

"If you're smart, you'll do the same," she says to me, then turns her eyes to Vigo. "I'll finally be free of you."

A certain and oddly peaceful grin spreads across her cheeks. It's a look that will haunt my dreams for years to come.

She lifts the knife, sets the edge of the blade against her throat, and slices herself open with composed determination.

I scream.

I scream as blood rushes from her gaping throat.

I scream as she falls to her knees.

And as the light leaves her eyes and she tumbles sideways to the ground, I sob.

I see red.

Red, red, red.

Everywhere.

It's splashed across my clothes.

It coats my skin.

It pools over my sneakers as it continues to *pulse, pulse, pulse* from her body, as her heart persists to beat it out of her severed veins.

I scream again.

As the pulsing spurts of blood slow, as my mind drifts back into my body, I turn my head to look at Vigo, who remains on the other side of the see-through cage.

And he's smiling.

Vigo is smiling the grin of a satisfied man, a blood-lusting man who knew this would be the outcome and has just been granted a most gratifying release.

My voice comes out as a shaky whisper as my body trembles and shakes out of control. "You're sick. You're sick, you're sick, you're sick."

He sucks in a long, slow, deep breath. "No, *schiava*. I am well. I am very, *very* well."

My new home is a transparent box, spattered and stained with blood, and decorated with a body.

Vigo left after the girl killed herself.

I haven't been able to move and I don't know how much time has passed. My back is still pressed against the plexiglass corner, as far away from the dead girl as I can get. I'm not sure whether I'm still breathing. I must be, but the only thing my mind is actively aware of is the sliced and bloody body on the floor, the stench of copper, the drying blood caked on my sneakers.

I don't know what's happening around me, if the other women in the other boxes are crying, screaming, or silent. I have no awareness other than blood and death before me.

Time must be passing as my legs grow weak and tired, and I slowly slip down to the mattress beneath my feet.

The blood of a dead slave coats the floor around my perch, an ocean of red surrounding my island mattress.

I close my eyes and try to force myself to think of something else, of anything other than this living nightmare, but my mind can't track a conscious thought.

My heart, though…My heart knows what I need.

It pumps an emerald green blaze through my veins, which ignites a flash fire vision beneath closed lids. Behind the fire blazing over my eyes is the man I fell desperately, tragically in love with; the man who both loved me and ruined me. The memory of his smile, of his snarky tone, and his warm embrace, holds me safely inside my mind.

My brow furrows as I squeeze my eyes shut tighter, imprisoning myself with Ezra inside the faraway pocket of my awareness. If I can stay here, I can stay safe. If I can keep the memory of him bright and vibrant in my thoughts, maybe I can survive here.

A twinge of pain in my ankle tries to pull me from my internal world to my external reality. My brain had shut down my pain receptors with the adrenaline rush in what I thought was going to be a fight for survival. But now that the immediate threat is gone, the physical agony returns full force.

Then I remember the pills from Kostya.

I had two left when we departed Mikhailov Manor.

I shift and dip my hand into my pocket. I don't have to dive far as my fingers find one twisted in the fabric near the opening.

Only one.

I move that pill to my other hand and dive back in, searching for the second, but it's gone. It must have fallen out in Vigo's haste to rip my jeans from me on the private jet.

Damnit.

I should save this one.

I should hang onto it until I urgently, frantically need it.

But I urgently, frantically need it now.

It's not so much the pain I need it for as it is the escape the strong drug brings for my mind. I *need* the escape.

Without another thought, I pop the white pill into my mouth and swallow it dry.

I close my eyes and breathe deeply, willing the medicine to shut me down, to take me from this nightmare and into a beautiful dreamworld with Ezra.

CHAPTER 9
EZRA

I RUSH TO my door in a heartbeat the moment I hear the metal key push into the lock from the outside.

I'm gonna pummel his ass the second he walks in here.

The night Anya was sold, Nikolai had set me free with just enough time to chase after the dust kicked up by the quickly retreating car. The piece of shit wanted it that way. He wanted to torment me by making me watch her leave. But the real kicker was that it was tormenting him to watch, too—whether he'd admit it or not. I'd seen the flash of regret in his eyes as the car turned off the manor grounds and drove out of sight.

I'd gone after him then, sought out a fight, but I was so blinded by my grief that he took me down with hardly an ounce of effort.

I wanted to kill him.

But there was something about the heartache of losing the person I love most in the world that took the fight right out of me.

My chest had ached, my heart had raced, my lungs had burned from the gasping breaths of shock that shut down my system. I had crumpled to my knees in front of Nikolai, feeling as if all the best parts of me had been scooped out, leaving me a hollow, empty shell of the man Anya loved.

Frankly, I'm surprised Nikolai hadn't killed me, with the way I sniveled on my knees. I was a pathetic, sad, broken man who had nothing else to lose. Perhaps he'd known there was nothing else he could do at that moment that would hurt me, there was no way to punish me further. But why he let me survive, why he kept *me* and sold *her*, was still a mystery to me.

I'd sat beside the front doors of the manor until Kostya returned from taking Anya away from me. Together, he and Nikolai herded my sad ass back to my room. I was a lump, a heavy brick to carry. They locked me in without shackling me to the bed, and I've been here for a day, maybe two, left to my own devices.

My grief caught fire in that time, burning in the pit of my stomach. It spread from limb to limb in a massive wildfire until my entire body succumbed to the relentless flames of rage.

I burned.

I seethed.

Fire licked over my soul, taking me straight to hell, showing me the lust that demons have for violence and depravity.

And the hellfire demon burns bright inside me now, ready to knock the devil off his fucking throne.

I have one palm pressed heavy against the wall beside the doorframe, the other on the knob, ready to pull and swing it wide the second the key turns. My chest heaves, sucking in a shaky breath as I prepare to wrestle the man who broke me to the ground.

But the second lock never turns.

Instead, something slides past my foot and I immediately look down to see something slip under the door. Just then, Nikolai's muffled voice comes through the closed door. "Just a reminder for you, *mal'chik*. If anything happens to me, she dies within a day. If you insist on fighting me, fine, fight me. But it will do you no good."

"*Mother*fucker." I grip my hand into a fist and slam it where it rests against the wall.

I bend and pick up what he's slid under the door. It's another picture of Emma, my ex-girlfriend, one of the few people who has been in my life for more than a season and would always have a piece of my heart. Though things didn't work out between us, she was one of the only people who knew the real me, someone who stuck by me when shit got tough, someone who would always be like family to me.

And he was holding me hostage by one of the only people I actually gave a shit about.

He's just adding fuel to my fire.

"I guess you should tell me what the fuck you want then before you open the door. 'Cause I'll tell you what, fucker, I'm ready to break your fucking nose the second this door opens. *Fuck,* would that feel good to my desperate fucking knuckles," I shout.

I can hear his amused chuckle, though it's faint through the door. "Could you fit anymore profanity into one sentence? At least you've found a way to make your anger entertaining."

"Open the *goddamn* door, you colossal *ass*hat, and say that to my face like a *fucking* man."

Breaths pass as we both wait for his response.

Adrenaline kicks up in my veins and whooshes through with speed and fury.

I hear the key turn in the second lock and I am *ready.* Grasping the knob again, I tug and tug until the lock clicks. I throw the door open, flinging it wide.

My brain can't even process what's happening as my body takes over. Nikolai is standing there, arms stretched out to his sides with a sinister *I-don't-give-a-shit* smile plastered to his face. I think Kostya is standing there, too, but my eyes are blinded and intent on Nikolai.

I charge forward, pull my elbow back, curl my fingers into a tight fist, and swing at his face. He ducks just in the nick of time like a goddamn ninja.

As he bends away from my right arm, I uppercut him with my left. Though he's quick, he's not quick enough to miss two in a row. The punch lands hard. He wobbles, taking a step back, and I take advantage to sucker punch him in the gut once, twice…

I collapse under his weight as he bends over my head, clawing at my back to find purchase as they scramble over the fabric of my black T-shirt. Somehow, he grips my waist and spins me with a grunt. Grabbing the collar of my shirt at the back of my neck, he forces me upright.

My head whips back as I try to assess my next best move. He pushes me toward the wall and my head flies forward. My forehead crashes into drywall and bounces off, throwing me back a step. I put my hands up in time to ease the next blow as he throws me against the wall again—luckily, I catch myself with my hands.

His hand clamps around the back of my neck and he pins me face-first to the wall with his body.

"Are you done now?" he asks.

"Not a chance," I spit.

I fling myself backward, my head tossing back and a bruising pain shoots through the back of my skull as I jam against his nose. He groans and steps back, and I whip around to see him doubled over. His fingers come up to touch his nose, then he looks down at them to see the blood I drew.

I huff to catch my breath after the frenzy and a smug

smile creeps across my cheeks. In that moment, I'm blissfully aware that I caused him an injury that made him *bleed*. It makes me pause in my fury to relish the moment. That brings me back to reality enough to notice that there are two other people in the hallway.

It's not just Kostya standing beside us, but a girl who looks scared shitless. Her hair is dark and long, like Anya's. She struggles against Kostya, who tries to lift her from the floor. She seems to have fallen to her knees in fear, curling around herself like a scared child, though she's at least as old as I am. My face drops at the look on hers.

This is a stolen girl.

An unwilling slave, just like me and Anya.

This sad young thing was stolen from her life. The newness of her circumstance is etched into her cheeks by the trails of her tears.

I bare my teeth at Nikolai, ready to knock him to the ground, but he holds up a palm to stop me as he straightens to his full height. "Touch me again and I'll hurt her," he threatens.

My agitation screams in my gut, shouting at me to hit and kick and hurt until he can't feel hurt anymore, until he's lying on the ground lifeless.

But a twinge of softness in my heart settles me.

I feel Anya grip my heart, like a ghost who haunts me. It's as though I can see her bright blue eyes in my mind, that look she would give me that told me to keep my mouth shut and follow the rules. She wanted me to keep the peace, not just for my benefit, but for hers, too. She needed me to do what I was supposed to do because it wasn't me he hurt.

It was *her*.

And now it's the unknown girl losing herself to sobs beside me.

I close my eyes and breathe, slowly, steadily, willing the violence that burns so bright beneath my skin to fade, willing the adrenaline in my veins to stop pulsing. The only thing that could ever calm me in this hell was Anya's sapphire blaze and the determination and strength in the husky tone of her sweet voice.

Yours, I say into my mind, and somehow, I find the peace to care about the well-being of this girl having a meltdown on her knees.

I lift my hands, palms facing Nikolai in a gesture of surrender.

"Your inability to control your impulses will someday destroy you," he tells me as if he's an older, wiser mentor.

He's certainly older.

Maybe wiser with experience.

Never anyone's fucking mentor, least of all mine.

"Maybe. But I've got nothing left to lose."

"Well, then. If you no longer care about Emma Mayfield's wellbeing, I'll put in the call now to end her. Of course," he cocks his head, "she is young...in good shape. Perhaps we can take her and sell her instead," he muses.

I bare my teeth. "Don't you fucking *dare*."

"What does it matter to you, *mal'chik*?" he asks with mock innocence. "You just informed me that you have nothing to lose." He waves a hand at Kostya. "Make the call."

Kostya reaches into his pocket with one hand while the other clings to the girl. He slips out his cell phone.

"No!" I reach out a hand as if I could halt him with some magical power through my palm. "Don't make any fucking calls. I'm done, okay?" I hold up my palms in surrender and lower slowly, begrudgingly, to my knees. "See? I'm done."

Nikolai tips his head at Kostya and he puts his phone back in his pocket. I sigh in relief, and in defeat.

"Good. I wanted to introduce you to your new dance partner."

"What?"

"Her name is Sasha. She's fresh to captivity, as you can see by her pathetic state." He casts a sideways glance in her direction with a look of disapproval. "I'm afraid we need to evict you from your room."

"Evict me?" My eyebrows knit together, then come apart again as I understand. "You're going to lock her in there."

"Yes. She needs to be situated close to Kostya and so, she needs your room."

The girl starts to speak in rapid succession, her words stuttering and starting between her cries. I don't understand a word she's saying, but it sounds like Russian. Nikolai affirms that it must be when he bites back at her, shouting something in his native tongue that makes Sasha flinch and sink back on her heels.

"She doesn't speak English," Nikolai tells me. "I imagine that will make dancing together a challenge, but you have a year before the next performance. Plenty of time for you both to learn enough about each other to dance together."

My head is shaking before he even finishes his sentence. "No. *No.* I'm not dancing with anyone else. Anya was my partner...*is* my partner. Always will be. I refuse to dance with anyone else."

"Don't be *fucking* stupid, Ezra. Anya is gone. She's not coming back. You will never dance with her again. The sooner you accept that, the better your days will be."

"Here? As if my days could be anything but shit living here with you."

He wraps his hand around my throat, sliding his grip up beneath my chin. He lifts with enough force that I'm made to stand, planting one foot, then the other, rising to my feet. I stumble backward as he pushes and slams my back into the wall behind me. He brings his face too fucking close to mine, close enough that I can smell the whiskey on his breath.

"Don't bite the hand that feeds you, *mal'chik*. I won't bother to threaten you with violence because it only drives you. But I will use your empathy against you. I will do terrible things to that girl to punish you. You know that I will."

He leans in closer to whisper to me and his stubble brushes against my cheek. The scratch of it triggers every violent molecule within me to attack the creep who is far too close to me.

I shove against his chest, but he doesn't budge. He shifts his hand, pressing his thumb over my windpipe and I freeze, knowing that if I fight him, if he presses too hard in the right spot, he could crush it and kill me.

"Show me respect or I will hurt you in all the ways I hurt Anya."

The way he hovers there, wavering deep in my personal space for more than an awkward beat, chills me, freezing my spine straight. He pulls his head back and gives me a secret grin, an expression that I'm sure will haunt my dreams.

And then he lets me go.

"Come," he says, turning and walking away. "You'll stay in Anya's room. Kostya will retrieve your belongings after he shackles Sasha for the night."

"Anya's room?"

He stops and looks down at the floor, hesitating before glancing back over his shoulder at me. "The room that *was* hers. She won't be coming back to claim it."

The hesitation was too obvious for him to hide.

Does some part of him miss her, too?

Does he regret making the worst mistake of his life?

Does he regret washing away the only color in this gray world?

Anya was that color.

She was bright sapphire eyes, rosy pink lips, burgundy and bronze cheeks. She was hickory and mocha hair, and honey skin. She was sparkling white and glacial blue, frozen beneath her protective layer of ice.

Anya.

Where are you?

What are they doing to you?

The reminder that my blue-eyed girl is gone slices across my heart, stopping it for several beats and suddenly, overwhelmingly weakening me. It makes me tired, too tired to fight anymore tonight. The ache of it lifts from my chest, rising to a lump in my throat, swirling around my mind and squeezing my brain in an aching vice.

My body takes over for my mind, my feet moving me forward to follow Nikolai down the hallway.

I hear Sasha scream, hear her fight Kostya, and then there's the slamming of the door that makes me jump.

I feel sad for the girl, I truly do. But I'm doing all I can for her by complying.

We reach Anya's room.

Not her room. Not anymore.

Nikolai unlocks it with a key. It had never been locked before, not as far as I knew. Anya had been with Nikolai for so many years that she'd earned his trust and the freedom to move about the manor as long as she obeyed.

But now he uses a key.

It's smart.

He shouldn't trust me.

He opens the door and lets me pass and I halt three steps

past the threshold. The room looks the same as the night we left it. The bed sheets are still rustled and twisted from the night of passion we shared. My tuxedo and her bright pink dress from the reception are still haphazardly discarded on the floor. The pillows I'd propped beneath her injured ankle are still piled on the bed.

Nikolai hasn't touched a damn thing since she left.

But why?

"She's gone." His voice behind me is far too soft. "She's not coming back. And it's because of you."

I whip around to face him but remain silent, brooding.

"I left the room alone. All of her possessions remain except for a few items that were sent with her to the Vittoris."

The fucking Vittoris.

"Why?" I asked.

"To remind you. To *punish* you. I want you to smell her on your pillow at night. I want you to see the last thing she wore. I want you to be reminded in every possible fucking way that she was here, you had the pleasure of her company, and now she's gone. Because you broke her. You stripped her of her obedience, willed her to misbehave, and tempted her to fall in love with you. I want you to live in that shame, that guilt. She's gone from both our lives now and it is all because of *you.*"

I open my mouth to speak, but he steps back and slams the door shut. I don't even react. I don't lunge for the door. I let him shut it and lock me in.

He wasn't wrong, but he wasn't right, either.

I had broken her...not her soul, but her armor.

I had tempted her...not to fall in love, but to hope.

I step forward, moving into the room and everything I see is Anya.

Unease strikes hard and fast in the center of my chest, causing my body to shake. I put my hands on top of my head, lacing my fingers together as I pace through my anxiety beside the wardrobe.

"Goddammit," I mutter under my breath, but I'm not satisfied with the intensity of my cursing. "*Fuck!*"

My fist comes down and slams against the closed wardrobe door. I pull my arm back immediately, shaking out my hand against the pain of instantly bruised knuckles. I instinctively wrap my hand around my aching fist and blink against a vision, a memory…Anya pinned to the wardrobe door with my body as I kissed her.

This is my fault.

This is all my own goddamn fault.

I was the one who suggested we come to her room to have sex that night. I wanted her to have a memory of me to hold onto in case Nikolai ended me.

That was so *fucking* stupid of me, and now Anya is paying the price for it.

"*Fuck!*"

I need her. I need her so desperately that I would offer up my own goddamn life if it meant I could spend one more minute with her. The universe is playing a sick joke on us— allowing us to find each other, giving each of us our soul mate under the worst of conditions, only to rip us apart again.

I feel empty.

Hollow.

My feet have me moving toward the dresser, wondering if he's left something of hers behind, some token or memento I can cling to. I open the top drawer and find that it's full. Everything is still here—her precisely folded panties, her tattered and worn pointe shoes.

I reach for the pale pink shoes, dingy and scuffed from endless practice. The ribbons that would tie them to her ankles are wrapped around the slippers, holding them together. I draw the pair closer, clutching them in tight hands, pressing them to my chest.

Shit.

It hurts.

I pause.

There's a full drawer of underwear here.

I set the ballet shoes on the top of the dresser and start pulling open drawers. Nearly all her belongings are still here. I go for the bottom right drawer and my heart falls into my stomach to see the same green and pink floral-patterned box that she'd shown to me in my early days here at Mikhailov Manor.

The pictures of her sister, Lidia, are all still here. Everything that held worth to her is still here.

He didn't even have the basic human decency to send her with her own goddamn underwear.

My heart leaps and rushes.

I move toward the bed of twisted sheets, eyeing the pile of pillows I had set for her to ease the swelling from her injury. I lower to sit on the edge and the fuchsia gown on the carpet calls for my attention.

I bend to pick up the dress from the floor, clutching it in both hands. I bring it close to my face, press it to my nose, and inhale deeply, slowly.

The scent of her remains.

Roses.

Sweet but strong.

Soft but heady.

My lungs stutter, forcing a burst of air that rushes out of me as a sob. The sob shakes me and forces unwanted tears to spill and I feel weak…so fucking weak without her.

I drag the dress along with me as I roll to lay on the bed. Hugging it close in my arms, I cry out my ache, breathe in her scent, and lose myself in the precious wreckage our love has left behind.

CHAPTER 10

Anya

I LAY AWAKE in my cage, looking up at the ugly gray ceiling. You could hardly call the thing I lie on a mattress. It's worn and thin, and I swear I'd probably be just as comfortable lying on the concrete floor.

I rest my arms behind my head as I stretch, flex, and rotate my foot. I kick my leg into the air, trying to work through the healing sprains and regain something resembling flexibility.

I've been nursing my injured ankle for the past week, forcing myself to rest it as much as I force myself to move it, knowing I need to engage the muscles and tendons to get them healing properly. It's getting better slowly. The swelling has gone down and the pain has decreased, though my mobility is still quite limited. I still wonder whether it might be fractured, though there isn't anything I can do if it is.

I'm not walking normally yet—not that I've had much opportunity to walk—but I practice as often as I can, pacing the three steps it takes me to get from one side of the box to the other.

Vigo has only taken me out of my box once since we arrived. He had left me inside with the dead slave while he slept comfortably in his room my first night here. He returned the next day to remove the dead body with the help of his younger cousin, Lorenzo, and the driver who brought us here from the helipad.

While they worked to dispose of the remains, Vigo had taken me to a walk-in shower behind the staircase, something I hadn't noticed—couldn't have noticed—when I'd first come down the stairs.

He'd stood and watched as I scrubbed myself clean of the blood that coated my skin. He took my clothes from me but never brought them back. Instead, he dressed me in a plain, baby-blue cotton dress. It has an empire waistline and flares out softly from beneath my breasts, which stops just above my knees. It has cap sleeves that draw tight around my bicep with elastic through the hems, causing the sleeves to pleat and puff over my shoulders in a youthful way.

I wasn't given a bra or underwear, just the blue dress that was a better fit for a child than a woman. And I've been wearing that same blue dress ever since.

There's another household slave who brings us food and water once a day. The uniform of his slavery is clear and consistent. It's always blue jeans, bare feet, naked chest, and a black leather dog collar.

Things here had been otherwise uneventful. Though every part of me still ached and seared with the burning need for space to walk and leap and dance, I found myself wondering why the girl had killed herself rather than use the knife to stab me, to attempt to survive.

She'd thought death was a better alternative.

As for me, I suppose I had already endured slavery and uncertainty for so long that I struggled to wrap my mind around why that girl so quickly chose death. It's not that the thought of taking my own life hadn't crossed my mind in the past.

It had—of *course*, it had. Especially on the worst days with Nikolai. But I couldn't imagine making a split-second decision to slit my throat.

What had Vigo done to her?

How much longer before he does it to me?

I have to force my mind away from the thought whenever it pops into my head. The vision of her body on the floor, blood spurting in pulses as her heart beat it out through the gash in her throat...it threatens to break my sanity.

As much as my mind wants to know, wants to be aware of what is to come to protect me when it finally does, I refuse to ask the other girls. I don't ask and they don't offer. Mostly, they cry or scream or try to talk with each other and with me about plotting an escape.

I have no interest in deluding myself into that false hope. I want *nothing* to do with an escape plan because I already know it's impossible. Escape will only lead to punishment and torture when they're inevitably caught.

Hoping is dangerous and these women are dangerous thinkers.

I'd learned that the blond in the first box next to the staircase had been here a month before I arrived. The brunette in the middle had been here for nearly three months. The girl who committed suicide before my very eyes had been here for a year.

That's all I know and all I care to know.

I'd belonged to Nikolai for three goddamn years. I'd left my childish misbeliefs about personal liberty behind long before these young women could even dream of the vileness of slavery.

I'm sure both women think I'm a cynical bitch for the way I scoff at their discussions of escape, for the way I balk at their sobbing fear and hopeful camaraderie. But I can't afford to lose myself again in caring for another slave's well-being, and I *refuse* to form any sort of attachment to these women.

Perhaps I've too easily accepted my fate, too easily given into the idea that I will be a slave for the remainder of my life.

Except...I know that I'm right.

The dark men are everywhere, and they own us—it's an epitaph written on the gravestones of women everywhere before they are even born into this world. The four families have a vast, worldwide reach, but they aren't the only ones who do this.

I wish it weren't true, but I know that it is. I have to survive it on my own.

"Anya?" the brunette in the middle box whispers to me.

Her palm is pressed to the plexiglass that connects our boxes as she sits on the floor.

I know her name is Bianca, but I don't let myself think of her as anything other than the brunette girl in the middle box. Connecting with another human being is what got me into this mess in the first place.

"What?" I reply, trying all at once to sound calm, but also as if I don't care that much to respond.

"If the three of us work together, I really think we can come up with a plan to—"

"*No*," I interrupt her with a forceful and determined answer.

"Why? Why won't you help us?"

"I promise you, escape from this is not possible. There's only survival or death. The sooner you accept that fate, the better off you'll be for it."

The girl shakes her head at me before turning to face the other direction, but I have one last thing to say to her.

"Hope is dangerous."

"It's *not*," she snaps back at me. "Hope is all we have. And if we just work together—"

I turn my head sharply to the side to look at her. "And if we just work together, then what? Do you know how to get out of this box? Even if you did, what would you have us do then? The metal door at the top of the stairs is locked from the outside."

Bianca opens her mouth to interject, but I keep going, pushing up from my prone position to lean back on my elbows, "Let's say, by some miracle, you get through it. Do you think you're just going to run off into the night?" I scoff. "Where will you go? How will you get off this island? You do know the only way on or off is by helicopter, right? What, do you plan to fling yourself off one of the massive cliffs and hope you don't bounce off a rock on the way down? Even if you didn't die from the fall alone, do you honestly think you could swim to safety?"

"I don't know, but—"

My eyes narrow on her. I know my building frustration is entirely misplaced, but it doesn't stop me. "Right. You don't know. It's not something we're going to figure out. Not on our own and not together. If you keep hoping there's a way out, it's only going to hurt more when you realize there isn't. This is *it* for us."

She mumbles something that sounds like, "Selfish bitch," before she turns her body away from me.

I internally flinch at the name calling, but I don't let it show. I just look away from her and lay back down, getting right back to my kicks and stretches. It's not the first time another girl has called me a bitch. I wasn't exactly the warmest or friendliest of people before my captivity and I've only grown colder over the years.

Ezra thawed me. It was tropical paradise when I was with him, but I've become arctic cold again. It's the way I have to be to protect myself. I have to shove any understanding or sympathy for these girls aside so I can focus on myself.

I *have* to.

It's the only way to survive.

I didn't have the means to pay the price of hoping for something better.

Entrechat. Pirouette.

Entrechat. Pirouette.

Entrechat—

"Would you fucking stop already? Christ!" Bianca shouts at me through our shared box wall.

I stop mid-jump, landing hard on my feet in exasperation. Pain shoots through my ankle with the rough landing—my healing tendons require control and precision. She paces in the cage beside me, her fingers digging into her hair and pulling.

"All day with the goddamn *dancing.* All fucking day!"

I glare at her, doing two more pirouettes on my good foot out of spite. I do feel bad for her frustration, but I would've lost my mind by now had I not been able to do what little dancing I can do inside my cage. We're all falling to pieces in this strange sort of isolation. We're only taken from our boxes twice a week to shower behind the staircase.

Vigo has taken the other two girls upstairs on some type of rotation system, once every couple of days. He hasn't taken me upstairs yet, but I've learned my place after only a month here.

We're Vigo's broken dolls.

You're not fucking broken, Anya, Ezra's voice shouts in my head.

It's jarring, making my muscles jerk. The shock of its

clarity lowers me to the floor, and I sit on the cold concrete with my legs stretched out in front of me.

My fingers touch my lips and I nibble on my thumbnail, feeling a jolt of lightning flash through my body at the sound of Ezra in my mind.

It's stirring the way he comes back to me so unexpectedly, so powerfully. If I close my eyes and inhale slowly, I can nearly smell the way his dance-induced sweat mingled with the soft peaches and cream scent of his soap. It was always the most intoxicating mixture of sweetness and masculinity.

I'm lost in that thought when Vigo comes down the stairs and I lift my head to look at him blankly. It takes me moments to blink back from memories of Ezra to reality, but as he walks past the first box, his eyes catch mine and lock me in.

He stalks past the middle box and my breath catches in my throat. He stops in front of my box—the third and final box—and cold sweat forms at the back of my neck.

I push slowly to my feet, tugging my stupid blue dress down to ensure it covers my bare bottom. He steps closer to the box and I step back on instinct. He enters a pin on the keypad entry, and I step back again, then again.

As the door pops open, he tugs on it, swinging it wide. "Come with me," he grins.

Oh, God.

Be strong, just be strong.

I pause for a beat, then lift my chin and move slowly toward him. I won't fight it like the other girls do with him every time he comes for them. I'd rather save my energy for when it's needed most.

And I have a feeling I'm going to need it once we're alone.

I can nearly sense Ezra's disappointment in my resignation, knowing he would've attacked, tried to fight, and run. But I quickly let go of that disappointment as I exhale. I know better than to fight the inevitable.

Still, my heart pumps wildly against my ribcage.

He holds his arm out toward the staircase. "Up you go. Stop and wait for me when you reach the kitchen."

No.

Don't go.

Don't go, don't go, don't go.

It's the first time I've been asked to go upstairs and my pulse beats steadily with the warning, *don't go, don't go.*

But I have no choice.

CHAPTER 11

Anya

I MOVE PAST Vigo to the staircase. Though I'm moving better now—I am even able to do some jumps and turns in my tiny cell—my foot is still stiff and a bit inflexible as I walk.

It feels immeasurably better to point my toes, to let the muscles and tendons extend and stretch—it's somehow easier to jump and turn. Walking, though, I feel pain where my ankle bends with each step. This staircase may as well have been a mountain for my aching, underused muscles, but I hide my pain and reach the top all the same.

The metal door is open and I step past it into the kitchen. There's a brief gut reaction that tells me to run, but I'm frozen in place as I come upon Renata Vittori. She's standing on the opposite side of the bright-white kitchen island. I keep my head lowered, but I look up at her from beneath my lashes.

The woman is wealth's goddess. She sips a sepia-colored liquid from a short, crystal glass, her free hand pressed to the countertop as she leans upon it. She wears a stunning, cream-colored dressing robe, all silk and long, with deep red outlining the hems of the sleeves. Intricately designed florals of burgundy and deep purple cover the creamy fabric. All she wears beneath is a matching silk red nightgown. Her jet-black hair, which matches her brother's, falls in pin straight pieces over one shoulder, shiny and clean and perfectly styled.

From her manner of dress, I gather that it's either late at night or early in the morning. There are no windows in the basement, so time is evasive. Given that she's drinking liquor rather than coffee, I'm guessing it's nighttime.

Vigo appears beside me and shuts the metal door, hiding it behind the hinged drywall as Renata greets me.

"Anya. I suppose I should say *welcome*. Are you behaving better these days? How long have you been with us now?"

I cast my shadowed eyes sideways toward where Vigo stands, my heart racing, wondering if I should respond, if I'm *supposed* to respond. It's the first time I've been upstairs since my arrival and I don't know the rules.

That makes me unsettled more than anything else.

"You may speak when spoken to," Vigo tells me as he shifts, pressing up against my backside.

His lips brush my shoulder casually as if we know each other, as if we are a couple.

Carefully, I respond to Renata, "Yes. I've been here several weeks, I think."

"Four weeks," Vigo clarifies.

His hand lands on my hip and he leans into me. I lurch forward with a gasp, my back arching to get away from him, but he harshly grabs both hips and yanks me back.

Taking a sip of her drink, Renata asks with a smug look on her face, "And how is your ankle healing?"

"Better," I say tersely. "Thank you."

Renata looks sharply down beside her. "Stop eating, Luca, that's enough. Up."

I jerk back in surprise as a young man rises from the floor behind the island next to Renata. I recognize him immediately.

It's the same shirtless, bronze-skinned, black-haired man who brings us our food and drink each day. She called him Luca. He always wears the black collar around his neck, but now there's a long, black leash attached to the C-ring at his throat. My eyes follow the leash to its end, finding that it's held in Renata's hand resting on the countertop. The young man wipes his mouth with the back of his hand as he stands, and Renata reaches out to scruff her hand through his hair.

I swallow hard, trying to take in all that I'm seeing, but I'm struggling to process. They behave as if everything that's happening is normal, just another day with the Vittoris. The collared boy seems almost content with the way he reacts, leaning into Renata's touch, dipping to press his lips to the curve of her neck.

Renata's smug grin widens as she returns her attention to me. "Do you think you will ever dance again? Pity what happened to you. The blond boy that Nikolai selected to dance with you so brilliantly showcased your talents. I thought he was quite appealing."

I don't speak at the reminder of Ezra, I just nod. I wish I could tell her that I *can* dance, that I *have* been dancing in my box, that I *will* dance for real again someday. But it would only come out of me with an Ezra-style snarky retort which most likely will get me in trouble so, I bite my tongue.

She turns to face her leashed slave as his lips dip down toward her collarbone. "I hope you two have a lovely evening," she says as she digs her fingers in his hair, lifting his head and letting him kiss her.

Is the Vittori island on another planet entirely?

Standing here in my child-like blue dress, watching a collared slave boy kiss his female master…It hurts my head to think about how bizarre and awful these people are.

And what bizarre thing does Vigo have planned for me?

Vigo puts his hands on my shoulders and pushes me forward, guiding me toward the arched opening up ahead on our left, leading out of the kitchen. Just as well, I feel like I'm in shock trying to understand what kind of rabbit hole of depravity I've fallen into.

Vigo shuffles me toward the staircase in the entryway. "Up you go."

I climb slowly, cautiously holding onto the metal railing that curves with the staircase, up and up to the balcony landing above.

Another mountain I've climbed and survived.

He guides me through the arched opening and leads me down a hallway to our right. We pass several doors, some open, some closed, some that are silent, some that carry voices speaking in Italian, a language I don't understand. Finally, we come to a stop.

Another keypad to gain entry. He unlocks and opens the door.

I start to suck in a deep breath to steel myself against whatever is about to happen to me in this room, but I only suck it in halfway before his hands slam against my back and shove me forward. I falter, stumbling past the threshold, but somehow manage to stay on my feet.

I whip back around to face him. I don't want to have my back turned to him anymore.

I back away as I watch him shut the door and he engages another lock from the inside with another pin. This one is meant to lock me *in* with him. I can't just turn the knob and run.

My heart is racing far too fast to process anything other than the fear for the unknown. Vigo stares at me, honey-brown eyes pulsing lasers that burn across my skin.

He licks his bottom lip and my body clenches unpleasantly, wanting to curl in around itself, wrap into a ball, and hide away from him in a dark corner.

He points to a spot behind me. "Sit. Brush out your hair."

What?

I look where he's pointing. Beside two windows covered with thick, brown curtains, I see a small vanity against the wall. It has a cream- and tan-marbled tabletop and it sits beneath a rectangular mirror on the wall.

On the marble tabletop there's a wooden jewelry box beside what is perhaps the most elegant-looking hairbrush I've ever seen—silver-plated and carved with some sort of raised design that I can't see from where I'm standing. A small cushioned stool rests in front of the vanity, inviting me to sit.

I move cautiously, casting my eyes back and forth to watch his movements until I reach the seat. I lower onto the stool and catch his eyes through the mirror as he approaches from behind.

His command was clear. I know what he expects me to do, so I don't bother questioning the odd request to brush out my hair.

I hear Nikolai's voice in my mind. *Good slaves don't ask questions, they just do.*

In a strange way, his voice is a comfort, only because it reminds me of a time when I knew the rules and the consequences for breaking them, a time when I understood.

I don't understand this newness with Vigo and his odd family.

I pick up the handle of the silver-plated brush and examine the backside of it. I draw my fingers over the elegant swirled floral design within the chrome. The bristles are soft, the color of wheat.

"Brush," he barks, and I jump from the unexpected

harshness of his tone.

"*Sì, Papà*," I nearly gag on the words.

The words he wants in response to his commands make me sick, but I'm thankful for the clarity, a rule I'm capable of following.

I shake out my long, tangled hair, letting it fall over my shoulders, and I begin to brush. There are knots and I have to pull the soft bristles through with some force.

I brush and brush until my hair is soft and sleek and smooth, until he tells me to stop. He approaches my side and reaches out to open the wooden jewelry box, pulling out a pair of elastic hair ties and two lengths of white, silky ribbon.

"Part your hair," he begins, and I lift my eyes to meet his in the mirror. "Tie each side just below your ears."

Pigtails.

Oh, God.

He really does want me to look like a child.

My chest heaves with a heavy breath and I swallow hard. I reach to pick up one of the elastic ties. I gather half of my hair together over one shoulder and tie it off with the elastic just beneath my ear, exactly as Vigo had instructed. I do the same with the other side.

"Tie on the ribbons," he says, and my hands shake as I reach for one.

With trembling fingers, I wrap the ribbon over the elastic, looping and tying it into as neat of a bow as I can manage, then I repeat it on the other side.

Looking at my reflection kickstarts my pulse.

The pigtails.

The innocent white bows.

The childish blue dress.

The cap sleeves that puff out in a juvenile way.

He's dressing me up to look like a goddamn child.
A doll.

The words that I said to him my first night here, before he left me to sleep with a dead body, bounce from dark corner to dark corner in my mind.

You're sick.
You're sick.
You're sick.

His eyes watch me in the mirror as I take in my reflection. *Can he hear how loudly my mind screams those words at him? You're sick!*

He's proud to have me think of him as a sick bastard. It's written all over his face with an arrogant smirk. He turns and walks to an ornate dresser on the other side of the room, near the door.

I swivel on my seat to look out at the space, taking in my surroundings with a rapidly beating heart. There's a king-sized bed to my right, neatly made with a comforter that looks more like a golden weaved tapestry. A short, tufted bench sits at the foot of the bed, resting on top of the massive, Oriental-style rug that's plush beneath my bare feet. Everything in the room is shades of gold and tan, an otherwise expected looking bedroom in a mansion of this size.

Vigo comes back to me carrying a pair of white socks. "Put these on."

I reluctantly take the socks from him, holding his gaze with my wary eyes.

"You know I've wanted you for years, Anya."

The statement freezes me, but I don't respond. I just bend and slip one sock on over my toes, rolling it up over my calf until it stops just below the knee.

He groans and I gag.

"When Nikolai let me use you as payment for my information about who killed his family, I knew I had to have you in my collection. Such a beautiful little doll. *La mia bambola Russa.* I've fantasized about you since that night."

I slip on the second sock and slowly lift, sitting up straight with a bowed head.

"Stop being such a good little girl," he snaps.

What?

"You're not a good little girl at all, are you?"

"I don't—"

"Don't talk back to me."

"I'm not—"

"Get up."

I stand, my forehead wrinkling in confusion. I don't understand the game he's playing.

What are the rules?

How do I follow them?

I don't know this dance, these steps, this performance.

How do I survive this?

He steps forward, suave and sleek in his pressed black slacks, crisp white button-up, and silk black tie. He grabs me by both shoulders, yanking me up to stand and whirling me around so he can sit on the stool instead. He lets go of me and begins to roll up his sleeves.

His eyes burn a hole through me. "Turn around. Lift your skirt."

I hesitate.

Suddenly, I feel more vulnerable and exposed than I've ever been. I've felt my fair share of exposure and vulnerability at Nikolai's hands, but fuck, everything here feels so wrong.

Wrong.

Wrong!

You're sick!

I spin around slowly, putting my back to him as he switches from one sleeve to the other. My fingertips brush my skin as I grasp the hem of my dress, lifting it slowly. Inch by inch, I expose my bare ass to him.

He lets out a low moan behind me and my gut rolls.

"Bend over."

Just do as you're told.

I bend.

His hands land on my hips, his thumbs rubbing circles on my cheeks.

"Tell *Papà* how naughty you've been."

"I don't understand what you want from me."

I yelp, wobbling in his hold as teeth sink into my ass, not playfully, but hard and bruising.

Nikolai's done that before. If this is all this will be, if all I have to do is serve as the unwilling subject for Vigo to play out his sick sexual fantasies with, then I can do this. I can survive this. I've done it for years before with Nikolai.

Except…

There was something about the way Nikolai wanted me as *me*, rather than a doll without a name, a fantasy, that somehow makes that seem as though it were reasonable.

Reasonable?

Nothing in my life is fucking reasonable.

Vigo's tongue runs over the deep bite and my muscles clench against it. He pulls back and a hand releases my hip to slap me there instead, making me shriek.

"Tell me," he says again. "Tell me you've been a naughty little girl who needs to be punished."

My lips purse, refusing to form the words, but his fingertips dig hard into my hip bones.

"I've been bad, *Papà*."

He growls, "*Sei una cattiva ragazza.*"

What did he say?

Should I respond?

Is that a command?

A question?

I don't speak fucking Italian!

I say the only thing I can think of that might appease him. "*Sì, Papà.*"

He responds with a heated groan and pulls me backward, forcing me to sit on his lap. His erection presses into my ass from beneath his tented trousers.

"I'm going to punish you." He kisses the back of my neck at the base of my spine using lips and tongue. "Does that scare you, little doll?"

My brain is screaming at him, wondering what the hell I'm supposed to say. I don't know what he wants. I don't know if he wants me to be scared or excited or some strange mixture of the two. I don't know if he wants me to fucking crawl like a baby and suck my goddamn thumb.

What do you want from me?

He brings his lips to my ear over one of my pigtails. "You don't need to be scared, little one. *Papà* only punishes you to make you better. Get down on your hands and knees."

I obey, more than happy to separate my ass from his erection. He adjusts my skirt to flip it all the way above my hips, ensuring all my private parts are on full view for him. It's quiet for a few stressful breaths, but then his hand lands with a smack against my cheek. I rock forward on the impact, but quickly readjust, knowing more spanks are to come.

And they do come, one after another after another.

But it's truly nothing for me, given all that I've been

through. He hasn't hit me all that hard and he stops rather quickly. I'm beginning to think Vigo might be survivable, but I know getting my hopes up too soon would be stupid.

"Tell me how sorry you are. Beg for forgiveness."

I swallow. "I'm so sorry, *Papà*. Please forgive me."

"Is that how you beg? With your back to me?"

I stifle a sigh, pushing back to sit on my heels. I take a quick moment to brush my skirt back down to cover myself before turning to face him. I scoot toward him on my knees.

"I'm sorry, *Papà*."

He grips my chin and tilts my head up, forcing our eyes to meet. "Beautiful little doll of mine, you know I don't want to hurt you."

I try to play his game to appease him, but I have to force the words out, stagnant and unfeeling. "I know, *Papà*. I'm sorry. I'll be a good girl."

God, how this nauseates me.

Vigo leans forward, pressing a soft kiss to my lips.

He lingers with his mouth on mine.

I watch him warily with open eyes and I'm surprised that his remain open, too; he's watching me just as carefully. There is a certain something in his uniquely honey-colored eyes that could easily set off a spark of attraction, a false feeling of trust with the allure of his good looks. He's a beautiful predator designed by the devil himself to tempt his prey with his charming good looks.

Just as I was tempted away from the world I knew by Nikolai.

Fuck, I hate him!

I hate them both!

I finally realize he's not holding me in place, so I yank my head back with force, angrily breaking the odd kiss that twisted a shameful pinch of lust in my belly.

Maybe I am just a whore like Nikolai says.

I don't deserve Ezra's love.

"Why don't you go and play with your rabbit, sweet girl?"

Vigo tilts his head toward the window beside us and I follow his eyes. I'm surprised I didn't notice it before, though I really didn't notice much of anything when I first walked in. There's an oversized, pink stuffed rabbit resting on the floor between the windows.

"You want me to…play with the rabbit." I'm careful to speak it as a statement, not as a question.

He grins at me and whispers, "Yes, go play. Crawl to your bunny."

I do as he tells me, getting back down on all fours. I crawl the short distance to the rabbit and sit back on my heels, lifting the plush toy from the rug. I look back at him over my shoulder, my eyes searching for some hint that I'm doing what I'm supposed to be doing. He gives me nothing but smoldering, sickening heat.

I look away quickly, glancing down at the bunny the size of a cocker spaniel in my grip. I have no idea what he wants me to do. I'm trying to sort out what this kind of fantasy entails with little direction from him. I think he must want to see me like a child playing with her toys, but I don't know if I can do this.

As sick as it makes me, I know this schoolgirl fantasy isn't all that uncommon. I should be able to do this. As far as the world of sex slavery goes, this is nothing more than a fetish, a kink.

I should be able to do this.

But then, the simplicity of this makes me wonder why the girls in the boxes beside mine fought Vigo so hard when he'd come to take them. They were *desperate* not to go with him. It makes me wonder why the woman who called my box hers before me was so willing to slit her throat and end her life the second the opportunity presented itself.

On the surface, this looks like nothing more than a fantasy, but as Vigo comes up behind me, the pulse of his aura tells me this isn't it—this fantasy isn't the thing the other girls fear.

There's something more coming.

My fingers dig into the velvety fur of the pink rabbit as my spine tingles in fearful anticipation.

"You love that pink bunny so much, don't you?"

My muscles tense. "*Si, Papà.*"

"How much do you love it?"

My brow furrows. "I…love it very much *Papà.*"

"Show your bunny how much you love it."

I hesitate for a moment and then bring the stuffed animal close, hugging it to my chest like a child would.

Is this what he wants?

"Yes, you love that toy so much. Why don't you give it a kiss?"

Odd.

So fucking odd.

I give the bunny a quick kiss on the nose.

He lets out a long, heated breath and out with it comes his sickness, rushing out into the room, swirling all around me, coiling me in its sinister hold.

"Now fuck it."

CHAPTER 12

Anya

"WHAT?" THE QUESTION shoots from my lips.

"Fuck it," he repeats. "Wrap your legs around it and fuck it. Rub your clit on it until you come."

Oh.

No.

No, no, no, no, no.

I know I can't say *no* to him for fear of how he'll hurt me if I do, but I can't do what he's asking me to do.

I won't do it.

I *won't.*

My head shakes back and forth, urgent in my protest, as he comes up behind me. He slips down to his knees, scoots in close, molding his body to my backside. My fingers squeeze around the bunny, drawing into tight fists through my agitation.

Vigo reaches around me, his hands clamping down on my wrists where I grasp the toy in my clenched fists. He pushes down, trying to force my hands and the bunny between my legs.

For the first time in a long time, I refuse. I absolutely, unwaveringly refuse to obey this order.

"No!" I shout, opening my fingers in hopes of dropping it. But his hands slide quickly over mine, lacing our fingers together, forcing me to grab hold of the stuffed toy as he shoves. I clamp my thighs together so he has nowhere to go but my lap. Vigo is so much stronger than me, though... forceful. He wiggles the toy as he presses, somehow managing to wedge the damn thing between my clamped thighs. He's got just enough of an opening to thrust it down hard between my legs.

I spread my knees apart, hoping he'll let go and it will fall, giving me a chance to toss it away.

But he doesn't let go.

He grips my fingers tighter, digging our hands into the bunny as he takes advantage of my spread knees, forcing it harshly against my naked sex. I lean backward, trying to get away from it, but his body is rigid, unyielding at my back. With my fingers still locked with his, he rubs the toy harshly against me.

"That's it. Fuck it, Anya. Fuck that bunny you love so much. Show Daddy how much you love it."

"Stop!"

My movements are frantic. I push my hands down harder, trying to break from his grip. I lean my body back, pushing against his.

I want this to stop, I want this plush, velvety symbol of innocent childhood far away from my sex. It's such a depraved thing he's forcing me to do, and it's all the more heinous that my stupid body could possibly have any response to any touch that doesn't belong to Ezra.

But it fucking does...and I couldn't be more ashamed.

My ass is held against his crotch as he holds me tighter against him, as I try to slip backward away from the bunny. He uses that to his advantage, and he begins to rock. He rocks our hips together, rolling them slowly forward and back, all the while holding the toy between my legs.

And no matter how much I hate it, no matter how I try

to fight this—to keep my body from responding and my mind safe from this nightmare—my body responds traitorously.

Wetness rushes to my core and my clit swells as his forceful rubbing turns to gentle rocking on the toy jammed between my thighs.

"Please, stop," I beg, though my voice loses its strength, it's determination, as he draws unwanted pleasure.

"Stop? Which part do you want me to stop? The way I'm moving you?" His lips fall to the side of my neck, beneath one of my pigtails. "Or the way I'm pleasing you? Tell *Papà* what you want."

"I...I want you to stop. All of it."

Weak.

I'm fucking weak.

My voice, my willpower, my sexual need.

I'm weak with all those things and I've never felt so deeply, brokenly ashamed of myself.

Except, I *have* felt this deeply, brokenly ashamed before. It was when Ezra had first arrived at Mikhailov Manor. When Nikolai fingered me in front of him, told me to come, but stopped before I could, just to humiliate me and leave me wanting. I'd felt shame then for the way my body responded to Nikolai's touch, for the way I tried so hard to get there, to come, to find my release simply because he'd wanted me to.

But Ezra had been turned on by the show of it, too. He'd always been turned on by the way Nikolai used me simply because our bodies are human, and they don't always react in the way we want them to.

I'm fed up with this nightmare, with letting other men control what my body does and doesn't do. I'm tired of responding because they make me respond. But if my body is going to take over anyway, if my body is going to let me feel pleasure from this sickness, then maybe I should just let it. Maybe if I let it, I'll take some of my power back.

I force my mind to jump the hurdle of shame and give the fuck in.

This is my life now.

No more Nikolai.

No more Ezra.

No more Ezra?

That thought fuels an indignant fire in my chest, burning through the barrier of my ribcage and ripping deep down into my belly. I let the blaze take over, my stomach clenching and drawing wanting into my swollen, aching pussy.

"You want me to fuck it?" I hardly recognize the sound of my voice, rising to a pitch of hysteria. "Then let me go and watch me fuck it."

He releases my fingers, though his hands only draw as far back as my wrists, resting there lightly. He stops rocking, but I take over for the both of us. Clamping my thighs around the stupid pink bunny, I roll my hips, holding it in place with my hands so my clit can rub against the soft surface.

"Tell *Papà* how you feel."

"Dirty." It was the sad, sorry truth.

"You feel like a dirty little girl?"

"*Sì, Papà.*"

"Don't stop, dirty girl."

His hands slide backward along my arms, though his body stays in place, his hips moving with me as mine rock. I'm thoroughly disgusted with myself, but I'm taking my fucking power back. He's gonna make me do this, like it or not, so I'll let myself like it because I have nothing else.

He pulls his hands away and I feel him shift behind me. At first, I think he's unbuckling his pants, but that's not what happens. He's shifted his body so that he's leaning a bit toward the left and he holds my hip with his left hand. I don't know where his right hand is.

Probably on his dick.

Though, I know it's not on his dick because I feel his hardness against the small of my back.

"Take a look at this…" I hear him say as I rock and rub. "Daddy's little doll. Sweet and dirty and aching for it. Do you like it, doll?"

"*Si, Papà,*" I hiss with sarcasm on a whisper.

I'm determined, so fucking determined to relieve this ache in my body. It's the ache of everything I've been through, everything that's been done to me, everything that's to come. It's the ache of finding hope, finding love with Ezra and having it ripped away from me so callously. It's the ache of knowing I may not see him again…

"Come on, Anya, get there."

Tears spring to my eyes and I shout at him, though I continue to defile this stupid toy. "Shut up, shut the fuck up!"

He lets me go and leaves me there, stepping back, and I know he's just standing there, watching me as I writhe like a whore, fucking for nothing more than a quick, fleeting release.

It coils in my pussy, throbbing, pulsing, screaming at me to rut and fuck and claim my release. It builds and builds before it crests and I feel the familiar break, the crippling tension just before, then the exploding release of an orgasm.

But it doesn't feel the same.

It doesn't feel good.

There's not an ounce of that pleasurable feeling through my clit. All I feel is a flood of painful emotion rushing through the released tension in my muscles with the absolutely ruined orgasm.

I remain powerless.

There was never any power for me to take back.

"Very nice, Anya, well done."

I whip my head to look at Vigo, tears painting stripes down my cheeks as fresh tears rush behind them to fill my eyes to the brim. But even through the sheen of liquid, I can see what he's doing. He's got his smart phone in his hands and he's holding it up, recording me.

"Anything you want to say to Nikolai? Or perhaps that slave boy you seem to have affection for? Maybe Nikolai will show it to him if you ask nicely."

Vigo laughs and it's filled with the black evil in his heart. My eyes narrow on him, my breaths are hard and shallow, my muscles burn to hit and kick and hurt him.

I jump to my feet and leap after him, knocking the phone from his hands, and it tumbles to the floor. As he bends to reach for it, I bring my knee up, hoping to catch him hard in the gut, but it's barely a nudge.

His hands latch around my wrists and he pushes them wide apart, dragging them down to our sides, bringing them together again in front of us. He puts both of my wrists in one of his large hands and grips the back of my neck with the other. He drags me close, pressing his forehead to mine as he bends down over me.

I'm held firm in his grasp, though I'm not done fighting him yet. I kick at his ankles, but he only chuckles as he burns me with the intensity of his gaze. I keep my eyes locked on his, determined not to give him my submission.

"Now there's that fight. I was wondering what happened to it."

I snarl, suddenly ravenous to hurt him as I try to thrash my wrists from his hold. "I know how to pick my battles."

"You've chosen the wrong battle," he says with a grin.

In one motion, he takes me down to the floor. He falls forward on top of me, causing my knees to buckle. My ass hits the ground first as he comes down on top of me, and the air is knocked free from my lungs as my back and head fall back against the carpet. I thrash my legs, wiggling, squirming, fighting to get out from under him, but he's relentless.

He's nothing like Nikolai.

Nikolai would punish me when I fell out of line. He would hurt me in his anger for my disobedience, but he did it to teach me a lesson. Normally, he took care of me afterward, or at least made sure I had what I needed to care for myself.

But this…Vigo forcing me to fuck a child's toy while he records it is just ruthless, reasonless debasement without any justification.

But Nikolai wasn't justified in hurting me, either.

What is wrong with my twisted mind?

With that same demonic grin, Vigo pins me beneath him, his body heavy on mine, taking my breath away.

"Take out my cock," he tells me, baring his teeth.

I shake my head. "No."

He bends, sucking my bottom lip between his teeth and clamping down *hard* until I scream from the pain of his blood-drawing bite.

"Take it out or I'll do that to your fucking nipple."

I huff, moving my hands between us to unbuckle his belt, part his zipper, and push down his slacks and underwear just enough to expose him. The moment it's out, he plunges inside me. It's as though his intrusion takes up too much space and forces my tears out to make room.

He fucks me hard and fast as I quietly cry beneath him. It's not about the pleasurable feeling of getting off for him, it's about controlling me, having that power over me. That's what he wants.

Any power I thought I could take back from selfishly and filthily seeking my own release has been sufficiently ripped from me.

He comes inside me with a grunt and a groan and that fucking smug grin. The mess of his ejaculation inside my body makes me want to scream and so, I do, like a mad woman.

I scream as he chuckles, gets to his feet, and tucks his cock safely behind his trousers again.

"Come with me." He easily returns to calm and collected, so unlike Nikolai. "You're a filthy, disgusting, slutty little mess. Let *Papà* give you a bath."

I stand naked and shivering in Vigo's en suite bathroom as he lets the clawfoot tub fill with lukewarm water.

The tan tile is chilly beneath my feet and the cold air whips around me like a wintry breeze. My pigtails are still in place with white ribbons, though haphazard pieces have fallen free and the back has matted and tangled from being fucked by Vigo on the floor of his bedroom.

Vigo dips a hand into the water when the tub is nearly full and turns off the faucet.

"It's ready, climb on in."

I glare at him, my arms crossed over my chest, trying to keep the warmth in. I don't want to get in that tub. I know that once I get into that tub, something terrible is going to happen and I don't want to know what it is.

"You can get in on your own or I can put you in. Your choice."

As if that's even a choice.

I step forward with hesitancy. I carefully lift my foot from the floor and sink it beneath the water's surface. Instant panic strikes my chest and I step back out, backing away.

I think Nikolai has done well giving me a healthy fear of water.

Vigo turns to me and plucks me from the floor with ease. He grips me by the waist with his two large hands and I naturally grab hold of his wrists, though I don't know if it's to push him away or to hold myself steady.

He whips me around and carries me to the tub. He's so tall and strong that he easily gets my feet above the tub's edge before I can protest. I kick mid-air, trying to grip the rounded edge with my toes, but he plops me down in the water with a splash before I can find purchase.

The whoosh of the water as it splashes with my landing, the feel of it rapidly rising from feet to knees prompts me into a fearful stillness. I stand, shivering and trembling harder than before, terrified to sit, terrified to put my face any closer to this substance that could drown me.

"Sit," he orders. All I can do is shake my head. "*Sit.*" His tone is sharper and he places his hands on my shoulders.

My fingers jump to fight him off, my eyes widening at the trigger that makes me feel as though he's going to push me beneath the surface—the way Nikolai had done three times before in the pool at Mikhailov Manor.

"Sit or I'll make you sit," he warns with an even tone. He removes his hands from my shoulders in a show of good faith.

Still, all I can do is shake my head and shiver.

He steps back and tilts his head coolly. "*Papà* only wants to give you a bath. You're filthy. Don't you want to feel clean again?"

He's baiting me to sit in the water and the bait he's dangling is inviting. I feel disgusting and want nothing more than to cleanse myself of every trace of him. Though my brain begs me to keep my head as far from the water as possible, my body forces me to bend. I slowly lower, taking sharp and shallow breaths as my body fights with my mind, tripping the wire of anxiety to a point of distress.

Tears are falling again, but somehow, I've managed to do the impossible—I'm sitting in a tub full of water. Though my hands grip the edges of the tub so hard my knuckles are white, my breaths are quick and my heart is racing, I'm sitting in the water.

With his sleeves rolled up, Vigo flips his black tie over his shoulder so it's not dangling in front of him. Dripping soap onto his hands from the bottle of wash beside him where he kneels on the tile, he dips his hands beneath the surface and I flinch. The water pulses, rolling out and back toward me as I move. My breath catches in my throat and I hold back a sob.

"I'm just cleaning you," he says with a smile, as if that should make everything better.

I try to steady my breathing through clenched teeth as his hands slide between my thighs. My eyes are wide, though I wish I could press them closed and find a safe space in my mind.

He gropes under the guise of cleansing me, though I'm feeling anything but clean as his fingers dance in and out of my pussy, circling around in-between my crack.

But then he stands, yanking his hands from the water so swiftly that I let out a scream as it splashes across my face, a droplet landing on my eyelash. I see him turn away, but when my panic sinks in, I can't care about what he's doing. I throw myself backward, away from the spray and start to push to my feet.

But Vigo is back at me in a flash.

He's there before I can shift my hands back along the edges of the tub to push off. I see his sinister smile as he spins around to face me, but I don't see the needle coming toward me until it's too late. Before I can find the strength to climb from the tub, he plunges the syringe that came from nowhere into the side of my neck .

"What did you do?" I demand to know as he tosses the syringe behind him onto the floor haphazardly. "What is that? What *is* it?"

Almost instantly the awareness of my sense of touch begins to fade.

Am I still gripping the edge?

I look at my hands to see that I am, though I can't really feel it. Then I see my fingers loosen, slowly losing their grip. I snap my head to look at him where he kneels beside me, his forearms leaning against the tub's edge, his chin resting on his arms, his head tilted, watching me with curiosity and amusement.

Sick amusement.

He speaks to me as if we're two old chums having a friendly conversation. "It's a paralytic agent. It's a fascinating drug. It freezes you inside yourself. Within a minute or two, you'll lose the ability to control your body. You won't be able to move. Completely paralyzed and at my mercy and it will last for *hours*. But here's the fun part. You'll remain conscious and awake and aware the entire time. Your eyes will stay open, unless I choose to press your lids closed, though I can't think of a reason why I would want to do that, *la mia bambola Russa.*"

Panic has taken hold of me entirely. My grip is weakening. My body is slipping. I open my mouth to speak, but I don't know if it opens. I try to scream, but no sound comes out. I'm slipping, slipping, sinking in the water.

"Before he sold you to me, Nikolai disclosed that he used water as a serious punishment for serious offenses and that it was quite effective with you. Disclosure of such things is standard in the paperwork when selling a slave, you understand. So, of course, I thought, *what a fun game that would be to play with you, Anya.* You didn't think I'd only play daddy with you and send you on your merry way, did you? Of course, you didn't. As you so rightly observed your first night here, *I'm sick.* It's true and I fucking love it. In moments, you'll become a real living doll and I will break your mind in ways you never imagined possible."

Slip.

Slip.

Slip.

My body drifts.

I fight to keep my head above water.

I thrash with every ounce of strength I can muster, but the water remains still. It's still and clear as my chin dips in. There's a ripple across the surface as my hands finally fall free from the side and drop into the water. My lips go under.

Somehow I'm able to remember to take a deep breath, inhaling through my nose, as I dig deep to my final reserves. I fight the paralyzing drug for one last moment, one last breath before my nose slips beneath the surface.

Vigo reaches one hand out above the water and waves at me, a demented grin plastered to his face. Then my eyes fall under, welcoming a rush of soapy water that stings.

I'm under.

I'm under and I can't move.

I'm under and I can't breathe.

I'm under and I can't fight, can't save myself.

I can't even close my eyes.

I have to watch above me as the distorted image of Vigo

leans over the water, watching me with an amused expression.

Pull me out!

Pull me out!

Pull me out!

I'm helpless.

God.

Please.

Pull me out!

I know I can make it to twelve. Twelve counts of eight before I slip into unconsciousness. It's all I can do—count. I can't fight, I can't scream. All I can do is drive myself mad with panic or force myself to focus and count, give my mind a task to take it from this madness.

One. Two. Three. Four. Five. Six. Seven. Eight.

One. Two. Three. Four. Five. Six. Seven. Eight.

One. Two. Three. Four. Five. Six. Seven. Eight.

I internally scream out in relief as Vigo's hands ripple the surface, slip beneath my head, and scoop me out of the water. My lungs scramble to take in air through my nose—I can't even part my lips to gasp. He lets me go again and I slide under.

One. Two. Three. Four. Five. Six. Seven. Eight.

One. Two. Three. Four. Five. Six. Seven. Eight.

He drops in a washcloth and presses it over my face, covering my eyes, my nose, my mouth.

Now I know why the other girls fought so hard to remain in their boxes in the basement. I know why the girl in my box had chosen her own death so easily. This isn't a punishment for poor behavior. This is nothing more than torture for torture's sake.

And like a hammer to a porcelain doll, he's going to shatter my mind into a million irreparable pieces.

CHAPTER 13

NIKOLAI

I LEAN BACK in my chair, letting my head fall back and my eyes drift shut. I try to relax and enjoy the feel of Sasha's pretty lips around my cock, but her softness simply isn't the same. She may have the same brown hair, dark eyebrows, and feminine frame as Anya, but she doesn't suck like her, doesn't taste like her, fuck like her, feel like her.

I comb my fingers into Sasha's hair at the back of her skull, grip firmly, and yank her head back. Her lips break free of my cock with a pop that's more annoying than satisfying. She looks up at me with puppy dog brown eyes, wanting to please her master and wondering how she's failed.

She's a weak piece of ass that I've already grown bored with. Still, my dick is hard. If I could just find a way to shut up the gnawing voice of my dead father, the voice who tells me that I'm an ambivalent, pansy-ass, pretty boy, then I could do what I really want to do and fuck *his* mouth.

I glance over at Ezra, who is fuming in the armchair beside mine in my bedroom. His knee bounces with his anxiety. He's a ball of furious energy that's constantly on the verge of exploding, especially when I force him to sit and watch as I do terrible things to Sasha.

I haven't involved him in the ways I did when Anya was here. I can't say for sure why. Perhaps it's because of Sasha. She's a weak little girl, eager to please. She fell into servitude so quickly and so easily that it has honestly put me off.

Anya was obedient and submissive, she followed my commands and aimed to please, but it wasn't for some delusion that she could make me fall in love with her. Sasha's eyes told me she was a hollow shell of a young woman with daddy issues; a girl who would crawl on her knees and beg for an ounce of affection.

Anya would crawl and beg, too, but it was for survival, not desire.

Fuck.

Sasha speaks to me in Russian, the only language she knows. She apologizes to me and offers me her pussy. She fucking *offers* it, just affirming to me that all women are sluts and whores.

Ezra's arms are crossed over his broad chest, a permanent scowl etched to his face, and his eyes are narrowed on the flames blazing in my fireplace. Fuck, I want to wipe that look off his face with my cock shoved in his mouth. But there's a buzz inside me, a painful vibration that ticks up every time I start thinking about how much I want him, and it shakes me right back to reality with my father's voice, the words that have haunted me for years.

Ambivalent.

Pansy-ass.

Pretty boy.

I toss Sasha away by the hair and she catches herself on her palms. She looks up at me with questions in her eyes, wondering what she's done wrong. It's pointless for her to question because she can't fix her failure. Her failure is simple—she's not Anya.

I tell her to get on all fours so I can fuck her from behind without having to look at her face, but my cell phone pings and buzzes in my back pocket, distracting me. Once, twice, three times in a row the texts ping through—I should've turned it off before I started fucking my slave's mouth.

I shift in my seat, reaching behind me to pull my phone from my back pocket. I look at the screen and narrow my eyes in curiosity.

I've got three new messages from Vigo Vittori.

We're not exactly friends, so this is unusual. Given that I sold him my girl a little over a month ago, the prickling on the back of my neck tells me this has something to do with her.

Not 'my girl.'

My slave.

I sold him my slave.

My thumb twitches, hovering over the screen as the thought of her death flashes across my mind. If he's killed her, there's no doubt in my mind he'd tell me about it. If he's killed her then…

Fuck.

I set my phone down on the side table between me and Ezra and shove my erection back into my pants. I stand, pat Sasha on the ass, and tell her to get the fuck out. Then, I pick up my phone and stride across to the far corner of my room beside the window.

The door closes behind Sasha as she leaves. There's no reason for doubt in my mind that she'll do anything but go right back to her room. It's so fucking pathetic the way she's bowed to me so quickly. I don't think I'd care if she offed herself or tried to escape into the wilderness.

I feel Ezra's eyes burning a hole in my back once she's gone. He wants to leave, too, and it's simply for that reason that

I make him stay while I open the messages Vigo has sent to me.

VIGO: Breaking in your girl. Thought you might enjoy this.

Below the text are two videos. The stills that show before I press play already have rage bubbling in my blood.

He knew it wasn't a choice for me.

He knew I'd have to watch.

Whatever vile things he's doing to her, they're no viler than what I've already done to her. There's one thing Vigo and I have always had in common—there's a sickness in our blood passed down through generations. It's a sickness shared by every member of the four families, dating all the way back to the four fathers who established our secret, conglomerate slave trade.

Those four villainous fathers had met by chance two centuries ago, fleeing their homelands against prosecution for the heinous, murderous crimes they had committed. They might have been some of the most prolific serial killers in history had the secret not been kept. But in their chance meeting, they chose to form a coalition, working together to evade charges of their various crime sprees by agreeing to provide alibis for each other in turn.

They were able to return to their homelands, build normal lives, breed children as depraved as they were, and the four families have carried on with the debauchery ever since. The partnership among the four fathers proved to be profitable for everyone. They quickly found themselves in the business of selling and trading human lives, which proved to be their most profitable and satisfying venture.

The descendants of those four fathers never stood a chance. *We were born sick.*

I rub my hand over my face, shake my head, and press play

for the first video.

It starts and my pulse thrums as Anya comes into the screen. She's on her knees, wearing a stupid blue dress that makes her look like a fucking child, and her hair is split into two ponytails, tied with ribbons. She's fucking—I narrow my eyes at the screen and then they widen in surprise.

She's fucking a goddamn child's toy.

Vigo is pressed up behind her, their bodies molded together, and he holds up his phone, high above their heads, angling it down to show them both rocking and grinding together. I didn't think to turn down the volume on my phone before clicking play so I get to hear their sordid dialogue.

"Take a look at this. Daddy's little doll. Sweet and dirty and aching for it. Do you like it, doll?"

"Si, Papà."

Ezra is leaping from his chair and running after me in a flash, practically stumbling across the room in his haste to get to me.

"That's Anya's voice. What is that?" he asks. "What the *fuck* is that?"

I growl at him, "Get on your knees, *mal'chik*. If I want you to see it, I'll show you."

He begrudgingly drops to his knees beside me, knowing that I'm his master and he'll obey immediately if he wants anything from me.

I'm still the goddamn king of this castle.

His bare chest heaves with the heavy breaths he's taking. Part of me wants to torture him by leaving him wondering. Part of me wants to torture him by showing him this video.

Either way, it will hurt him.

Hurting him makes me feel like I'm in control.

But the video continues.

Vigo is no longer rocking behind her, he's standing back, filming her fuck herself to completion on a toy. Then, she's looking at the camera, tears streaking down her pretty cheeks, and my gut rolls with something resembling nausea. It's an uneasy feeling I'm not accustomed to and don't really care for.

I flinch to see her launch herself at him so unexpectedly. She attacks him and the phone falls to the floor. Though all it manages to capture visually is the ceiling, it still records the sound.

Ezra falters, his shoulders rounding and slumping, one hand landing over his heart as the other presses down into one of his strong thighs, holding himself up lest he should crumble to the floor. He hears what I'm hearing, the sounds of Vigo and Anya struggling and fighting, exchanging words.

"Take out my cock."

"No."

"Take it out or I'll do that to your fucking nipple."

The sound of Vigo fucking her, coming inside her.

The sound of Anya letting out a single, sharp scream.

"Come with me. You're a filthy, disgusting, slutty little mess. Let Papà give you a bath."

That's where the first video ends. I run a shaking hand through my hair.

Why am I shaking?

This is what I wanted.

I sold her knowing he'd do this to her.

I click on the second video and stare at it for exactly five seconds before my hand opens inexplicably and my phone tumbles to the floor.

Anya underwater.

Her blue eyes wide and wild.

Motionless.

Drowning.

Ezra scrambles to grab my phone as Vigo says something on the clip about the fucking paralytic drug he's always used with his broken dolls. Anya is one of them now, because of me.

I pace away, not giving a shit that Ezra has picked up my phone, that he screams in pain seeing Anya underwater. I don't care when he clicks back to watch the first video. I don't flinch when he throws my phone at the wall and it crashes to the floor.

It's not necessary for me to punish him for touching my property. What he has seen on my phone is proving to be punishment enough.

He screams, his fingers digging into his hair as he curls forward on his knees, as if the heartache in his chest is a dense, dying star, pulling every other part of him toward its center as what he's seen slowly destroys him.

I should be glad.

It's what I wanted—to offload the bitch who betrayed my trust and fucked her pet when I gave her an inch of freedom for one fucking night. I wanted to hurt them both for hurting me so effectively, for her refusal to give me a spoonful of love for all the years I took care of her, for his refusal to look at me with anything other than hatred and disgust.

I don't need his disgust.

My father gave me enough to last a lifetime.

My throat gathers a lump. My heart pounds. My hands tremble. My eyes burn.

I don't know why, but suddenly I feel like I've made a mistake. *I don't make mistakes.*

I have to sit. I go back to my armchair and slowly lower. My elbows fall to my knees and my head falls into my hands.

"You did this." It's a quiet hiss of truth from Ezra after several quiet moments. "You did this to her. You sold her to a fucking sociopath, and he's going to ruin her in ways you never could've dreamed of."

I lift my head slightly from my hands, turning to look toward him. "Is that meant to compliment or insult me?"

"Neither." He chuckles behind a sob. "It's just the fucking truth."

"I know what I did."

"Do you? Do you really? Do you understand that you signed her death certificate when you sold her to that monster?"

"He's no more of a monster than I am," I try to convince the both of us.

"You're right," he concedes, his head bobbing lightly. "You're worse."

He pushes to his feet and my armor locks into place. I stand and square off with him as he steps toward me. I force a sneer, though I'm aching as much as he is.

I don't ache.

Nothing hurts me.

My father's voice echoes around me. *Ambivalent, pansy-ass, pretty boy.*

"You handed her over to him. Whatever happens to her now is your fault." His fists clench at his sides.

"Of course it is," I agree. "I own her, I choose what happens in her life."

"You don't own her anymore. He does!" Ezra shouts. He points a finger behind him through his outstretched hand, aiming toward where he left the phone, as if Vigo were standing there himself. "He chooses if she lives or dies now! He chooses if he hurts her, helps her, treats her like a fucking toy. And it's all because you weren't man enough to face the fact that she doesn't love you, doesn't want you. She knows how weak you really are. Beneath the orders and the threats, you're nothing, and she knew that."

I feel like a cornered wolf and that's how I behave. I bare my teeth at him, practically growling a warning at him before I attack. I rise from my chair and he stands as I swiftly move toward him. I slap both my palms against his chest and slam him hard against the wall behind him.

He flips his wrists between my arms, knocking my hands off, but I come right back, pressing my forearm against his neck. I shift my arm to jab my elbow into the hollow of his throat before he tries to throw me off again. I press in.

My face is an inch from his as I dig into the spot. "I'm not nothing. I am *everything*. Everything you wish you could be, everything she wishes she could come back to now. Maybe with Vigo, the bitch will understand how good she had it with me. I'm happy for her to live with the regret of her choices for the rest of her life."

"I don't even know how to respond to such bullshit. You're a bullshitting, motherfucking, son of a bitch, Nikolai. You're pathetic."

I tilt my head, pressing harder with my elbow. "What the fuck is wrong with you? You're a fucking slave. I can kill you and no one would care. Yet you still push and push and *fucking* push me."

Ezra's eyes narrow to slits and mine do the same as he snarls, "You took away the best thing that ever happened to me. I have nothing left to lose."

I'm rage filled.

Indignant.

My blood boils and hates and loathes.

And it pulses that shameful lust through my veins.

My mouth crashes on Ezra's before I even know what the hell I'm doing. I've taken him off guard and he stills, rigid in my hold as I press my lips to his. I kiss him long enough to inhale and exhale one trembling breath. Then I step back and whirl away from him, stalking across the room as he stands there in a stupor. I bend, pick up my phone from the floor, and type out a text on the newly cracked screen.

NIKOLAI: Bring her to the next quarterly meeting. I'll bring the boy. Let them torture each other with their pathetic longing. They deserve it.

CHAPTER 14

Anya

I'VE BEEN ONE of Vigo's broken dolls for a total of three months now. I only know this because I'm on my way to the next quarterly meeting of the four families as Vigo's escort.

The Campbells' estate is nestled and hidden away safely in the Louisiana bayou, somewhere near New Orleans. Though I'm told it doesn't belong to the Campbells anymore. The American family is now headed by the Leblancs—still descendants of the founding Campbell family by blood, but no longer by name. They'd given power to the son of a Campbell sister whose name had changed to Leblanc by marriage.

There was a reason females weren't allowed to be the Head of House for their family, and it was because they might marry off and change their names. It would be an upheaval to the family name that held its reputation with the powerful elite— from buyers and sellers, politicians and law enforcement. Of course, any logical person might ask why the women simply choose not to change their names when they marry. The only answer that would be given was that it's because of tradition.

Thus, this change from Campbell to Leblanc strikes me as unexpected. It's unusual—an uncharacteristically dramatic change in leadership. I don't know the details of why it happened or what it means or if it means anything at all.

Honestly, I couldn't care less.

The only thing I care about right now is the fact that I'm clean, fed, out of that godforsaken box with the ability to move and walk and talk. As Vigo's escort, I'm at least given the grace of being cared for enough to look decent for the Leblancs' talent and reception. I'm only ever out of the box when Vigo wants to play with me. That *always* means being drugged.

I suppose I should be grateful that he gives each of his dolls time enough to recover between doses, though recovery only involves wallowing in fear trapped inside a clear, plastic box.

In three months' time, he's stripped all substance from within me, leaving me a broken, hollow shell of a woman who wishes daily for the release of death.

I'm not entirely sure why Vigo is bringing me with him to this quarterly meeting. Having been stripped of my talent, I'm no longer considered a talent slave. Talent slaves travel with their family to the meetings, but I suppose I didn't really know what to expect belonging to the Vittoris. They're the only family who keeps multiple slaves in their home for themselves. I think they enjoy creating their own rules.

It's taken nearly two days to travel from Palermo to New Orleans with the stop off in Lisbon for fuel on the Vittoris' private jet. And with so many people on board, Vigo has managed to keep his cock in his pants.

There's Renata and her slave Luca, their younger cousin Lorenzo, and one of the family's talent slaves, a pianist named Olivia. She's the blond girl I remember seeing with Vigo and Renata at Nikolai's talent reception three months ago. She looks healthier now than she did then. I guess she used to belong to Vigo until Lorenzo took a liking to her.

Vigo's mostly ignored me on the flight, constantly staring

down at his phone. I'm glad for that because it keeps his interest off defiling me.

Much to Renata's dismay, we have to travel via airboat to get from the airstrip in Louisiana to the Leblancs' estate. It's hidden away and only accessible through the bayou.

Renata fusses with her long, black hair as the boat whirs forward, whipping it behind her. The boat scurries and splashes through the muddy water, and I take in the swampy air with gratitude. The brush of the wind over my cheeks feels divine. Renata has the privilege of snobbery, fussing over her tangled hair and ruined clothes. I hide a secret smile that the cream-colored Prada suit she was stupid enough to wear is spattered with mud.

She should've known better as she's been to the estate before. Why she would choose such impractical travel wear is beyond me. I didn't have a choice in my travel wear, but Vigo at least had the foresight for practicality, I suppose. He had given me the same skinny jeans and plain shirt I had worn the day he took me from Nikolai, though the jeans feel a little looser now.

We whip through the eerie bayou landscape where water has risen high, making the trees appear as though they were drowning. The dreamlike landscape—where we sail through a hazy, watery forest—almost feels magical, almost like freedom.

Almost.

The Leblancs' estate appears from the parting swamp fog like a haunted daydream. The home is tall, foundation high above the overflow of the water line. White columns run all the way across the square-shaped front profile of the estate. The spaces between the columns on the top floor are fenced with black lattice work, which match the black shutters around its many windows. The left and right sides of the home are set back a bit, framing the center square of the house, making it look proud and ostentatious.

There's a narrow, paved stone walkway leading from the dock where the airboat lets us off. It's another thing for Renata to fuss over when one of her stiletto heels gets caught between two uneven stones. She utters a string of Italian curse words, prompting a petty, almost normal looking argument between her and Vigo.

Vigo points at her feet when he speaks, shaking his head, presumably judging her choice of footwear. She yells back at him and eventually, he pockets his phone with a huff, going back to help her yank her shoe from between the pavers as she leans on Luca for support. I stand and wait for my masters to end their petty squabbling.

Renata, refusing to lose face again, removes both of her shoes and strides ahead of the group—fearlessly barefoot—toward the main entrance of the estate. It's a good fifty yards to walk to the entrance.

As we approach, we're greeted by an anxious looking man. He jogs down the front porch steps, watching his feet, pushing out a nervous breath from between rounded lips as he straightens the lapels of his navy-blue jacket.

His tousled, thick, blond hair reminds me of Ezra's. From a distance, I suffer a beat of hoping. But I quickly set aside any foolish ideas that Ezra might be here. Nikolai always brought me, not my partners, to the quarterly meetings with him. Though, I suppose Ezra must be his only slave now.

Unless he killed him, too.

I stop dead in my tracks at the thought, pressing a hand over my heart, pressing hard until I can feel the beat through my palm.

No one notices that I've halted, not right away, because we're slaves. We walk behind our masters.

The man from the house greets Renata first, holding out an outstretched hand, as she charges ahead. She doesn't take it. Instead, she leans in for him to kiss one cheek, then the other, in greeting.

"Vittoris," the blond man says. "Welcome!"

"Leo." Renata turns on her pleasant business persona. "How are you adjusting to becoming the new Head of House for the Leblancs?"

His brows lift and lower as he huffs out a breath and tilts his head. "About as well as you'd expect, I suppose. I didn't… Well, I didn't know much about the Campbells, er, their legacy, with the four families. The family trade. My mom never shared much and well, I understand now. So, here we are." He holds out his hands.

He looks far too young to be a Head of House.

He behaves far too anxiously to be a Head of House.

The others are Nikolai, Vigo, and Murphy O'Shea, each as ruthless, arrogant, and unambiguously sociopathic as the last. This man, Leo, is going to be eaten alive if he doesn't pull his shit together, and quick.

We're welcomed into the home and shown to our rooms. I'm to stay in a room with Vigo. The dark-gray space we're given feels as oppressive as it looks from the moment we cross the threshold. The four-post bed of the relatively small space is draped with off-white fabric. The hardwood floor beneath our feet creaks with each step, and the dark walls make it feel like a cave. There's a length of chain attached to an ankle cuff resting on the floor. The chain is secured to a metal loop that's been bolted down through the flooring next to the bed.

That chain is for me—to keep me locked up when my master attends the board meeting later.

Vigo asks me to shower and prepare for the talent and

reception that will begin in just a few hours. I'm both surprised and thankful that he gives me some time alone in the connected bathroom.

I'm also thankful there's no bathtub here, only a walk-in shower. The thought of him drugging me and tossing me into the swamp water still crosses my mind, making my heart skip a beat. I can only hope the events of this quarterly meeting will keep him occupied enough to spare me his torment. At least until we have to return to the Vittori mansion in Italy.

I sigh, shaking out my long, damp hair. I have a make-up bag full of unfamiliar products and I've been directed to make myself look presentable, though I don't really know what that means to the Vittoris. I knew how to prep when I belonged to a Mikhailov, but everything feels foreign now.

I look over at the dress Vigo has given me to wear this evening for the talent and reception. A floor-length, golden silk gown hangs on the back of the bathroom door. It's a beautiful dress, and a part of me looks forward to putting it on, to play dress-up, to pretend life is as good as the dress looks.

Digging through the make-up bag, I find a palette of eye shadow and decide upon subtlety. I brush on soft brown and shimmery gold eye shadow. I add a bronzing blush over my foundation to highlight my cheeks, and I choose a deep burgundy lipstick.

As I finish up my make-up, Vigo opens the bathroom door without warning and it startles me. He barges in, though I stand nude in front of the sink.

He looks me up and down. "This is a good look for you."

I swipe on another unnecessary layer of lipstick as I ignore him. I look the worst I have ever looked. I've lost weight since I've been in his care, weight I didn't need to lose. My body feels week. I haven't truly danced in months and my muscles have lost their strength such that every movement requires a great deal of effort. I used to move with such ease and now, I'm just a fragile little doll.

Vigo smacks my ass as he moves toward the toilet and undoes his zipper, standing just behind me as he relieves himself. I take my dress from the hook on the door and carry it into the bedroom, just to get away from him.

I put it on and move to the standing, full-length mirror in the corner of the room to look at my reflection. I can't help but see myself as a sickly, thin shell of the girl I used to be. The dress should cling nicely to my curves, but it hangs off me in places it shouldn't. The spaghetti straps keep slipping from my shoulders and I know I'll be fussing with them all night. At least my face looks like my own, though I'm starting to see the lines where my cheeks will hollow out if I lose any more weight.

If I broke this mirror, could I slice my throat open with one of the shards of glass before Vigo stops me?

The thought bursts into my mind with force. My breath catches in my throat and tears fill up my eyes because now I'm thinking about it.

I'm really thinking about it.

If there's no hope for change, for freedom, I wonder how much longer I can survive in this life.

"Tell me what you think," Vigo asks with his hand on the small of my back.

He leads me around the Leblancs' estate ballroom that's been setup as an art exhibit. Four oversized windows line the long outside wall, letting the pink and red hues of the sunset filter the space in an eerie glow.

Two ornate crystalline chandeliers hang overhead, giving the room an austere mood. The golden hue of the light complements the golds and reds and tans in the floral-patterned carpet that spans the space.

At first glance, the event looks normal. A group of wealthy socialites gathering in a grand ballroom to view an artist's work.

The Leblancs' talent slave—a tall, slim brunette who looks utterly exhausted—stands near one of her many paintings decorating the walls of the ballroom.

Vigo slips his hand upward to grasp the ends of my hair and gives them a tug, awaiting my response.

"I think...I think these paintings are sad."

Vigo chuckles softly. "They are rather boring to look at, hmm? I would prefer to watch you dance over looking at these stupid paintings. Perhaps without your clothes on, around a pole. Maybe I'll have one put in your cage so you can practice for me."

"You disgust me," I tell him boldly, stupidly.

His hand slips down my backside, coming to rest over one cheek, as he bends to whisper in my ear, "Mind your manners with me or you'll regret it."

I swallow, backing down, because I believe him.

We move around the outer wall, observing the painting slave's works of art. The paintings are rather beautiful in a tragic sort of way. If I could paint my slavery and everything I've felt over the years, I imagine it would look similar.

Dark colors.

Abstract with menacing strokes.

A mixture of intention and improvisation—just the way Ezra and I had danced.

My intention mixed with his improvisation.

I would give my life just to see him again.

I might give it anyway.

I observe the social niceties and expectations Vigo has for me, keeping the essence of myself firmly inside my mind. I'm lost in my head, staring blankly at one of the paintings as Vigo speaks to someone behind me. They talk about business and other inane things as I drift.

But then a sudden spark, like static electricity, prickles across my skin. I think nothing of it at first, but then there's a gradual awareness, a tingle of response to a familiar aura. It forces me from the dark corner of my mind and drags me back to reality.

"Vigo." Nikolai's voice dances into my ears.

For the first time, I don't fear the sound, I welcome it.

My heart thuds as I whirl around. Nikolai's presence may be oddly welcome, but his isn't the aura that sparked awareness, the aura that crawls over my skin, begging to be noticed.

"Ezra." His name slips unintentionally from my lips.

Their eyes fall upon me for the way I speak out of turn. But I don't care, *can't* care, because Ezra is here and he's caught me in his sparkling green eyes, full of happiness, wonder, and worry all at once. It's as if the Earth has taken a breath at the unexpected sight of him and I feel the land shudder beneath my feet.

Three months.

Three months since I've seen his face.

Three months since I've heard his voice.

Three months since I've felt the rush that comes from being near him.

I had cursed myself for falling in love with him when Vigo became my master. I tried to write him off, tried to think of him as the man I loved for a season, never to be seen again. But all this time has passed, and I still want him, love him, *need* him.

We both step toward each other, moving together like a dying star and its lonely planet, eager to find our orbit together again. But Nikolai slams a hand against Ezra's chest, pushing him back, and Vigo snatches me by the wrist, pulling me swiftly against his side.

How can that spark still exist between us after all this time?

I need to touch him, hold him, kiss him.

My stomach aches for him. A hollow spot I didn't know existed opens wide and begs me to fill it with the love I can only feel in his arms.

"Where's your new girl?" Vigo asks Nikolai, nudging me in the side with his elbow. "Did you hear he's replaced you with another ballerina?"

My jaw sets as I jerk my stomach away from him.

"It's almost as if he had someone lined up to replace you before he even sold you, *schiava*. You're lucky I wanted you, don't you think?"

Vigo bends to kiss my cheek and I try to pull away. He grabs my chin and forces me to look up at him, planting a firm kiss on my lips. I want to spit on him, but I wouldn't dare. He slaps my cheek for my struggle nonetheless, and I wish I *had* spit on him.

Nikolai's arm whips out to slam against Ezra's chest once more, holding him back when he lurches forward. Then he continues the conversation coolly, as if no movement had occurred.

"Sasha is in our room with Kostya," Nikolai replies with civility, though his eyes narrow on Vigo. "She's not quite ready to make an appearance yet."

"Ah, you've found a fighter then?"

"Quite the opposite, actually. She bores me." I can feel Nikolai's eyes on me.

Mine are on Ezra.

"So strange seeing you at a reception without Anya at your side." Vigo baits Nikolai's anger, putting his arm around my waist and tugging me closer into his side. "She's been your faithful companion for years."

Vigo steals my attention, his hand sliding up the side of my waist. He stretches his long fingers across my breast. I still myself in his hold, knowing better than to fight.

Ezra is ready to pounce and part of me wishes he would. He could start a fight and get us both killed, but then at least our shared torment would be over for good.

What's wrong with me?

Nikolai's lips purse into a straight line. "And now she'll be your companion."

Vigo laughs and it's menacing in its coolness. "I doubt that. She's neither faithful nor a companion to me. And my girls don't survive years. You know that, Nikolai." Vigo claps him on the shoulder.

Nikolai shrugs him off. "They might survive years if you took better care of them."

Vigo tilts his head. "Are you so concerned now with Anya's survival? You were rather flippant about her well-being when you sold her to me."

"The contract you signed with me is anything but flippant. Perhaps you need to review the well-being clause you agreed to."

Vigo shrugs and I stare up at him, wondering what the hell Nikolai could be talking about.

Well-being?

Since when has my well-being been of anyone's concern?

I suppose I can't deny that Nikolai did provide far more toward my care than Vigo has ever attempted to do. That didn't mean he cared about my life now. Nikolai was the one who sold me to such a neglectful and despicable master as Vigo. In many ways, that makes him worse—Nikolai chose this for me.

My eyes turn to him, shooting icy cold daggers straight from my soul.

"I urge you to consider the importance of being a man of your word, Vigo. You know how the board will lean on such matters. Lovely catching up with you." Nikolai smiles as charming as the devil himself, then he nods to me, *acknowledges* me. "Anya."

I suck in a sharp breath at the way his eyes cast an appraising glance over my body. He's glanced a million times before, but this glance is filled with disappointment, anguish, perhaps even…regret? He snaps for Ezra to follow as he turns to walk away.

There's a moment, only a brief, tragic moment, where Ezra meets my eyes before he's forced to move. In that moment, we speak silently, hurriedly through looks and electric sparks which only exist between the two of us.

I love you.

I miss you.

I need you.

I'm going to save you.

The last message is from his eyes to mine and it meets me with such ferocity and truth that it almost feels as though he can save me.

I can't control myself and I speak without thinking. "Mine?"

Ezra rushes toward me. It's stupid for me not to, but I can't seem to fight the pull. I drag myself from Vigo's grip as Ezra's hand latches around my wrist, tugging me into the warmth of his embrace.

We wrap our arms around each other for no more than a

moment, but it's the most fulfilling moment of my life.

"Yours. Always yours," he whispers just before Vigo and Nikolai rip us apart.

Ezra turns with Nikolai's rough hands on his shoulders, guiding him away. Looking back at me, he grants me a small smile. That small smile lights me on fire. I have to fight every part of my body to remain in place rather than run after him again. We've already tested our luck and it failed us.

When Vigo commands me away, I'm forced to tear my attention from Ezra. It's painful, forceful, like being ripped from orbit. I feel colder with each step he takes, only just realizing how cold I have been for the past three months without him.

Ezra has always been my sunshine. My life may cease to exist without his warmth. It *doesn't* exist without his warmth. I've been brutally reminded of everything I need, and its everything I can never have.

The hollow spot inside me will never be filled.

Another hour or so passes as we wander listlessly about the space. I tail behind Vigo as he engages in small talk with other members of the four families. My eyes are vigilant, constantly searching the room for Ezra, but I don't see him or Nikolai again in the ballroom.

Vigo doesn't seem to care when I lag behind a few paces, giving myself a small reprieve from the overwhelming pulse of his evil aura. Perhaps he does care, perhaps he intends to punish me later for trailing behind, though I can't bring myself to care.

What worse could he possibly do to me?

Give me death?

A reprieve from the pain of existence?

I'm within his periphery. It's not as though I could escape the home unnoticed. Even so, I know from years of experience that the exits are closely guarded for that very reason. Still, it doesn't stop me from contemplating an escape plan.

I could sneak up to the second floor.

Hurl myself over the balcony's edge.

It's a morbid thought, but it comes naturally.

It's a stupid thought, though. I'd probably survive the fall, only to injure myself further and suffer more in Vigo's captivity.

But there are other ways to do it…other ways to end it.

Oh, God.

Ezra can't save me.

No one can.

I want to spare us both further misery.

Fighting for my survival is only prolonging our pain.

I don't know if I can keep fighting.

I'm exhausted, hollow, and just fucking tired of this captive existence.

I want to be done.

I want to end it all.

CHAPTER 15

Anya

I RESENTFULLY PUT a hand on Vigo's shoulder for balance as he bends before me, latching the metal cuff around my ankle and locking the padlock that secures it to my leg. The standing mirror shows our reflection and I see how empty my soul is through my eyes. They used to be a vibrant shade of sapphire and now they are a cool, gray-blue, open wide and vacant.

Did they look that way before I saw Ezra tonight?

Vigo stands, turning to face the mirror and blocking my reflection as he combs his fingers through his wavy hair. Then, he straightens his jacket.

I can't help but to think that mirror would shatter nicely into sharp edges.

"I'll return in a couple of hours. Just keep quiet and don't do anything stupid, hmm?"

Vigo turns to me, slipping an arm around my waist and drawing me close. I turn my head away so I don't have to look at him, but he grabs my chin and forces me to regardless.

"Do not worry, little doll. *Papà* will return to take care of you." His hand slips down over my ass and squeezes. "I might even be generous tonight and let you come on my cock if you behave yourself."

I'm tempted to laugh.

To think that the pleasure of coming on Vigo Vittori's cock should be incentive enough to change my mind about killing myself is absurd.

Kill myself?

Have I decided to kill myself?

I swallow the retort that threatens. I don't really have it in me anymore to spare the energy and I'm just ready to be done.

But am I really ready?

He's disappointed in my lack of response, though he doesn't let on. He enjoys knowing he's tormented me into responding out of anger or fear or frustration, and I've learned that denying him that gratification makes *me* feel better on some level.

He shoves me backward and I stumble, landing roughly on the bed behind me. He gives me a look, almost as if he knows what I've been thinking about, but thankfully, he leaves without another word.

I rise to sit on the edge of the bed where he's left me. I feel a certain sense of satisfaction in that final look he's given me. It was a look of confusion, frustration, morbid curiosity.

He knew death was on my mind.

I breathe deeply and weigh my survival on a scale of truth.

Am I so certain that no one can save me? Yes.

Will ending my life take the pain away? Yes.

How horribly will Ezra mourn my loss when he hears about it? Terribly, but then he can focus on saving himself.

Tears well at the thought of what this will do to him, but I know he'll be better off when I'm no longer a concern. Though the thought of leaving him permanently feels like a dagger to my gut, I know I want this.

I want death.

I want this horror story to end.

The affirmation in my mind brings me a strange sort of calm—the peace of knowing that I've made a decision, right or wrong.

Break the mirror.

Cut your wrists.

Be done before he returns.

If I act now, it can all be over soon. I would no longer feel the pain of loving and losing the only person who made me feel truly alive. Seeing him tonight only reminded me of how dead I already am on the inside—I died three months ago when we were ripped apart.

There is no rescue, no salvation for us. Only crippling heartache and tormenting longing.

My hands grip the bed at my sides as I look into the mirror. My breaths quicken as I envision my macabre plan. In my mind, I can see the glass shattering, breaking into a thousand pieces and spilling to the floor. I envision picking up a piece of my own broken reflection and sliding it across my wrists.

A shiver crawls up my spine and I close my eyes. Immediately I feel like I'm underwater again, looking up at Vigo through waves and ripples as my temporarily paralyzed body slumps deeper beneath the surface.

I gasp as my eyes snap open.

I can't go through that, not again.

Never again.

I bend and take off my shoes. I leave one where it rests on the floor and pick up the other as I stand. I move in front of the mirror and stare at my reflection.

Am I the same girl I was with Nikolai?

Am I the same girl Ezra fell in love with?

Somewhere inside I think I'm that same girl, but my

strength has been stripped from me in Vigo's ownership. I know I would've died a long time ago had I been with Vigo from the beginning…If it had been Vigo who had served as my benefactor since the age of eleven…If Vigo had been the one to steal me away over three years ago.

It was all a cruel joke of fate. It was by chance that Nikolai found me in that dance studio when I was a child. It was by chance that he picked me. It could have been anyone else, but fate had chosen me, and it had been breaking me into smaller and smaller pieces ever since. Ezra had managed to put some of them back together for a while, but seeing him tonight just reminded me of how impossible a task that is. It broke me all over again.

I'm not the same girl I used to be. The girl I am now is so desperate for freedom that she's willing to do whatever it takes to get it the only way she knows how.

I hammer hard against the mirror with the stiletto point of my shoe. It cracks, splintering across the reflective glass. Though no pieces have fallen to the floor yet, it effectively shatters my reflection.

I don't even want to see my reflection anymore.

I slam my shoe again, hitting the same spot I hit before, and a few small pieces above it fall to the floor. I hit again, farther down the mirror, and the entire top half falls with a whoosh to the floor. I jump back as the sharp edges pool on the floor beside my feet.

I lower to my knees slowly, eyes searching the remnants for a suitable sliver. Light reflects off a triangular piece on the floor and I reach for it. I'm careful, shaking off the tiny, dusty shambles that rained down over it like glass snowfall.

I shake my head and laugh to myself.

Why should I be careful given my intentions?

My hands are trembling because of my intentions.

Because I can't believe I'm intent on doing this.

Can I really do this?

Just do it.

Get it over with.

I tap the sharp tip of the glass piece on the side of my left wrist. Without even pressing, I can feel the sharpness of the triangular shard. This is going to hurt—I wonder if I'll be able to push through the pain to cut deep enough. My heart races.

I push down on the spot, just a little, just to test.

A little more.

A little deeper.

My face scrunches in pain as I drag it, slicing hardly a hair's width into my skin. A large drop of blood pools and falls, followed by a trickle that lasts for only a few seconds. I haven't done any damage.

I exhale, pushing out the breath I'd been holding, and out with it, tears begin to flow. I don't think I can push through the pain of this enough to sever the veins, to let blood flow free from my body until there's none left for my heart to pump to my organs.

The *pulse, pulse, pulsing* spurts of blood from the neck of the woman who lived in my box before me suddenly flood my memory. She'd sliced her throat, fast and easy, and was dead in no time at all. Her blood had spurted from her body with each final beat of her heart.

Perhaps that would be easier...

I lift the sharp tip and place it against the side of my neck.

I press in, drag a microscopic amount, and feel the small line of blood trickle down the side of my neck.

With the blood comes the tears.

Tears for everything I've been through.

Tears for the life I'll never have.

Tears for the pain of what I'm about to do.

Tears for the love I've lost forever.

Ezra.

Those emerald green eyes of his flash across my mind, just like they had the last time I'd almost died, when Nikolai held a gun to my head. Just like they had when Nikolai drowned me in the pool.

Here they are again. Emerald gems that sparkle and mesmerize and give me an inexplicable sense of peace, calm, tranquility. It strengthens my resolve to end my suffering now. At least I can chase those green eyes into the bliss of unconsciousness.

I pull the make-shift blade just a little farther, testing the pressure and depth and more blood trickles down my neck. But I know this is only surface bleeding. I need to press in harder—a quick draw across my throat and I'll meet my end.

Do it.

Don't do it.

Just do it.

You shouldn't...

Just do it now!

I dig the tip into my skin.

The door crashes against the wall as it's flung open wide.

I turn my head to look, pulling an unintentional, shallow stripe across my neck with the blade, hardly nicking the surface as Vigo bursts into the room.

"Did you think no one heard you break the fucking mirror?" He points his finger at the wall right beside the mirror. "Renata's on the other side of that wall, you stupid girl."

He marches across the room and hovers over me before I can decide how to react. It's not instinct to kill oneself, so I don't have the impulse to quickly slice my throat open before he reaches me—though I wish I had. Instead, I waver, frozen, waiting stupidly until he decides for me. He bends and frees me from the ankle cuff. He snatches my wrist, twisting and yanking me upright, forcing me to drop the shard as he pulls me to my feet.

"You really should have been quicker about it, baby doll. Now you've given me something to look forward to."

My mind is so muddled, confused by the swift change of events. "What?"

"Your punishment."

Fuck, fuck, fuck.

He's right.

I should've been faster.

I shouldn't have hesitated.

I should've been braver, stronger, more determined in choosing my fate. Because now another fate was going to be chosen for me.

I plant my bare feet as he yanks back on my arms. He manages to drag me out into the hallway. "Just let me *die*, Vigo. Let me do it, let me go!"

His grip slips from my wrist, the blood he's smeared around creating a thin, slippery coating. Free from his grasp, I spin, ready to run back into the room, grab that piece of glass, and finish what I started before he can catch me, but when I turn, I slam hard into a solid brick wall of a man who catches me with both hands on my waist.

Nikolai.

Nikolai?

I look up to meet his cold, gray eyes and they regard me with curiosity, concern, and the same familiar hunger that was always there from the beginning.

His eyes lower, surely observing the blood that's now

dripping down my chest, staining the top of the fabric of my gown.

His voice is eerily quiet when he speaks. "What did you do, *rabynya?*

CHAPTER 16
EZRA

MY BLUE-EYED GIRL is fractured, splintered right down the middle from the untold horrors of her servitude to Vigo.

I don't see her at first, but I hear her voice. I hear her yell, "Just let me *die*, Vigo!" and the words rebound painfully around my skull.

Our timing is somehow perfect to run into them and witness this moment. Nikolai was bringing me back to the room to shackle me in for the night before heading off to the boardroom. I was coming down the hall behind him when Vigo tore from his room just in front of us, dragging out a girl in a flash of gold.

The flash of gold was Anya in the gown she'd worn at the reception.

"Just let me die, Vigo!"

My adrenaline spiked, muscles twitching, everything within my veins pounding with the message to grab her, run with her, *save* her.

But I've learned that my adrenaline doesn't have the privilege of conscious thought. It doesn't understand that I can grab her, I can run with her, but I don't have a way to *save* her.

Not yet.

My heart hurts to see the state of her as she crashes into Nikolai. She looks thin, frail, exhausted, but more horrifyingly, she looks determined...determined as she tries to run back into the room after begging for death.

It punches into my gut when my mind clears enough to see the red. The disturbing crimson smears on her left wrist and hand. More smears across her chest as it drips from a short line on her neck.

"What the fuck..." My voice is quiet at first until I make sense of what's happening, of what she tried to do. "What the fuck, Anya?!"

I don't care about my place in this fucked up world. I storm past Nikolai and reach for Anya's bloody wrist, taking it in my hand. Her eyes fall to where I hold her for a beat, then lift to meet mine with a look of resignation mixed with shame. The look shows me a fissure in her existence that threatens to split her soul apart. It has me ready to set off a fucking bomb in this place.

But then she's pulled from my grip as I'm pulled from her. Vigo takes me by the shoulders and spins me before slamming me face-first into the wall.

"Don't touch my slave," he sneers before releasing me.

I spin to face him, but before I can punch the look off his entitled face, Anya's sobs draw me away.

"Let me go," she cries, fighting against Nikolai's hold. "Let me go, let me go, let me *go!*"

"Why would I let you go, *rabynya*? So you can attempt the coward's way out again? Try to kill yourself?" Nikolai pulls his hand back and slaps her. "How *dare* you do something so goddamn selfish."

Nikolai's shoulders shake, his expression an unusual mixture of rage and fear as Anya crumbles before my eyes, devolving into sobs of heartache so deafening that it brings me to my knees.

Vigo grabs Anya away from Nikolai. "She needs to be punished for this. I'm taking her to the board. She's been with the four families far too long to allow this sort of behavior, and I will *not* give her the satisfaction of death. She hasn't earned it because I haven't finished with her yet."

Anya chuckles darkly. "He hasn't finished with me yet, Nikolai. I haven't *earned* death." Her joyless laugh twists her features into a grim scowl.

Nikolai's brow furrows, his eyes narrowing in concentration as he looks at Anya. She's sinking away from Vigo, her body limp and exhausted in her sobbing, like a wilted rose trying to sink back into the Earth from which it sprouted.

Nikolai's eyes flicker, his brow line straightens out, and he looks at me pointedly, though he speaks to Vigo.

"Good. I'll bring the boy, then, too. Lock them together. I guarantee he won't allow her to attempt this again while her punishment is being decided."

Only a man as fucking arrogant as Nikolai Mikhailov would put his slaves alone together, knowing that one would prevent the other from committing suicide.

He wasn't wrong.

Anya cries, "Please, please punish me, but don't hurt him anymore. Don't hurt him. Don't hurt Ezra."

That hurts me.

I hurt so badly because of her, *for* her.

I feel everything she's feeling as if I were feeling it myself, and it's the most fucking painful thing I've ever known.

Vigo's already dragging her away down the hallway. I follow as Nikolai stalks after them. We head back downstairs to the ground level and pass the empty ballroom on our right.

Just past the ballroom, we turn right down a hallway, but it dead ends about five strides ahead. At the end, there's a pair of wooden, double doors propped open—the entrance to the boardroom.

This alcove in front of the doors is brown and bleak and formal. Leo Leblanc appears from behind the doors, sensing the presence of some of his guests.

"Come on in," he says to Nikolai and Vigo, but tilts his head looking at me and Anya. "I'm sorry, was there something wrong with their shackles, or..."

The poor guy wracks his brain trying to figure out why Nikolai and Vigo brought their slaves along with them.

"No," Nikolai says. "We have a matter of punishment to arrange for a slave. Is there a room nearby we can lock them in until the meeting is over? She cannot be left alone."

Leo looks Anya up and down, seeing her bloodied, sobbing form and seems to have trouble sorting out what's going on. I just want to get to her so I can hold her but these giant pieces of shit stand in my way.

"She tried to commit suicide," Nikolai clarifies impatiently.

"Oh. *Oh*. Yes. Actually..." Leo brushes past and gestures for the group to follow where he leads.

Vigo grabs Anya by the elbow, dragging her along beside him roughly, and I seethe as I follow behind Nikolai. Turning right from the alcove, we walk in the opposite direction of the ballroom. We turn left into a room two doors down.

It looks like a home office space, though it's rather small considering the size of the estate.

Leo crosses the room, dodging furniture in close quarters, and moves behind the wooden desk that rests in the center. He bends to reach beneath it and the bookcase beside us suddenly swings open—a hidden door.

"We can put them down there. No need for supervision."

"Show us." Nikolai waves a hand, waiting for Leo to lead the way.

Leo gives a quick nod then rushes around toward us. He pulls the hidden door open wide, crosses the threshold, and we follow.

We're cloaked in darkness just a few steps past the hidden entrance. When we come upon light again, it's from a lantern-style fixture on the wall, lighting a path down a cement spiral staircase.

It's like we've stepped back in time and entered a medieval fucking torture chamber. Coming off the staircase is literally like walking into a dungeon. It's a wide square room with concrete walls and floors all around us.

Leo moves across the room and bends, picking up two large metal cuffs, much larger than the ankle cuffs in the bedrooms.

"These go around the neck safely," Leo explains. "Will that do?"

Vigo puts his hand between Anya's shoulder blades and shoves her forward, stepping after her as she stumbles. "Yes."

"Don't fucking put that on her," I practically growl.

Nikolai pushes me forward after her. "Shut up."

Anya is quiet and still, her tears and her blood slowing to a trickle as Leo positions the metal cuff. He closes it around her neck and secures it with a padlock in the front. A long, heavy chain dangles from the back, attached to a hook in the floor. It's at least as long as she is tall.

Her hands come up to touch the metal collar, her fingers gripping around it, trying to slip in from the top and bottom— it looks like there's at least some give and she won't be strangled by it.

That grants me one small reason for relief, but it's short

lived to see how far she's fallen into resignation. She doesn't fight or complain. She just backs up against the wall and slumps, slowly sliding down the wall until she sits on the floor.

She's given up and it fucking kills me.

I won't fucking let her go through this alone.

I don't fight, I don't stall, I don't argue.

I step forward, take the cuff from Leo, and put it around my own damn neck. I let him secure it with the padlock and immediately lower to sit beside my blue-eyed girl.

Fuck everyone.

"In a few hours, after we've taken care of business and decided collectively upon the appropriate measure, we will return to deliver Anya's punishment."

I wave my hand dismissively toward the staircase. "Fine. Fuck. *Go.*"

Vigo turns and stalks up the staircase without another beat. But Nikolai hesitates, looking at the both of us. My hand is twitching, aching to cross the two inches of space between us to touch her, hold her, hug her, kiss her.

But I won't until they're gone.

I won't put her at risk like that.

Nikolai's eyes narrow, flicking back and forth between us. There's a contemplative look there that I don't think he knows he's sharing, but I see it.

He's lost in the stare for a few moments before he finally shakes off the look. He turns away slowly and heads back up the spiral staircase. Leo finally follows after. I wait until I hear the hidden door at the top of the staircase click shut, and when I hear it, the lights lower to a faded dimness. They remain on, just faint, and Anya looks like a shadow beside me.

I reach my hand out to touch her, but she beats me to it. She falls sideways, leaning heavily against my shoulder. I feel heavier and lighter all at once. The air rushes out of my lungs as I angle toward her, wrapping my arms around her and pulling her close.

Even when everything in the world is wrong, it's all made right when she's in my arms.

She cries, her face falling to my chest as her skinny arms sneak around my waist. "I'm sorry," she says. "I'm sorry. I can't do it anymore. I can't live like this. I just want it all to end."

I'm stalled on the tracks and her words are a freight train barreling into me. I don't know what to say to her to make it better, so I just tell her the truth.

"My life means nothing without you in it, Anya. If your life ends, my life ends."

She stills.

She raises her head slowly and I can see the blue of her eyes in the dim light. The shade is dull in this lighting, but it's my blue-eyed girl all the same. Everything that makes her Anya is still right there behind the cloak of color. Seeing her again, after all this time, reminds me how hard I fell for her.

I told her once that my heart beats for her, but I didn't understand the absolute truth in that until this moment. I feel like I've just been resurrected in her arms.

Her fragile, malnourished, too thin for her arms.

"I'm yours," I tell her, picking up her tiny arm to inspect the bloody cut she made on her wrist—it's small and seems to have stopped bleeding. I let go and lift both of my hands to hold her cheeks, to brush the tears from them with my thumbs. "Always yours."

Her eyes flicker as they search mine, the familiar flicker they've always had whenever she's looked at me seeking honesty, rawness, and truth. Truth is exactly what I'll give her.

"If you die, I die," I tell her.

Her head tilts, falling heavy into my palm and her expression softens.

"Ezra, I…I wanted to hate you," she says, and I wait for her to continue, though her silence stretches through several beats. "I wanted to hate you for making me fall for you, for disrupting the predictability of my captivity with Nikolai, for making me fall so hard and so deep that I risked everything to be with you, just for that one night in my bed. But I don't hate you. I could never hate you. My life without you is meaningless pain. And that's all it's been since he sold me." Her voice cracks as fresh tears spill.

I press my forehead to hers. "But…wasn't that one night with me worth everything? I'm really good in bed."

The sound she makes is magic. It's a sob, but there's a laugh behind it that forces her to smile and fuck, I can't help but grin at her. I lick my lips before tilting my chin forward, pressing my lips softly against hers.

I don't know why it surprises me that she kisses me back, that she parts her lips and invites me to kiss her deeper, but it does. It surprises and calms me, and it excites me and scares me.

Anya makes me feel everything more intensely than anyone else ever could.

She tried to kill herself.

My breaths quicken with the deepening kiss, the intimacy with the woman I love who has been gone from my life for months.

She tried to kill herself.

My heartbeat races with the passion I feel for her and the passion beats out a pulse of wanting, but even more so, of anger.

I'm angry.

I'm angry with *her*.

She tried to kill herself.

I pull my head back, though my grip remains firm on her cheeks.

"Why the fuck did you do this, Anya? Did you really try to kill yourself? Why? Why would you do that to me?"

I press my lips to hers again, unable to dampen this fiery mixture of love and rage that's starting to boil in my blood.

"I'm sorry," she says between heated kisses. "I just need it to end, I need it to be over."

"Over? No. No, it's not over. Not like that. I promised you, didn't I?" I kiss the corner of her lips. "I promised you that if there was a way for us to escape this nightmare, I'd find it."

Her eyes narrow and she yanks backward, dragging herself free of my grip. "There's nothing for you to find. There never was. The only escape is death."

I throw my head back against the wall, digging my fingers into my hair from the roots. "Fuck. That's not...it's not—" I stumble over my words. "Death isn't the only escape. I have faith in that. And I need you to have faith in me. Don't you have faith in me?"

She turns toward me, moving to sit on her knees. She reaches out to brush her thumb along my jawline.

"I have faith in you, Ezra. All the faith in the world. But I can't have faith in you finding a way out when I know there isn't one." She sighs, her head falling to the side as she watches my expression shift. "I can't believe how much I..."

"What?"

"How much I need you. All my reasons made so much sense to me when I cut myself. But now, alone with you...the only thing that I *know* is how much I need you."

Everything in me softens.

I reach for her and she reaches for me. She climbs onto my lap, hiking her dress up toward her hips to straddle me.

Both her hands grip my cheeks and she bends to kiss me with a fierceness I couldn't have expected in her current state. But I meet her with fierceness of my own, a heated passion for her that's been bottled up deep inside for far too long.

Her tongue seeks mine out, battling to taste me as if she's been starved and is finally being fed. If I thought her fragile body could take it, if these stupid chains weren't so goddamn heavy on our necks, I would flip her, slam her to the floor, and bury myself deep inside her until someone forcefully dragged me away.

I need to be inside her—as shitty as it is to admit in this hell—and I would feel bad for feeling that way if I didn't know how much she needs it, too. Every part of her body hums for it, a tingling, pulsing aura that flows from her and electrifies me with every brush of skin on skin.

She and I are meant to touch.

Our souls demand it.

Our hearts beat for it.

Maybe it's arrogant or cocky even to think it, but I know that our separation did this to her—more than Vigo's torment, whatever it is he did to her, because our separation was worse. And seeing each other before, in the ballroom, knowing we would only be torn apart again…that's what broke her.

My heart can't handle that.

I need to mend her, put her back together, make her whole again.

Her lips break from mine only to land on my face where she presses fevered kisses on every inch of exposed skin.

"Mine?" she whispers, her voice suddenly heavy, powerful with desire and need.

"Yours," I reply, sliding my hands across her back.

I hold her close as I sit up straighter, scooting my ass all the way back against the wall. Her arched back presses her body against mine as I move my hands to run up her thighs, slipping beneath the bunched fabric and reaching for her hips. My fingers skim across skin, nothing but skin, even where the fabric of her panties should be.

If this were the real world, I'd think it was hot, but it's not the real world.

This is all real.

It's just not the real you want to know.

"He doesn't let you wear—"

"Shut up," she snaps, leaning back to look at me. "Don't finish that sentence. Don't say another word about him."

She snatches my wrists in both her small hands and yanks them away from her body. I think she's going to scold me, yell at me, move away and stop touching me.

Instead, she grips my wrists tighter, pushes my hands to the wall on either side of my head, and bends to kiss me, holding me in place.

Fuck.

I won't say another fucking word.

She leans into my hands, letting the wall support her weight. Our kiss becomes a frantic, heated devouring of each other, and I'm losing my mind with how much I need her, every part of her.

Her hands slowly loosen their grip on my wrists. Her palms slip over my palms and our fingers lace together. Her hips move as she inhales deep through her nose and our lips break. She drops her forehead to mine.

"What's wrong with me? How is it that hardly ten minutes ago I wanted to die, and now all I can think about is making love to you?"

I lick my lips. "The same thing that's wrong with me. We

fell in love."

Her body rolls, rocking forward and back with all the grace of a dancer. "You're the only thing that makes me feel alive. I want you."

"So have me, Anya. I promise you, whatever you want from me, I want it from you, too."

Anya bites her lip for an adorable microsecond before letting go of my hands. She reaches between us and works at my buckle. Sitting back on my thighs, she unbuttons, unzips, undoes me completely so she can have what's hers.

God, she makes me hard.

In literal hell, she has the power to turn me on.

She lets out a shaky breath as she fists my shaft and shifts her body. The tip has barely brushed across her warmth and wetness before she sinks down, taking me inside her completely. We groan in unison, both feeling the same relief of being two broken pieces that have just been put back together.

I don't give a shit whether she moves or stays still, just the feeling of being inside her is like being home. Nevertheless, it feels fucking amazing when she moves, grinding slowly. She gives me her eyes instead of her lips and somehow, that feels even more amazing.

The brightness of her blue irises is returning. The fight in her is coming back with her desire, with our connection.

Our connection is everything.

Without it, we're nothing.

"I'm better when I'm with you," she says.

"We're better together." I kiss the corner of her lips.

She reaches for my hands again, our fingers braiding together and holding tight. I bring her knuckles to my lips and kiss each finger with sensual softness, earning gentle puffs of breath from her lips as she gives me her soul-deep gaze.

She rolls her hips slowly, an erotic dance that only she could ever perform for me so spectacularly, and it feels so fucking good. She's building me up, so excruciatingly hard, making me desperate, making me want to take and take from her until she's given me every piece of her soul.

I'll keep the pieces within my own soul, protect them, keep them safe.

Her eyes flutter as she fucks, her thick eyelashes fanning over the blue and making her look otherworldly, like a fairy or a forest nymph or a goddamn mermaid.

Fuck.

I don't even know how to describe it.

She's just fucking magical to watch, especially as my name falls from between her plump, burgundy lips.

I drop her hands and grab her face, holding her steady while I kiss her with force. My mouth presses hard to hers, forcing her to open for me, to let me in for a taste. Her hands cover mine as she obliges, giving me her tongue to suck on. She whimpers and her body sinks, conceding to the pleasure I know is coiling in her belly.

I sit up taller, forcing her to lean back while she fucks me. She puts one hand behind her, gripping my thigh just above my knee for support as I kiss her roughly.

If I thought she could take the pressure of a man laying on top of her, if I thought she could mentally handle giving me the control and letting me climb over her, I'd throw her down, fuck her roughly, make her feel so wet and so good that she'd never let me stop.

But she's been hurt too many times and letting her ride me feels just as damn good.

She moans into my mouth and her ass swirls as she changes her angle. Our kiss breaks as she digs her hand down hard, almost painfully on my knee, and she's fucking me in short, quick strokes. Her eyes lock on mine and I'm letting go. That vibrancy is turning up like a dial with every second that passes, her brightness rising and radiating light into the room.

Nothing could be more intimate, more sexy, more ethereal and beautiful as the expression on her face as she uses me for her pleasure.

And thank *God* for the sounds she makes. The same puffed out little "*oh*" sounds I remember from the times before when she came with me.

Not ever when she came for Nikolai.

Only when she came for *me*.

It felt like a goddamn privilege that only I knew what her true pleasure looked like, sounded like, felt like.

It feels so fucking good.

Just like before, the "*oh*" sounds lengthen, lose the harshness in their tone, become more like rushed breaths that have to come out each time she exhales. When she's jerking more than rocking, I feel her pulsing pussy drag my orgasm out of me. She's pulsing and squeezing around me until she lets out one last, long, purely satisfied "*oh*."

I lower my hands from her jawline to her waist. I grip her hard, holding her in place. I bend my knees, plant my feet, lift my hips from the floor, and fuck and fuck and fuck until I explode inside her. I come long, slow, with a final groan as her spasming muscles clench tight around me.

We don't move.

We just breathe and exist together.

The bubble of serenity we were granted the privilege of hiding inside while we made love to each other gradually fades away.

In its place returns the cold concrete beneath my ass, the

damp and musty smell of a basement in a house in the bayou, the noisy clank of our chains as we shift into more comfortable positions.

Anya's inner thighs are slippery and soaking wet from the both of us. I don't want her to wear the evidence of our indiscretion, so I pull out my stupid blue pocket square and reach between us as my cock slips out from its place in heaven. I press it against her to soak up the liquid that's dripping from her and it feels almost more intimate to take care of her this way than it did to fuck her.

She sucks on her bottom lip for a beat, watching me as I wipe away the wet evidence of our fucking.

"I love you, Ezra," she says.

I breathe in the words as she climbs off me slowly, adjusting her dress and sitting beside me again. I put my cock away and I shove the pocket square down into my pants pocket as deep as it will go.

"If you love me, then promise you won't try to leave me again. You're strong enough to survive this. You owe yourself that chance."

I turn to look at her as she slips her hand in mine and I lock our fingers together. I look deep into her eyes and see her there; I see her strength coming back, her survival instinct reviving and renewing itself.

I don't kid myself to believe that the thought of ending all of this with her death won't come across her mind again. I know it will. It will be present until I get her the fuck out of here, until I save her. I just need her to keep her strength long enough for me to figure a way out of all this.

"I don't think I can promise you that," she says so bluntly that it twists in my gut.

"Fine. You don't have to promise me that. As long as you

promise me that you'll give me enough time to try, that you'll stay alive long enough to give me a chance to save you."

She sighs. "Ezra, I can't—"

"You *can*," I tell her, "and you will. I know you will. Even if you don't think you can right now. Just…tell me you'll give me time, Anya. Please."

She closes her eyes before her head falls to my shoulder. "I'll give you as much time as I can."

I don't feel great about the way she says it, but it's agreement so I'll take it. In truth, I don't know how much time she has. I don't know how long it will take for Vigo to grow bored with her or lose his temper and kill her or sell her to someone else. I don't know how long she can continue to survive the kind of torture he inflicts upon her.

I lean over to kiss the top of her head. "I don't blame you for wanting to end it all. Really, I don't. But you went and made me fall in love with you, so I feel like you kind of owe me."

There's humor in my tone and I know she hears it. I can feel the joy from her smile even if I can't see it all that well.

"If I owe you, then you owe me, too."

"Hell yes, I owe you. I owe you too much to ever pay back."

She looks up at me, her tone turning serious again. "Debt forgiven. I don't think either of us stood a chance." She smiles softly, but sadly. "We were doomed from the start."

I hesitate before I ask, "Do you regret it?"

Her eyes brighten, shining a light in the dark space. "No. I don't regret anything."

I have a fight ahead of me.

I don't know how I'll do it, but one way or another, I'm gonna save my girl before she loses herself again.

CHAPTER 17

NIKOLAI

"ANYA'S BEEN QUITE the little rebel in recent months, hasn't she?" Renata notes unnecessarily. "First letting Nikolai's boy into her bed and now this. Perhaps she should be sold outside of the families to a client."

"Selling her would only be offloading the problem to a customer," Cordelia O'Shea says. "I would never sell a rebellious commodity to one of our loyals—unless they requested it, of course, which in my experience, is rare. It might be best to decommission her and be done with it. Or let her do it herself if she's so desperate for death."

My head snaps toward Delia sitting on my left. "No. Her transgression doesn't warrant decommissioning."

"Agreed," Vigo adds. "Why should we give her exactly what she wants? Regardless, I'm not done with her yet."

"Then what do you propose?" Renata asks.

Vigo straightens in his seat, spreading a sadistic grin across his face. He opens his mouth to speak, but I don't give him a chance.

"Give her to me tonight," I say.

"Are you serious?" Renata chuckles.

"Yes. She needs to be put in her place. Clearly, Vigo has

pushed her too far." I give him an admonishing look. "I can put her right again."

Vigo leans forward, pressing his elbows to the table and steepling his fingers beneath his chin. "And what makes you think that?"

I lean back in my seat, feigning a disinterested sigh. "Because I know her better than you do, Vigo. And let's not fool ourselves. She never once tried to end her life in my care. You've broken her to pieces, and someone needs to put them back together if you intend to keep her."

"What makes you think—"

I lean forward with a snap. "You signed a contract with me, and I expect you to honor the agreement. You've already breached several clauses you agreed to for her welfare, so I suggest you stop pretending that I'm *asking* for a night with her. Your lack of decorum necessitates it."

Renata tilts her head at Vigo, her dark eyes narrowed. "Is that true? Have you neglected to abide by your contract?"

Vigo's lips twist into a slow, wide smile as he leans back from the table. "It depends on how you look at it."

"Bullshit." Murphy, the O'Shea family Head of House, sits back, crossing his tattooed arms across his broad chest.

"Aye," Delia agrees, and her words drip with sarcasm, "I'd be happy to review the contract with you if you're having trouble interpreting it, Vigo. I'm sure Nikolai has laid out clear terms for you in his sale." Vigo's smile fades as Delia speaks. "What are the consequences set forth for breach of contract, or has that not been laid out? I assure you that the board would lay out an appropriate consequence if Nikolai neglected to write one into the contract."

Vigo has always had a bit of a soft spot for Delia. She had successfully seduced him once—more than a decade ago when they were in their twenties—to gain a favorable trade deal through Lisbon. If anyone could shut him up, it would certainly be Cordelia O'Shea. And she seems to have done just that.

Vigo's eyes don't leave her as she tosses her soft, strawberry blonde hair over one shoulder. She plays him like a fiddle with her intentional flirtation. It's a skill the women of the four families develop carefully from the time they begin to blossom in their teens. Our business decisions are made by men and men alone, though that doesn't mean we haven't all suffered the influence of one of the powerful women in our ranks. They're as ruthless as the men, though they have the finesse of womanhood.

"Fine," Vigo finally says to me, though he looks at Delia. "Have her for the night. Straighten her out and set her right."

"And?" Delia tilts her head.

Vigo leans forward, licking his lips before he responds, "I'll sit with you to review the contract. Let you straighten me out and set me right."

She smiles. "My pleasure."

Vigo leans back slowly in his seat, placing his arms on the rests and smoldering at the woman.

I refuse to let relief touch the features of my face that I'll have a night with Anya. I don't need to feel relief for it. Fuck, I don't even know why I suggested it.

You know why.

"Very well," Renata says, jumping in to take the lead like she always does. "Nikolai will have Anya tonight and return her to Vigo in the morning. Leo, why don't you move us along to the next agenda item?"

Leo Leblanc may be the Head of House for his family, but he was never meant to be. Since the four fathers began their cooperation generations ago, the American family has always been the Campbells.

But then they went and killed my family, and I got my retribution at the last quarterly meeting hosted in my home. I killed the previous Head of House, Chandler Campbell, along with Leo Leblanc's parents. Three from their family for the three of mine whose lives were stolen. With no other suitable male Campbell in the line, our board agreed to appoint Leo, making a major change that was unprecedented.

The Leblancs were distant relatives, and though they knew of our world, they weren't living in it. Furthermore, Leo was relatively young to be thrust into this role with no previous knowledge of our criminal dealings—not that he had a choice. At only twenty-seven years old, he became the Head of House for a family he knew little about.

Murphy, Vigo, and I had our whole lives to prepare for our roles, and at thirty-five, thirty-eight, and thirty-nine respectively, our life experience far exceeded Leo's. Nevertheless, he was Head of House for his family and he has to make decisions as such.

Leo swallows and clears his throat, leaning forward on his elbows on the table. "Yes. Next item is the matter of Murphy's…" He looks down at his notes on the table in front of him. "His bride?"

I roll my eyes at Leo's apparent lack of preparation, but more so at his seeming inability to appear confident *despite* his lack of preparation.

Thankfully, Renata has more patience for the young, blond-haired protégé she seems to have taken under her wing. She's managed a rather impressive collection of young boys in her care over the years, so it's unsurprising that she's taken a liking to him. She takes over the agenda item on Leo's behalf.

"Murphy has petitioned for an early bride," Renata says.

My eyebrows raise in surprise. "Really?"

"I'm impatient." Murphy shrugs, speaking in his Irish accent. "What's the point in waiting until I'm forty to find a suitable wife?"

A cold reminder that in five months' time, I will be forty and forced to discuss the selection of my own wife. My argument against which is untenable, though the secret I've been keeping for nearly three years will be forced to come to light. It's not as though the revelation of which would be an outright surprise to anyone here. What I've done is not entirely unheard of within the bounds of the four families, but my recent decisions—decisions I might perhaps be willing to admit I have some regret for—will make the conversation of my future bride difficult to say the least.

Delia sighs. "I've tried to talk him into waiting until it's his time," she sends a chastising look to her cousin, "but he insists he wants a bride now."

"All of the Heads of House must agree for us to move forward with an early petition. What are your votes?" Renata asks.

"Agreed," I reply.

Vigo follows, "Agreed."

All eyes fall to Leo and he straightens in his seat. "You're petitioning to get married?" he asks for clarification.

My impatience grows and I sink back into my seat, crossing my arms over my chest.

"Aye," Murphy replies, exasperation lifting his eyebrows in a manner of mockery.

Leo clears his throat, finally realizing he should fall in step and vote as the other Heads of House. "Agreed."

"Petition granted. Congratulations." Renata's smooth, thick voice pours out like honey. "I'll prepare you a portfolio of suitable women to join the four families."

"Actually..." Murphy uncrosses his arms, leaning forward

on his elbows on the table, "I already have someone in mind. A fiery little thing I had the pleasure of meeting by chance last time I visited the States."

"Murphy." Renata folds her hands. "You know your bride must be approved."

"And she will be." He flashes a grin at Renata. "I'll send her details to you for approval and you can pass it along to the Heads of House for the final vote."

Renata watches his features carefully, a stare of truth-seeking. She waits for his grin to falter and fade, but of course, it doesn't. Murphy O'Shea is not one to back down.

"Fine, then. Send me the details and we'll make a decision at the next quarterly meeting. Fair?"

"Fair." His grin broadens and he leans back in his chair.

One thing our women get the first say in is the choice of brides for the Heads of House. Our women need to be vetted carefully before brought to marry into the family. They need to be an appropriate blend of submissive wife and ruthless leader.

Someone like Anya.

It's a combination that, for obvious reasons, isn't easy to come by. I'm actually quite intrigued to learn more about this bride Murphy intends to wed.

The intrigue, however, is fleeting.

My mind drifts as Renata assists Leo in moving forward with the agenda—discussing family sales figures over the last quarter.

It wanders to the sight of Anya, bleeding and begging for death in the hallway. I'd be lying to say it wasn't a shock to my system to see her unraveled. I'd unraveled her myself more times than I can count, but never so completely.

Vigo has ruined her.

My jealousy has reached its peak, aiding my imagination

in drawing up all the vile things Vigo must have done to her. It's not that he's done anything to her that bothers me, it's that he has broken her enough to attempt to find death on her own. She was apathetic about life when she was mine, but she hadn't actively sought the escape of death. She still had that fight left in her, even if it had been slowly fading over the years.

Just when I thought it was coming back, that I was about to have everything I wanted with my *rabynya* and her precious pet, they went behind my back and fucked each other. More than that, they fell in love. Not with me, but with each other.

They were both supposed to be mine—my faithful companions…my willing slaves to offer me comfort on the nights when my grief kicked up and switched on my rage. They were meant to be my reprieve, my outlet for the sexually violent release I needed to get my head back in the fucking game. But they'd ruined it before it even began.

I hate Anya for her betrayal, but there is this nagging, shrill voice from somewhere deep inside me that saw her bleeding in the hallway tonight for what I'd wanted her to be from the beginning.

She'd been there for me, however unwillingly. Her presence had always been a constant which dampened my evil spirit and kept it in check. When she finally broke as my slave and gave me her constant submission, she was the willing angel from heaven who let me clip her wings and use her in all the vile ways I wanted to use her. In doing so, she saved countless others that the devil inside me would have destroyed.

Since she's been gone, the blackness has been seeping in, swallowing my soul bit by bit. I no longer have her goodness to balance my evil, and her absence has forced me to recognize it. The recognition requires gratitude, though I'm loathed to grant it.

Still, I have a mission with her tonight. A mission based on a longshot and a lie that I told Vigo when I sold her to him. A lie that's listed in the very contract I used to barter my time with her tonight. Personally, I don't give a shit about any consequences I might earn for fraud or breach of contract. I only care that Vigo does as he promised when he signed it, and I know the lovely Cordelia O'Shea will keep him in line for that.

My hopeful outcome from this evening is highly unlikely from a statistical standpoint and it may make no difference to Anya, or to myself, in the long run.

But my attempt will absolve me of the burden of gratitude I somehow feel is owed to her for the years she granted me her submission so willingly.

I wish to owe no debt.

I wish to make my attempt at granting her an insurance policy from our night together, then wash my hands of her.

Then I wish to take Ezra home, to find a way to make him and Sasha the companions they need to be to satisfy the demonic urges within me.

CHAPTER 18

Anya

BEING WITH EZRA again has both energized and drained me. To think of how determined I was to end my own life only to be brought face to face with him just after my failed attempt…

I'm embarrassed.

I'm ashamed.

I'm guilt-ridden.

Perhaps it was fated for us to be reunited when we were. I don't know, it's difficult for me to believe when fate has made my life so miserable.

Miserable until Ezra.

Every moment I'd shared with him alone, from the day I met him, has been filled with passion. Whether it came out as hatred, anger, lust, or fierce and powerful love, every memory I had of him with me was passionate. Our passion fueled me to keep fighting for another moment with him; though at the same time, it drained me of my last dregs of energy so that I felt hopeless and exhausted in his absence.

I need him to be with me forever.

I need him to feed me that fuel every moment so it doesn't burn out when he's gone.

I'd nearly snuffed it out myself tonight, and I know I'll only try again when it dies down to a flicker, a sparking ember.

I made him a promise, though, a promise to try, to give him time to save me. And while I don't believe it's possible, I'll keep my promise to him. I'll try my best because having his love is the only thing that matters to me.

I'm thankful for the fire he's lit inside me when Vigo and Nikolai come to retrieve us from the dungeon. I hope and pray that neither man will smell the sex on us. I suppose it doesn't matter because I know I'm going to be punished for trying to kill myself regardless…I just don't know how.

Leo is with them and he unlocks the metal choker from around my neck, freeing me. I bring my hands up to rub the sides of my sore neck, relishing the freedom from such an oppressive chain. Ezra stands but Nikolai holds up a palm to stop him.

"You'll remain here tonight, Ezra."

I whip around to look at him and his eyes blaze, narrowing at Nikolai.

"Excuse me?" Ezra says.

"Anya will be with me tonight. She and I will need our time…uninterrupted. But don't worry, I'll have Sasha brought down to keep you company."

Ezra's nostrils flare. "What are you going to do to her?"

Nikolai shakes his head. "That's none of your business. Say goodbye to your pet, *rabynya*, you won't be seeing each other again for quite a long time."

"No," I say and dash toward Ezra at the exact moment Nikolai reaches out to grab my wrist.

I fly into Ezra's reaching arms and he clamps them tight around my body before Nikolai can touch me. The shackle of Ezra's embrace is the only binding I want.

His lips brush across my ear. "Remember you promised me. Give me time. Please."

I press my face into his shoulder, sucking in a long, deep breath to inhale the sweet scent of him one last time. Then I'm violently taken from him with Nikolai's fierce hands gripping my waist and tearing me away.

I nod at Ezra, acknowledging my promise to him.

Nikolai drags me toward the steps by my wrist and I manage to twist back around to steal one more glance. Ezra's brightness shines and threatens to knock me off my feet with the way he grins and winks at me. He could almost have me fooled that everything is okay. I smile in return before I'm pulled out of sight.

Oh, God…the way he makes me feel.

My palm crushes against my bloody chest, over my heart, and I mourn the rush of him fading with each melancholy beat of my hopeless, helpless heart.

I stand beside the locked door in the room Nikolai has been given for the evening. My back is pressed against the wall as I wait for direction on the manner in which I will be punished by my former master.

I was granted the unfortunate privilege of meeting my replacement, Sasha. A girl who looked similar to me, for all intents and purposes, but who was nothing like me at all. She bowed to Nikolai with a needy, desperate sort of submission, not in the way I had learned to submit over time. I learned it was best for my survival, but I had always abhorred my own behavior when I had to bow.

Unlike me, it's clear this girl wants Nikolai's approval, not for her safety, but for her self-esteem. I almost feel sorry for her naivety, but my heart just doesn't have the space to concern myself with her. In any case, she was taken out of the room soon after I arrived and I'm left alone with Nikolai, locked in the room with no way out.

I watch as he pours a drink from a bar cart near an unlit fireplace. A sitting area with a couch and two armchairs separates us across the large space, and a traditional, mahogany four post bed sits threatening on the opposite side of the room.

He turns as he lifts a glass of whiskey to his lips and I'm surprised to find that his eyes aren't immediately filled with lust and violence.

"Come sit, Anya. Let's talk." He tilts his head toward the sofa. "Would you like a drink?"

My eyes are wide as I subtly shake my head. "No."

He stills, watching me, waiting for me to obey. Though I wish to stay right here, with my back pressed firmly to the wall, I know I must submit and do as he wishes. Slowly, I push away from the wall and walk forward. I circle around one of the armchairs with my eyes plastered to his. I reach the couch and lower to sit as he takes a long, slow drink from his glass, then sets it back down on the bar cart.

He moves swiftly, crossing to sit on the couch beside me, and I jolt at his sudden movement. There's still a cushion's length between us, but I'm wary for how long that will last. I'm sitting straight and stiff, my spine rigid and chin lifted, and I have to turn my entire body to face him. He settles into the corner, lifting his arm to rest along the back of the couch and crosses one ankle over his knee. Though I'm tense and terrified, there's also some strange part of me that feels a sense of relief, only for the reason that I've been spared a night with Vigo.

But have I really been spared?

Boldly, I ask the question that begs to be answered, knowing he may punish me worse than ever simply for asking. But I need to know, and this silence is overwhelming.

"What is my punishment and why are you giving it?"

I brace myself for his violent outburst, drawing my body back toward the arm rest behind me, but it never comes.

His head tilts. "Do you wish Vigo were giving it?"

"No," I reply truthfully.

His forehead wrinkles. "Why is that?"

"Because—"

"Have you found that I'm a kinder master than he is?"

I swallow thickly, my eyes turning toward the unlit fireplace. "You're no kinder."

"Don't lie to me, Anya," he hisses. "You attempted to take your own life tonight."

I suck in a sharp breath, turning to face him with the full force of my confidence returning, self-preservation be damned. "He may have driven me to it faster, Nikolai, but you were driving me there all the same."

There.

I've done it.

I've brought the devil out of him.

His crossed leg comes down as his face twists to rage. He throws himself across the couch at me and snatches me around the throat before I can protest.

"You had everything you wanted with me. Everything you needed. I even let you keep your fucking pet."

Incredulity overcomes me and I'm lost to it, neglecting my sensibilities that tell me to succumb, to give in, to submit.

"He's *your* pet, Nikolai. Don't play me for a fool. The dance partners weren't for me, they were for *you.*"

His gray eyes flash with a lightning strike that sets fire to his features, a puff of black smoke sweeping across his irises.

"They were for *both* of us, Anya. I was building a life for us, regardless of how you choose to see it."

He keeps saying my name and I hate it. He acts as though he thinks of me as a person when all I've ever been to him is his talent slave.

His *rabynya.*

His *slave girl.*

I choke against his grip as he drags my body down the couch, pulling me beneath him until I'm flat on my back. He pins me there with his hips settled on mine and I cough when he finally loosens his grip on my throat.

His nose touches mine as he bends over me. "I would've kept you forever."

The edges of his voice soften in a way I've never heard before. I gasp, flinching at the sound of it, his hot breath dancing across my skin. His eyes spark with the truth of his admission and it's as though he's stabbing me in the heart with it.

I take in a deep breath, my chest and belly rising to meet his as I fill my lungs. "But you didn't keep me. You sold me."

His eyes flicker to my lips. "Because you betrayed me."

"You hurt me, tortured me, used me for years, Nikolai. What would you have gotten out of keeping me forever? How long would that forever have been? Every time I looked at you, I hated you more. I hate you now more than ever."

My eyes burn as I speak my truth openly, no longer fearful of his retribution because it doesn't matter. He has me for the night, but no punishment he could serve would compare to the torment to come—the torment of waiting for Ezra to save me before my lust for death returns, too overpowering to deny.

"You disgust me," I tell him, tempted to spit on him, baring my teeth.

His nostrils flare as the corners of his mouth lift into a snarl. I open my mouth to insult him more, but he smothers my words with his open mouth on mine. His kiss crashes down on me so ferociously that it freezes me, still as a statue. His tongue sweeps inside my mouth, seeking mine, and my anger ticks. I slam my hands against his chest and by some miracle, take him off guard. I push hard enough that he topples off the couch and I take the opportunity to rise and flee.

Except, there's nowhere for me to go.

And I've just denied the devil.

I move to the far corner of the room, expecting him to already be upon me before I spin and press my back against it. But he hasn't chased me. He stands, hovering in front of the couch where he fell, fists clenched at his sides, stance wide and domineering.

"Your punishment, *rabynya*," he begins, and I brace myself to hear the worst, "will not involve pain or fear. Your punishment is pleasure."

What?

He stalks toward me as I work to make sense of what he's telling me.

My punishment is…pleasure?

"You betrayed me. You gave your body to someone it didn't belong to with careless regard for your master's wishes. Tonight you tried to take your own life. Your body and your life do not belong to you, they belong to your master." He arrives in front of me and I hold my breath as he presses in close, his body molding to mine. "Your punishment will be your own body's betrayal against your heart and mind."

I turn my head as he leans in close, just to avoid his piercing stare.

"I intend to seduce you, Anya. I'm going to touch you in

all the ways you wished I would touch you before. I'm going to make you wet with need. I'm going to bring you to the point of aching for my touch until you willingly drop to your knees and crawl to me."

His fingertips gently trail over the tops of my thighs, slowly gathering the fabric of my gown. "And then I'll remind you of Ezra because then you will know how you have betrayed him. I'll return you to Vigo, sexually satisfied, though your heart will ache with the weight of your disloyalty knowing what you and I have done, knowing how you dripped with need for me as you begged for my cock."

My breathing grows rapid and shallow as he speaks, as his fingers reach beneath the gathered hem at my knees and creep upward. If he were to succeed in the punishment he proposes, the aftermath would truly be the worst punishment I could ever endure.

He knew I'd given my heart entirely to Ezra and he wished to use it against me now. If I'd ever felt anything for Nikolai, one ounce of caring or concern, one hope for his humanity, it no longer—

Oh.

His fingers graze upward across my flesh and his hands turn sensually to grip the crease where my thighs meet my hip bones. He breathes lightly against my neck as he runs his nose along my skin and his thumbs rub gentle circles over my sensitive flesh.

My whimper is involuntary.

I don't want to want this.

At least, my mind and my heart don't.

But my body betrays me as always, especially in the aftermath of my sexual experience with Ezra when we were chained in that secret room. Once with Ezra didn't feel like enough, and my body continues to hum with need for him after coming on his lap so spectacularly.

Ezra had primed me for more sexual touch and now I'm receiving it from Nikolai.

This makes me hate Nikolai so much more as my skin prickles with awareness, my body excited for this touch that isn't harming or hurting. Sensation is deceitful in the way it clouds my mind in the moment, even knowing how it will hurt my heart when it's gone.

Maybe I am just a horrible slut.

I don't deserve Ezra.

"Do you recall the one time you came to me willingly, Anya? It was not so long after your first partnership with Jamal ended…a few months before I brought you Erik to dance with." His lips caress the skin behind my ear. "I was in the shower when you came to find me in my room. Do you remember?"

Did I remember?

Of course, I remembered. He'd taken Jamal after our performance failed to meet his standards. He was my first partner and I was so lost after Nikolai took him away. I'd developed a connection with him—not the same as my soulmate connection with Ezra, nothing could compare to that. But I'd been distraught, heartbroken, struggling to come to terms with the reality of my captivity.

The day he's asking me about held the only halfway decent memory of Nikolai that I had. It was the memory I'd had to conjure up time and time again, each time he forced me into sex that I didn't want. It was the only orgasm I had with him by choice and it was only because I was desperately lonely that day.

I'd been naïve in my loneliness then, just seeking comfort, and his behavior that day might've changed the course of our entire relationship as master and slave. There was a part of me that thought we could be something more.

But I'd been wrong.

He'd only used my willingness that day as a means to study my sexuality so he could use it against me—like he's planning to do now—to force me into pleasure that I don't want and didn't ask for.

"I remember," I tell him plainly, forcing my focus to the unlit fireplace, trying to imagine flames as a distraction to the way he touches me.

"Do you remember how I made you come on my fingers?"

I swallow as his lips skim across my skin to kiss the hollow of my throat. "You used me." My voice is monotone, detached. "You didn't want me the way I wanted you that day. You used my willingness against me."

He pulls his head back to look at me, his gray gaze piercing mine as he grips my chin and turns my face toward his.

"And you're so fucking sure that's all it was for me?"

He smacks his palm against my cheek, not hard, but hard enough that it shoots a sting across my face and startles me.

I narrow my eyes at him. "Yes."

His fingers move until both hands hold my face at my jawline. He holds me there as he leans in to kiss me, bruising my lips with his. He pulls his mouth from mine with a smack of his lips and rests his forehead against mine.

"You're as inobservant as you are beautiful, Anya."

He's such a filthy, goddamn liar.

"You'll have to try harder if you wish to seduce me into thinking you ever wanted more from me than unwavering obedience to bend to your sadistic will."

A smirk tilts his lips. "I missed this version of you...the one that fought me."

"How could you possibly miss it? You literally beat it out

of me, Nikolai. I have the scars to show for it."

"You don't remember what happened the day after you came to me, do you?"

"I don't know what you're talking about."

He licks his tongue across the flat line of my mouth, then bites my bottom lip, tugging it hard, causing me to whimper. Both of his hands move to grab me by the waist as he walks backward toward the bed, pulling me with him. He lowers to sit when he reaches the side and spreads his legs wide, dragging me in to stand between them.

My brow furrows as his fingers slip beneath the straps of my dress, sliding them off my shoulders. I wait for him to say more as he tugs on the dress, encouraging it to fall from my figure and tumble to the floor. I wait as his rough palms test the weight of my bare breasts, the tops of which are covered with my dried blood. I wait as his thumbs brush the peak of my nipples, coaxing them to harden, spreading warmth through my stomach. I wait as his eyes latch onto mine, sending me a look that burrows into my soul.

He sighs, uncharacteristically and dangerously calm. "It's just as well you don't remember."

The sexuality he draws over my skin seeps into my pores and lights a flame of physical desire that I don't want. I fan the flame, turning it toward my anger instead.

"Remember *what?* Do you wish to pique my curiosity? You have it. So tell me."

"It doesn't matter anymore. I sold you to Vigo. You're not mine…not anymore."

"Except that I'm here with you now and you're behaving as if you still hold ownership over me."

"You weren't even mine when I had you."

He says it smoothly, calmly, in a way that takes me

completely off guard. Nikolai has never been smooth or calm with me; he's been angry and jealous, lust-driven and violent. He's been aggressive and hateful and unpredictably brutal. This is so off-character that the back of my neck prickles with baffled and cautious awareness.

I could almost believe his sincerity with the look of his eyes as they soften, but I've never known a soft side to him. Except for the day he mentioned when I came to him willingly—but that was years ago. It was all a rouse to study me. It might have felt sincere at the time, but I know him better now.

So, what happened the day after and why can't I remember?

I have to know.

I drop to my knees between his wide-open legs and grip each of his muscular thighs. I slide my hands forward until they meet his hips, turning the tables on this seduction.

"Tell me what happened the day after." I bring temptation to my tone. "Please, *moy khozyain.*"

I bring my hands together to meet at his buckle and his hands snap to mine in a flash, snatching them in both his large hands and leaning forward. He brings my hands to his lips to kiss my knuckles and nausea strikes in my belly.

He's not allowed to be gentle with me.

Only Ezra has earned that right.

"If you don't recall then there's no point in telling you. No one else of importance knows. Don't ask me again."

I stare at him with ferocity as my brain works to go backward in time.

What happened the day after?

What the hell happened?

I vaguely remember Nikolai's brother bringing me to his office.

But why was I with Nikolai's brother?

We were drinking.

Yes.

His brother had forced me to partake until I reached a point of total inebriation before taking me to Nikolai's office. They were both there, so was Kostya. And there was another man, too...someone I'd never seen before and haven't seen since.

But why was he there?

"We signed something," I say slowly, testing the words for myself more than to ask him.

Nikolai grabs the back of my head and yanks me toward him in a flash. His lips fall against mine to silence me and he's successful because I'm too lost in searching my memory to fight him off. He moans against my mouth, parting my lips with a sweep of his tongue. I kiss back, an old habit from when I was his obedient little fuck girl.

Nikolai stops kissing for a beat and speaks with his lips brushing against mine. "Sit on my cock, Anya, sink me deep inside you."

My brain stops searching for the memory and snaps me back into the moment. My heart beats faster, pulsing an old, familiar danger signal through my veins. My eyebrows slant toward my nose in determination as I yank my hands away from his grip.

"No," I tell him and my heart races, knowing how stupid it is to refuse him, but feeling compelled to all the same.

I sit back on my heels, turning my face away and brace for his rage, his outburst, his violent attack against my bold disobedience.

But it doesn't come.

Instead, his hands rush to remove his clothes. He stands, his hips only inches from my face as he loosens and removes his tie before working the buttons of his shirt. He tosses them both aside and rushes to his buckle. I'm frozen, shocked, overwhelmed, dangerously curious that he hasn't beaten me, cut me, bent me over and fucked me painfully from behind for my refusal.

In moments, he's naked before me, cock standing proud and thick, heavy with lust. He lowers quickly to sit on the edge of the bed again, grabbing my hair on the way down and dragging me forward. I think he's going to force me to take him inside my mouth and I swallow hard. But he surprises me yet again; instead, he lifts up on my hair, pulling a thick section high above my head and tugging painfully until I'm scrambling to get on my feet to lessen the pressure.

My breaths quicken, my heart thumping hard. I see the Nikolai I once knew return now that he's descended into a feral, sexually desperate state.

He releases my hair once I'm standing and grasps my hips. He pulls me forward, wrapping his arms around my waist and kissing my belly button. His tongue sweeps out, drawing flat across my skin and my body responds. He breathes out harshly through his nose, the rush of air heating my flesh, and I watch his shoulders tremble as he inhales my scent.

He *trembles*.

I've seen him in the throes of passion, but I've never seen him tremble with need. I struggle to make sense of that as his fingers reach down to cup my bottom, squeezing and pulling me closer. His lips graze lower, traveling down until he reaches the curls above my sex, and the heat of his breath drags sensation down with it. I feel the rush of need dampen my core and sadness rushes with it, too.

Nikolai lifts me with his strong arms, slipping his knee between my legs, forcing them apart. He shifts me until I'm straddling him. With one arm wrapped firmly around my back, he reaches between us with the other, grasping his thick erection and positioning me to take it.

I press my eyes shut and feel a tear slip from the corner, gliding slowly down my cheek. He lines me up and pushes me down, making me take his cock all the way, deep inside me. I let him take my weight, let him hold me against him because I've lost the strength to hold myself up.

This is too much.

It was only hours ago that I made love to Ezra, just like this. And Nikolai is taking that moment from me now. It hurts so much more that he's behaving differently than I've ever known him to be.

He pushes my hair over my shoulder so it drapes behind my back before he kisses the nick on my neck where I attempted to cut myself.

"I dare you not to move," he says to me. "I dare you not to fuck me, to hold still while I touch you, kiss you, lick you, drive you to the point of madness."

Bastard.

Anger replaces my sadness and it kickstarts my pulse, racing a fever of rage through my veins that threatens to explode from my pores. I can't stop myself from lashing out, not now, not while he tricks my body into wanting pleasure from him.

I shove my hands against his bare chest, pushing as I arch my back away from him. He doesn't budge and I remain firmly in his grasp with his arms tight around me. I shout out my anger and beat my fists against his chest, but it doesn't faze him. Instead, it only heightens his awareness and feeds his lust.

His mouth clamps over the crook of my neck and he sucks in a gentle, sensual rhythm—not his usual biting fervor; this time it's softer and more sexual. I could cry with the way he worships my skin with his mouth, drawing across my collarbone to the hollow of my throat as I lean away.

I thrash and pull as his head dips for my breast, sucking my nipple into his mouth and rolling his tongue around it.

"Stop," I plead, my palms landing flat on his chest to try to shove him away one last time.

But then he groans as he sucks, sending a shivering vibration like a lightning bolt from my nipple straight through to my clit.

"Stop," I say again, but my voice is softer, weaker.

My hands slip from his chest, my body melting to the good feelings that ripple from my core. I look down at Nikolai and he releases my nipple to look up at me. He's panting in need as he watches me and I realize I'm panting, too. It's from the exertion of fighting him.

No, it's the feeling of his swollen cock shoved inside my throbbing cunt.

I am a slut, a whore—just like Nikolai said.

"I can't..." I say, but it's more for me than for him.

I wish he would just take me and be done with it. I wish he would slam me to the ground, fuck me until he comes, then leave me to pick up my broken pieces on my own. But instead, he watches me, caresses me, heats my skin with his desperate breathing, and fills me with dirty, wanton need.

I need to move.

I need to fuck.

I need to come.

I need, but I don't want. It will tear me apart to hold that burden of guilt, for being the woman who made the choice to fuck another for her own pleasure. I can't do that to Ezra.

I can't.

"I hate you," I whisper.

"You can hate me while you fuck me," he breathes against

my throat, turning his head to kiss a line along my jaw all the way back to my ear.

His tongue flicks my earlobe and I jolt, surprised by the feel of it, and the movement rocks me forward. We both groan with the small movement of my hips over his. Only his groan is pure pleasure where mine is tinged with a thousand painful emotions.

I push out a heavy breath, dropping my head to look down between us, forcing myself to see the shame of our physical connection. Somehow I hope to convince my body to stop this madness, this nightmare where I want to rock and grind and fuck Nikolai until I come.

But looking is a mistake because the bastard is so tragically attractive. I feel torn apart. My mind screams for this to stop, my heart pounds with sadness and shame, my body swells and slickens and begs for a release at any cost.

This is when I realize how little strength I have left—at the moment I rock back then forward with intention.

Goddammit.

Nikolai groans, holding me tighter, burying his face in the side of my neck, and I shudder.

He's not supposed to hold me like this, touch me like this, let me fuck him like this. I hate him more than ever before— yet I need this release so much. I need to fuck, to take all the good feelings he stole from me.

My hips move of their own free will, rocking forward and back, forward and back. I press down, slackening in his hold to ensure he's sunk inside me as deep as he can be because the swell of him feeds my pleasure.

"I hate you," I pant out as I move. "I hate everything about you."

"Show me how much you hate me, Anya. Fuck me with

every ounce of hatred you possess."

Why is there a hint of weakness in his voice?

His hand finds its way to my breast and he pinches the hard peak between his fingers, rolling it sensually. The roll sends pleasure tumbling around my insides, falling down, down, down to my throbbing clit, making me clench with desperate need for release.

I grip his shoulders in my palms and I fuck. I fuck hard and dirty like the slutty slave he's reduced me to.

"I want it back," I huff. "Give it back."

Surely, what I'm saying makes no sense to him, but I don't care. It doesn't matter. I want him to give back everything he's stolen from me.

Happiness.

Security.

Freedom.

Ezra.

He took Ezra from me by selling me.

Ezra's green eyes and smile break through the cloud of brokenness in my mind. Though I know it should halt me, should stop me from fucking, instead it sparks an explosion inside me.

I scream out my relief as I come with visions of Ezra swirling through my mind. The release is so strong that it's nearly painful. It clenches every muscle in my body until every part of me bursts with pleasure and relaxes into dopamine-induced bliss.

I'm only barely aware as Nikolai flips me onto the mattress, slamming me down on my back and rutting inside me until he comes, spilling a rush of warm liquid inside me.

My entire body is limp, lax from the overwhelming orgasm, and I feel as though I have nothing left in me to give.

Exhausted and defeated, I begin to cry.

Nikolai kisses the tears that stream down my cheeks, licking them away.

"That's a good girl, *rabynya*. Don't worry. I'll be sure to tell Ezra that I didn't hurt you tonight. I'll let him know how you fucked me and came harder than I've ever felt before."

I let my head fall to the side, looking at the wall. "Tell him what you want. He knows me and loves me all the same…" I turn back to look him in the eye. "Not that you would know anything of love."

He stills and a flicker of something passes across his eyes only to disappear into the abyss of his soul. "I know more than you think."

He climbs off me and crosses to the fireplace, lifting the half full glass of whiskey he'd set down before.

"Don't move," he instructs. "I intend to fill you at least three more times tonight."

I press my eyes shut, letting tears pour from beneath my lashes until there aren't any more to spill.

CHAPTER 19

Anya

I'M ORDERED TO put my dress back on and sit quietly in the chair when someone knocks on the door. It's early morning, the sun just beginning to rise and casting an orange and yellow glow from the windows.

Nikolai is still in a state of undress, fresh from our morning shower together. He promised me three, but he fucked me five more times. The final session ended only ten minutes ago in the shower.

He'd bent me over and rammed into me from behind with my hands against the wall. It felt like it went on forever, my pussy sore and overused. He insisted that I come again on his cock and I'd run out of carnal energy to force my body to submit beyond my mind's will. But Nikolai insisted, and he always gets what he wants. As a result, my pussy is swollen, painful, and rubbed raw.

I feel like dying now just as much as I did before.

I perch on an armchair near the fireplace, wearing last night's golden gown. The blood stains remain along the neckline, but the dried blood has been washed clean from my skin. The slices I made in my neck and wrist stopped bleeding, though the fresh marks serve as an immediate reminder of what I've done.

Nikolai pulls the door open, revealing Vigo standing there and panicked nausea coils around my insides like a snake. I pull my legs up to tuck them beneath me and I curl into a tiny ball on the chair.

"I've come to collect my pretty little doll," Vigo says.

Nikolai works to fasten the buttons on his shirt as he tilts his head to beckon him inside, only it's not just Vigo. Kostya and Leo have come along, too, escorting Sasha and...Ezra.

Ezra's eyes search the room. I lift my head and straighten my spine at the tingle of awareness I feel. Our eyes meet and he moves, rushing past the others as though his life depends on touching me.

Maybe it does.

I feel that way about him, too.

I stand, whipping around the chair in a flash. My arms open for him and our bodies crash together with force.

No one protests or stops him, but naturally, he's taking me away from them, pushing me backward as he holds me tight, walking me to the farthest wall in the room. He doesn't stop moving until he has my back to the wall. He holds me tight, refusing to move.

My heart is pounding for no other reason than his body pressed against mine. My current and former master are in this room with no escape. Danger swirls around us like a dark cloud. But being in his arms feels like constant lightning strikes, shocking me with a relentless fire of desperate need.

"I love you," I whisper into the side of his neck. "I love you, I love you."

My hands slip up to catch his cheeks, and I look at him, giving him all the sadness and hurt and love and longing that's twisted and tangled in my soul for him. His green eyes give it all back to me in equal measure and it's how I know he's the only man that ever would've been for me.

"Made for each other," he says to me.

The perfection of his words—reflecting exactly what I'm feeling inside—crushes my heart in all the beautiful, tragic ways love ever possibly could.

Urgency washes across the reverie and he dips his head to kiss me. I hold nothing back, swiftly seeking his tongue to mingle with mine, to speak that language without words that only the two of us know. It takes only seconds to lose myself in him, to forget the world around us and drown in the pure satisfaction of his lips on mine.

But then I open my eyes and I see Vigo.

He stands just behind Ezra's back, hardly a foot away.

It startles me to see him so close and I pull my head back too harshly, breaking our kiss. The back of my head lands with a thud against the wall behind me and my eyes narrow on the demon himself, angry with the way he so cruelly pulled me back to reality.

Ezra registers my unease, his face falling as he sees my expression. He spins around, pinning me between his back and the wall.

"Well, isn't this a precious moment? It really is too bad that no one gives a fuck about a slave who can make love to them sweetly. We might've been able to sell you two as a package deal." Vigo clicks his tongue and Ezra presses harder against me, protective in his stance. "As it were, my clients prefer something a little more extreme. So, I guess it's time for me to take back my sad, broken little doll so I can rent her out for what she's useful for—dark, dirty, heathen fucking."

I gasp as I see Nikolai rush toward Vigo from behind. He reaches him quickly and drags him away by the back of his shirt. I grip Ezra's biceps, willing him not to react and flee when all I need is him right in front of me, keeping me safe. I turn my head and rest my cheek against his back, breathing in his scent.

Nikolai drags Vigo across the room and they stop in the corner farthest from us. They speak in hushed tones, though we can hear them all the same.

"I thought you understood the terms of your contract," Nikolai seethes. "You spent the night reviewing it with Cordelia, didn't you? Or were you too busy fucking each other to handle business?"

"Relax," Vigo tells him with a knowing smile. "I'm only trying to get a rise out of them."

"Anya is *not* to be shared. Have you been renting her out to your clients?"

"No, though she has had a fair number of offers since the video of her fucking that stuffed rabbit in her sweet little pigtails and blue dress. I'm losing money off the bitch by following your terms, Nikolai. You should be grateful she's still alive."

"How much?"

"How much?" Vigo cocks his head to the side. "How much *what?* How much have I lost?"

Nikolai inhales a thick breath and speaks through bared teeth. "How much to buy her back?"

"*What?*" Ezra says and they both snap their heads to look at us.

Their tempers flare, heating their discussion.

"I'm not selling her back to you, Nikolai," Vigo tells him. "I enjoy tormenting her far too much to give that up for money. In fact, the torment it causes *you* makes her priceless to me." I can hear the smile in Vigo's tone.

Cocky bastard.

"You said you're losing money on her," Nikolai asserts.

"Sell her back and cut your losses."

Vigo laughs. "You make it easier and easier to deny you every time you open your mouth. Every ounce of passion for her that you show me strengthens my desire to keep her and do awful, *awful* things to her. This conversation is over, Nikolai. Unless you want to go to the board and waste their time asking them to reaffirm what you already know. She is *mine* now. I purchased her fairly and that's that."

I hear the way Nikolai hisses through his teeth. "Then you can go and take her back from my slave."

Ezra straightens to his full height and widens his stance.

"Order him to move aside," Vigo requests.

"I have no interest in doing that. You want to take her back with you, so take her back. Fight him if you must. I don't care."

Kostya barks out harsh words to Nikolai, asking him in Russian if he's lost his damn mind, though not in those exact words. Nikolai only orders Kostya to be quiet.

I think Kostya might be right.

I think Nikolai *has* lost his damn mind.

Vigo whips around and charges across the room toward us, stopping just in front of Ezra.

Ezra presses back into me, protecting me, though I can feel his muscles twitch, ready for a fight.

"Move," Vigo orders him.

My heart skips and stutters, then bursts into a pounding rhythm. My hands squeeze around Ezra's arms. I know my fingers are digging into his flesh, but he lets me dig, thank God.

I don't want to go back with Vigo.

But I also don't want Ezra to get himself into trouble. Vigo grins as he postures, sending out notice with his stance that he's prepared to fight Ezra.

Between the two of them, the air rumbles with the

anticipation of combat. Two overwhelming forces, one darkness and one light; their auras sizzle and crackle where they crash together in the space between.

It's overwhelming.

It feels almost inevitable that these two forces should collide and explode to release the searing tension.

Ezra has gone rigid, every muscle in his body tense and braced for attack. The way he covers me, protects me, stands up to fight for me melts my icy heart all over again. He's putting himself at risk of future consequences, yet he does it for me.

Damnit, if that doesn't make me love him so much more.

Ezra reaches back to tap the side of my hip with his hand. I know without words that he's encouraging me to let go of his arms. He wants me to remove my touch so he can focus on fighting for me.

This fight won't end well. One of them will get hurt, probably both, and it won't resolve anything. Whether Ezra fights Vigo or not, Vigo is taking me back to my box. I will still belong to the Vittoris. I will still be tortured and brutalized. I will still be without Ezra.

Let him fight.

In resignation and in love, I force my fingers to loosen their grip and slip away from his arms.

Ezra steps forward, tilting his head from side to side to stretch his neck. He pushes his navy-blue suit jacket to fall off his shoulders and onto the ground. He tosses the dangling end of his necktie over his shoulder and clenches his fists, sending Vigo a clear message.

"You're gonna have to go through me to get to her."

The look of Ezra bristling with rage and readying himself to fight also sends *me* a clear message. It rushes straight past my senses and clenches deep within my core. Pride and wonder and a deep, primal need spiral around my insides and it makes me feel…everything. I feel everything for him.

Vigo lifts his chin, an upward nod of acknowledgment, with a sadistic grin of entertained delight. He pauses, taking his time to remove his precious cufflinks. He casually rolls up his sleeves as Ezra rolls his shoulders, clenching and unclenching his fists, preparing to deliver a beating.

Then there's a silent beat of waiting.

Nikolai remains in the far corner of the room with his arms crossed over his chest, his head tipped to the side with a look of curiosity on his face. He shows no signs of interference.

Is he hoping Ezra will start this fight so Nikolai will have an excuse to punish him later?

Why hasn't Nikolai stopped him yet?

Why haven't I stopped him yet?

Because I don't want to.

I lift my hand to graze down Ezra's spine. Though it should be, it's not a touch meant to soothe him, to calm him, to encourage him to back down. It's not a touch that tells him to keep his cool so he doesn't make things worse. It's a touch of finality, a touch of acceptance, of encouragement, because I've had enough of this shit, too.

That seems to be all the encouragement he needs. I can nearly hear his overused adrenaline pump whirring into action. He steps forward and Vigo lurches.

They collide in fists and fury.

They're both snarling wolves snapping and clawing with brute force.

Ezra swings a side jab that collides with Vigo's skull, just to the side of his left eye. Vigo turns out of the hit, spinning around and charging toward Ezra like a linebacker, catching him in the gut with his shoulder and pushing him back. They're quickly coming toward me. Ezra manages to hold steady for a few beats, but I yelp when he stumbles, jumping and scrambling away after he lands on his ass in front of my feet. Ezra doesn't fall to his back, though. He fights to sit upright, reaching over Vigo's back and punching his sides, over and over.

Vigo climbs, trying to push Ezra down on his back so he can get on top and pummel him, but Ezra is strong. He grabs Vigo's skinny hips and flips him sideways, rolling on top of him as quickly as he can. Straddling him, Ezra squeezes his knees in against Vigo's hips to grip him in place. Ezra grabs Vigo's tie and wraps it around his fist, pulling just enough to lift his head off the floor. Ezra punches and punches and punches at Vigo's face until blood spurts from his broken nose.

I can only see the side of Ezra's face in his manic beating, but it looks like he's smiling down at Vigo as the red spatters his pristine white button-down shirt and stains the carpet beneath them.

Ezra hits.

And hits.

And hits.

I've never felt so many things at once. Watching Ezra defend me makes me feel proud and powerful. It makes me feel love and deep respect for him. It makes me feel horror and fear for the consequences to follow. It makes me feel strangely aroused and desperately needy for this formidable man who gave me his heart.

"I hope you die, motherfucker!" Ezra screams down at Vigo, lost in his violent rage. "I'll fucking kill you!"

"*Mal'chik!*" My head snaps up at the sound of Nikolai's voice, but Ezra doesn't stop, doesn't even acknowledge that he heard it. "That's enough. Stop."

Ezra punches.

He hits.

He pounds.

Nikolai's nostrils flare and he storms forward—I know I have to stop Ezra before Nikolai gets to him. Ezra might start swinging at Nikolai and only God knows what would happen to him then.

"Ezra." I say his name softly but firmly, as a command of my own, because he is mine as much as I am his.

Only a second passes before Ezra stops. He lets go of Vigo's tie and drops his head onto the carpet with a thump. Ezra's chest heaves as he inhales and exhales heavy breaths.

Confident that Ezra is no threat to me, even in his violent fury, I step forward and reach out to touch him. My fingers only brush his shoulder before he snatches my hand in his bloodied ones. He stands in a flash, whirling around to face me and throws his arms around me. This time I'm pulling *him* backward, wanting to protect him from the consequences to come if he'd been given seconds or minutes longer. He might've beaten Vigo to death given more time.

I don't even know what the punishment would be for a slave killing a Head of House.

I wanted Ezra to kill Vigo.

Then Nikolai.

Even Leo Leblanc and Murphy O'Shea.

But killing them probably wouldn't matter to our freedom. Their reach is so vast that I don't even know how we could ever fully escape if we were lucky enough to get away.

Regardless, my love and loyalty to Ezra has strengthened immeasurably over these short moments. He would do anything for me. He would put his life at risk for me. I know I have to keep my promise to him—I just don't know how. There's still a nagging voice in the back of my mind that tells me death would ease all my suffering.

Maybe that voice will never go away.

If that's true, then I have to find a way to silence it.

"I'm sorry," Ezra whispers to me, holding me tight in his vice-like embrace. "I shouldn't have done that. I know." He kisses the crook of my neck, silently telling me of his regret.

"No regrets," I tell him plainly, squeezing him. "I love you. I love you so much."

"God, I love you, Anya." He spreads his legs apart to sink to my height so he can be closer to me. "I love you. I'm yours."

"I know you're mine. Always."

"I'll save you. I promise." He grabs my cheeks and kisses me with an explosive passion in the aftermath of his rage. I want nothing more than this—his lips on mine, his tongue aggressively seeking the taste of me as I open for him. I don't even care about the blood on his hands that smudge my cheeks. It's Vigo's blood and that makes me feel somehow more powerful, more capable of survival.

He pulls back and gives me his gaze. I relish the vibrancy of his eyes, knowing that he'll be taken from me at any moment. His green eyes and my blue mingle. Between the two of us we are green earth and blue ocean—forces formidable on their own, but together entirely unmovable, unshakeable, significant, and mighty.

Ezra is the savior who rescued me, then destroyed me. He is the lover who showed me pleasure that made the pain more profound. He is the soul mate who completed me, then ripped me apart with his absence. He is the end and the beginning and everything in-between.

Then Nikolai rips him away from me and I fear our in-between may be done too soon.

Our end may be coming.

The Vittoris stay an extra day at the Leblancs' estate to allow Vigo time to recover. He'd suffered cuts and scrapes and bruises, though the worst injury he received was a broken nose. He would be fine.

As a slave, I'd suffered the same injuries, though not necessarily all at once. Still, if a tiny, insignificant woman such as myself could continue vigorous dance rehearsals with a broken nose, surely Vigo could quit whining like a small child and pull himself out of bed.

Who's weak and pathetic now?

Renata sends me to the Leblanc kitchen to get more ice for Vigo's swollen jaw. She sends her slave, Luca, with me to ensure I don't try anything stupid.

Like grab a kitchen knife and finally cut my throat open wide.

She doesn't understand that I don't require suicide watch because I'd made a promise to Ezra to try—to do my best to stay alive while he tried to find a way to save me. No such way existed, but Ezra deserved to hang onto his hope, even if mine had been lost. He *needs* that hope—he needs to hope and dream and believe in something more. It's part of what makes him Ezra, and I love that about him. So I'll pretend I haven't given up on a future for as long as I can… for his sake.

When we reach the kitchen, I'm surprised to run into Kostya. I would have thought Nikolai would have left when the O'Sheas had, and that was hours ago. Kostya catches my eye with a fearful yet determined sort of look that draws my curiosity.

I do my best to be surreptitious, telling Luca to go on through the large kitchen and look in the walk-in pantry for some plastic bags to put the ice in. He's so used to blind obedience with Renata that he immediately walks away.

Kostya takes advantage of Luca's absence and rushes toward me. I take a step back, unnerved by his eagerness. But we both stop and still when he's just in front of me. He looks left and right, checking for anyone who might be watching, and my eyebrows draw together.

He reaches into his pocket and pulls out an object. Reaching for my hand, he places the object on my palm and closes my fingers around it.

Kostya whispers to me in Russian. He tells me to use it when all feels lost, that Ezra will be given one as well. He tells me to hide it, keep it silent, and only use it when it's absolutely necessary. Because when the battery dies, that's it. He has no way to get me another.

I look down at my hand, jaw dropped open at what he's given me.

A cell phone.

A small, cheap texting-and-phone-calls-only kind of phone.

I ask him why.

He tells me he made a promise to Nikolai a long time ago—a promise to keep my heart beating even if Nikolai stopped it himself.

Kostya promised Nikolai he'd keep me alive?

Kostya knows how much I need Ezra to get me through hell with Vigo. He tells me I'll find only one contact listed on the phone when I turn it on, but I should wait until I'm home with the Vittoris and the phone can be hidden.

I'm baffled speechless.

I had distrusted Kostya for all these years.

But he'd given me pills when I was in pain, and now he's

giving me a phone to text Ezra.

Only, he looks conflicted about it. I ask him if Nikolai told him to do this and he tells me no, rather emphatically. I know he's telling the truth by the way his eyes dart around the room, watching for anyone who might see or hear us.

Luca returns rather abruptly and Kostya turns on his heel, vanishing down the hallway before I can thank him.

Once again I'm grateful for Luca's blind obedience as I send him back inside the kitchen to fill one of the plastic bags with ice. I take that time to stuff the phone deep inside my jeans pocket, thankful the bottom of my shirt flares out loosely, just enough to hide the bulge until I can secure it safely beneath my mattress in my box at the Vittoris.

Luca and I return to our masters with the ice requested and my heart twitters with a flurry of excitement. There's something to look forward to, though it may be short lived. The phone battery will lose its charge at some point. But sometime soon, when I need him the most, I'll be able to reach out and contact Ezra.

Perhaps all is not lost.

Not yet.

CHAPTER 20
EZRA

SEEING ANYA—ONLY TO be taken from her again—was almost as hard as not seeing her at all. Her rosy scent is starting to fade from the pink evening gown I sleep beside in her room at Mikhailov Manor. Each night it fades a little more, only sinking me further into fear.

Fear of forgetting her scent, her smile, the electric crackle of her touch.

Fear of losing her entirely.

It's only been a week since I saw her last at the Leblancs' and every minute that passes without a plan to save her makes me more fearful. Saving her and doing it soon is all I can think about now. My mind has spun its way through thousands of escape plans—a thousand possibilities and all of them are shitty. I know the odds are stacked against us—the probability of me actually finding a way to save her is next to nothing—but it won't stop me from trying.

I run my brain through a new train of thought while I sit on her armchair by the window and flip through the box of pictures of her sister Lidia. I've started keeping my pictures of Emma here as a reminder that any escape plan comes with high stakes for all of us.

Anya had received and placed the last picture of Lidia in the box the week before Nikolai sold her to Vigo. Looking at it now, I can see how they have the same smile. It's bright and true and has the sort of quality that makes you feel like you're special if you get to see it. On the back, as with all the pictures, are two numbers.

Eighteen.

Thirty.

Lidia's eighteen years old now. She looks happy in this picture, bright and cheerful. She looks more like her big sister now than she did in her younger pictures. Though it hurts my heart to see these—to look at Anya's sister, to see Emma, and know they're being stalked just for a weekly photo—it humbles my more outrageous ideas for escape. These pictures remind me that I can't just improvise, I can't be reckless, I can't fuck this up.

The picture I hold is the last one of Lidia. Nikolai hasn't brought anymore of her since Anya was sold months ago, though I continue to get new pictures of Emma.

Is Anya getting pictures of Lidia from Vigo?

Is Lidia alive?

Have they stopped watching her?

Maybe she's safe.

Of course, she's not safe…none of us are safe.

When the door to my room—Anya's room—bursts open wide without warning, I merely glance up from the picture in my hand. Though I was certain I'd see Nikolai standing there, I tilt my head in curiosity to see Kostya instead. Nikolai rather enjoys being unexpected company, so I'm surprised it's not him standing at my door. He's been gone a lot lately, though. He left again on business travel only a day or so after we returned from the quarterly meeting in Louisiana. Here we are, a week later, and I have yet to see him make an appearance.

Kostya steps inside without invitation and shuts the door behind him. My heart starts thumping against my ribcage, though I can't really place the feeling. I'm not exactly fearful of Kostya, not in the way I am for Nikolai and his unpredictable rage. But I am uncomfortable with him since I don't really have him figured out, which makes me nervous.

Kostya hurries across the room toward me and I sit up straighter, confused by what he's doing. But then he stops right in front of me. We pause in a weird kind of stillness as he looks down at me and I look up at him. A look of uncertainty flickers across his face, as if he's not sure why he came in here in the first place, or perhaps he's second guessing himself.

I don't ask the question, I just wait.

After a moment, a decisive expression wipes away his uncertainty and he reaches into his jacket pocket. In one motion, I set the box of pictures down on the ottoman in front of me and stand, curling my fists, ready to fight if he's come here to kill me or—

Why would Kostya kill me?

Why wouldn't he?

He holds out his hand in front of me and I freeze.

There's a cell phone in his palm. One of those small, prepaid things you can grab and pay cash for on your way through the checkout lane.

"I take a big risk for you," Kostya says in his thick Russian accent and broken English.

I realize then that I've never really spoken to this man. He's just kind of existed in the background.

My eyes dart between the phone and his face, trying to figure out what the fuck he's doing and *why*.

"We have many of these. Paid in cash. Business done this way. I stole two."

"Two? You stole two phones? From who?"

"*Khozyain.*"

There's a Russian word I'll never fucking forget.

He stole them from my *master*.

"Why?"

He sighs, setting the phone down on the ottoman. He rubs a hand over the back of his neck and turns his head to look at the door with urgency.

"You do not tell him."

"I won't tell him," I affirm, my heart thumping harder. "Is this a way out?"

He shakes his head. "Not for escape. Do not call the police. They will not come here. Mikhailovs pay for silence."

Well, fuck.

I know he's not bluffing. I'd be surprised if Nikolai *didn't* have the local police in his pocket—though local would probably be a relative term considering how far we are from anything even resembling civilization.

"Then what is this for?"

"I give one to Anya at the Leblancs'. One phone. One battery. I do not think she can charge it. But I give it to her."

"But *why?*"

"I make promise to Nikolai long time ago. Keep her heart beating even if he hurt her. Stop him from killing her when he lose control. I know she will hurt self again if she does not talk to you."

My heart stops.

"I can call her on this?"

"No," he says firmly, stepping closer. "No, you cannot speak. Only text. You cannot risk the phones being found. Keep silent. You understand?"

I nod though I'm stunned into silence. .

"She sent text, ten minutes ago. You should reply soon."

"She texted?"

He nods, taking a backward step.

"Keep it silent. Keep it hidden. He finds it and I will say you stole it."

I reach down, lifting the small, black phone from the ottoman as if it were a precious, fragile jewel. "Understood."

He turns and walks toward the door, but I stop him just as he grips the knob.

"Hey. I don't know if this is some kind of sadistic trick you and Nikolai have masterminded just to fuck with me, but if it's not…thank you."

"It is not trick," he says pulling the door open. "You are welcome."

He leaves and I fall back into my seat as I stare at the small screen. There's one unread text. I sigh, swiping a hand over my face. I know this could be fake. Hell, it's more likely some sick plan for Nikolai to torment me further by making me think I'm texting Anya.

Yeah, this might be a setup…but what if it's not?

It's a simple phone. A few click-throughs show me immediately that there's no internet, no apps, nothing helpful at all. It's not a touch screen and certainly not a smartphone. It's made just for phone calls and texts.

Without giving it another thought, I open the message that's waiting. It's from a phone number that has already been entered as a contact on this phone. In fact, it's the only contact listed.

Plain and simple, the text is from A.

Kostya must have set that up before giving us the phones to make sure no one texted from another number that I might mistake as Anya.

A: Mine?

I sink back in my chair, lifting my hand to grip my hair as I stare at the screen in disbelief.

Only Anya would send that text.

I know it.

It's that punch in the gut feeling of just *knowing* it's her that makes me unintentionally hold my breath.

She sent her message twelve minutes ago. I have to hurry with my reply. I don't know what her living conditions are like—whether she has privacy to text me without someone catching her, whether her time to do this is limited.

E: Yours.

My knee bounces as I hold the phone in front of my face, staring, waiting more anxiously than I ever have been before, just hoping for a reply.

"Come on…please, Anya," I whisper at the phone.

Two full panic-inducing minutes pass before a reply pops up on the screen. The phone is already set to silent and it will have to stay that way, meaning I'm going to drive myself insane waiting and staring at this thing.

A: Is it really you?

I laugh, the breath I'd been holding rushes forcefully from my lungs. I feel relief, happiness, sadness, fear, and joy all at once. I know anybody could text that simple message, but I know it's her. I *know* it in the pit of my stomach.

E: Who else would it be?
A: It's really you.

My legs spread wide and I lean forward, resting my elbows

on my knees as I type.

E: Are you okay? Are you safe?

Our conversation continues, one reply after the next.

A: Safe? Really?
E: You know what I mean. Can you do this without getting caught?
A: I think so. But I can't charge it. When the battery dies, that's it.
E: Then we should make the most of our time.
A: What are you suggesting, E?

I reason that Kostya must have entered my number in her contacts, too. He put her in mine as A, so naturally, she sees my messages as being sent from E.

E: Your tone suggests a wandering mind, A.
A: You're imagining my tone, E.
E: Am I?
A: Not entirely…I miss you.
E: I miss you. So fucking much.

A couple of minutes pass without a reply. Though my fingers twitch to send another message, I wait. I wait because I don't know her situation or circumstances. I don't know where Vigo keeps her, whether it's safe for her to be texting me right now. I'm not going to risk her being found out by incessantly sending her texts—even though I think I could write her a goddamn novel right now and still not tell her everything I need to.

A: I'm really trying, E. I'm trying to keep my promise.

Shit.

There's an implication with this message. She's trying to keep the promise she made me at the Leblancs', her promise to stay alive, to give me time to work out a way to save her. But this message tells me she's struggling because she has to *try* not to kill herself.

Fuck.

She has to *try.*

I shoot to my feet and pace the floor, pent up energy springing my legs into action.

What do I say to her?

What can I possibly say to that?

E: I know you are and I love you more for it. Just for trying.

I squeeze my eyes shut after I press send. I think I can nearly feel her sigh from wherever the hell she is tonight.

A: I don't want to be morbid. Distract me. Give me some peace.
E: Just tell me what you need. You know I've got you.
A: I don't even know what I need.
E: Dick pic, maybe?

There's a pause.

I almost think that was a stupid thing to say, but I also know Anya. Sometimes she just needs a reminder that she's allowed to smile over something ridiculous, that she's allowed to take a break from being so damn serious. Though I am second-guessing it now because this situation has earned seriousness to the highest degree. And I know my sarcasm tends to get lost in translation, so...

A: Send it.

E: Seriously?

A: NO! I don't think I've ever laughed out loud here. Not until just now.

Snark met with snark. I've met my match with her. My cheeks hurt from the wide fucking grin on my face.

E: Damn. I had my pants off and everything for you.

A: Did you really?

E: I guess you'll never know.

A: I wouldn't be offended if you did. Actually, I'd be offended to find out that you didn't.

E: Take my pants off for you?

A: Yes.

Every message sends excitement rushing through every part of me.

Anya excites me.

Face to face or through secret texts on a prepaid phone. My body tingles just to know it's her on the other end of the line. She's fucking *everything* to me.

I pause halfway through typing out a reply when she sends another message.

A: Do you remember the first time we kissed?

Of course, I remembered.

It was the night that Nikolai forced me to help him rape her. I'd carried her back to her room that night, took care of her, cleansed her in the shower. We both admitted that night that we felt something connecting us. I'd told her that my heart raced for her. It was true then and it's true now, and I know that will never change.

E: Of course I remember. How could I ever forget?

A: I wanted you that night.

A: I dreamed about you that night.

A: I woke up, soaking wet between my legs and aching for you.

Jesus.

I lick my lips, running a hand across my mouth. Three texts sent from God knows where and this woman already has me half-hard.

E: I dreamed about you that night, too. I woke up hard.

A: Is that unusual for you? ;)

Did she just send me a fucking winking face?
Jesus Christ.
That's adorable.

E: Not unusual since I met you. Did you touch yourself? After dreaming about me?

A: I wanted to.

E: But you didn't?

A: It was the first time in three years I felt like I wanted to be touched. I just wasn't ready that night.

E: But two days later in Nobility Hall...

We dry fucked like two horny teenagers, I want to write, but I don't.

A: I was ready for it then. I felt safe with you.

E: That means everything to me.

A: That I felt safe with you?

E: Yes.

A: I always feel safe with you. I wish you were with me now.
E: I'm so sorry. I feel like I've failed you, A.
A: He's coming.

"Shit."

I burn a path into the rug with my panicked pacing. My veins pulse with adrenaline I can't resolve. If Vigo's coming for her now, I can't help her. I can't do a goddamn thing. If I thought it was hard before, it's nothing compared to the fear I have now.

He's coming, she wrote.

He's coming.

And I can't help her.

He's coming.

The last text I got from Anya was a haunting message sent a month ago.

He's coming.

I've all but died inside, not knowing what happened to her, where she is, if she's okay. I've devolved into a shell of a man who can hardly get out of bed.

I only eat when Nikolai forces me to, threatening to hurt Sasha if I refuse. I only sleep when I'm so beyond exhaustion—from dance rehearsals and being involved in Nikolai's sadistic torture-fuck sessions with poor Sasha—that my body forces itself to shut down.

I'm not the man Anya fell for right now, and I don't think I have it in me to become that man again until I know she's okay.

He's coming.

He was coming for her a goddamn month ago.

Did he find the phone?

Does he have her tied up somewhere?

Has she been tortured endlessly since the day we last texted?

Is she even fucking alive?

I know she's still alive. I know I would feel it in my soul if she were dead. Maybe that would be preferable to the alternative in my mind—where she's been locked up, tied down, fucked, beaten, and tortured for a goddamn month.

If she's going through half the shit I have nightmares about every time I collapse on her pillow, I wouldn't even blame her for breaking her promise to me and ending it all. I'd even pray she gets the opportunity and the courage to do it. And then I'd do the same thing because there's nothing left for me in this world if she's gone.

Fifty-two days.

Fifty-two days of waiting.

Fifty-two days of incessant, secret phone checking.

Every time I pick up the damn thing, I hope, pray, sacrifice my soul to whatever god in the universe wishes to take it, that I'll see that divine notification that I've got one new message.

That's all I want.

One new message.

I get up from the bed I can't seem to fall asleep in and wander to the dresser. I pull out the pink and green floral box of photographs and sit on the armchair. I sigh, deciding whether it's worth pulling out the phone to check. It'll only depress me further to see there aren't any new messages.

Still, I reach for it.

I'd never forgive myself if she had texted and I didn't see it just because I was too depressed to check. I was grateful that Kostya helped me keep it charged. I knew she couldn't charge hers, but at least my phone was ready to receive a message from her. I brace myself for disappointment.

I lift the basic-as-fuck cell phone from where I keep it hidden in the box of photographs and click the button on the side to illuminate the screen. My spine shoots straight and I fumble with the phone, doing a double take.

One.

New.

Message.

I jump to my feet, the box of photos flipping off my lap and crashing to the floor, the pictures spilling out into a jumbled pile of rectangles. I step over it, pacing forward a few strides from the sheer burst of energy provoked by that little envelope icon on the screen.

I click to open it.

A: Mine?

She sent it to me five minutes ago. My fingers type faster than my brain can work.

E: Yours.

E: Are you okay? Tell me you're okay.

E: Wtf happened?

A: I'm alive. I wouldn't say I'm okay.

E: I've been so fucking worried about you.

It takes her two minutes to reply. Two minutes that threaten to make my head explode and my heart collapse like a dying star.

A: Has it really been nearly two months? That's what it says above my text. God, it feels like a year. He came for me unexpectedly when we last texted and I had to hide the phone. Didn't have time to turn it off. By the time I got back to my box, the battery had died. Got lucky. Risked my life to use Vigo's charger today, but only got 30%. Tell me you love me, quick.

E: I fucking love you.

A: Was the 'fucking' really necessary?

E: Yes. Tell me you love me, quick.

A: I love you more than my own life. I hope you know how true that is. I'm only alive because I made you a promise.

I run a shaking hand through my hair, trying to figure out how to respond. I read that last line three times in a row. *She's only alive because of her promise.* That means that she's thought about—

E: I'm gonna find a way. I'm gonna save you.

I feel like I'm lying to her because I've failed her. I'm not any closer to figuring out how to save her, and I feel my own hope slipping. But selfishly, I keep promising that I'll save her, just to keep her alive, just because I can't stomach the thought of a world without Anya, even when she's suffering a fate worse than hell.

If I were a better man, a *good* man, I would let her go. I would tell her she didn't owe me anything. That she didn't need to keep any promises to me. I don't know what kind of hell she's living in, but I know the feeling I get from Vigo.

What kind of monster am I to ask her to live that hell for me?

I guess I'm not a good man because I can't let her go. I won't let her off the hook. I have to make her keep her promise.

> **E:** Just hang on for me. Just a little longer. I'll convince Nikolai to bring me to the next quarterly meeting at the Vittoris. One month. I'll find a way to take you away from this nightmare.
> **A:** I just want to be with you. That's all I want.
> **E:** Soon, baby. You and me. It's the only thing that matters.

CHAPTER 21

Anya

TIME PASSES BOTH slowly and quickly in this particular level of hell. I can hardly believe it's been two and a half months since I last saw Ezra at the Leblancs' estate; two and a half months since I last tried to end my life.

The few text message exchanges we had are the only thing that keeps me going. It's the only bright spot in the darkness of what my life has become. Even so, day by day, little by little, my strength is waning.

The battery on my phone is dead and I won't get lucky twice. I'd only been able to charge it the last time by risking everything. I had smuggled the phone from my box to his room when he took me one night. I plugged it into Vigo's charger when he left me locked alone in his room—Renata had come to him with an urgent need before he began his playtime with me. He hadn't injected me with his paralytic agent yet, and I was so damn lucky his charger even fit in the cheap, basic phone Kostya had smuggled to me.

My last exchange with Ezra had taken the battery life down to fifteen percent, so it's off and hidden beneath my mattress. It's just enough to have one more text exchange before the next quarterly meeting in a few weeks—when, hopefully, I can see my Ezra again.

I desperately need to see him because I think about ending my life daily. Some days I curse myself for promising Ezra I'd wait, that I would stay alive for him. But because I promised him, I try to keep my word.

It's past sunset and I haven't eaten today, but there's a buffet table in the piano room covered with platters of various finger foods. My mouth waters to see it as Vigo brings me and Bianca, the girl from the middle box, inside the open space. The girl in the first box died.

At least, I think she died.

He took her one night last week and she never came back. He hasn't replaced her, so that just leaves me and Bianca. It's not a comfort to have Bianca living beside me in this torment. She hates me because I won't entertain the idea of working together on an impossible escape plan. She has more hope than I do and sometimes I feel jealous for that. Her disdain for me only adds an additional layer of discomfort and unease to our shared slavery.

The black, grand piano that sits in the room beside the entrance of the Vittori home reminds me of the one in the dance studio at Mikhailov Manor—the piano that was never used, but sat there simply for appearance.

Olivia, the Vittoris' talent slave, stands beside the grand instrument with her hands demurely behind her back. Her eyes focus on a spot on the floor, her head bowed in servitude. She looks much healthier since Lorenzo has started to care for her. Vigo undoubtedly treated her as horribly as he treats me when she was his responsibility.

I think it's lucky for her that Lorenzo has taken an interest. I think he loves her. I can only guess, based on the way he looks at her, and I'm not entirely certain that she loves him back.

Though she's healthier now in Lorenzo's care, there's no telling how he behaves with her behind closed doors.

She's still a slave.

Renata stands beside the buffet table, selecting an appetizer and popping it into her mouth. She says something to her collared slave boy, and he opens a bottle of champagne sitting on the tabletop. It pops when he uncorks it and my body jerks at being startled.

Vigo stops, spinning around to face me and Bianca. My eyes beg me to linger upon the sight of nourishment just ahead of us, but I force my head to bow.

"You're here to watch our talent slave rehearse. She needs an audience for practice," Vigo says. "Help yourself to food and drink, then sit on the couch so she can start. Go."

Neither of us wait for a second command. There's food and I've been given permission to eat. Wasting no time, I head over to the table and lift a small plate to fill with appetizers. This might be my only meal for a while, and my appetite has been especially voracious as of late. Normally, I could trick my mind away from focusing on the emptiness of my belly, but that's been harder and harder to do as of late.

I don't bother with a drink—water has been regularly supplied to us, so I'm not concerned with thirst. When my tiny plate is stacked full, I rush to the couch to sit and unceremoniously shovel food into my mouth.

The rest of the group settles on the couch and the armchairs beside it. Vigo plants his ass next to me with his hip touching mine. I wish to recoil, to pull away, but I'm already pressed as close to the armrest as I can be. He reaches to take a bite from my plate, plucking a morsel away and shoving it between his lips before I can protest.

Internally, I seethe.

I turn to glare at him, my eyes cold and hard, but he just smiles at me as he swallows.

I have never loathed someone as much as I loathe Vigo.

Lorenzo appears at Olivia's side and she turns to face him as he touches her arms gently. She tucks a strand of her straight, golden-blond hair behind her ear and her cheeks flush pink as she bows her head toward him.

He taps two fingers under her chin and she lifts. I can't hear what he says to her, but whatever it is elicits a tiny, cautious smile from her. It's so subtle, I can hardly call it a smile, but it's there.

It makes my heart ache for the way one touch from Ezra, one look, one word, could melt the entirety of my icy exterior and turn me into someone even *I* didn't recognize. One moment with him could bring all the best parts of me that I've hidden away for so long to the surface.

He makes me better when I'm with him.

It's painful the way I have to miss him now.

With Lorenzo's encouragement, Olivia moves to sit at the piano bench. He steps away, moving to stand behind the couch as Olivia begins to play. The piece she's selected is somber. The music is melancholy and hauntingly perfect—an eerie soundtrack for the nightmare of my life with the four families.

I only really listen for a few eight counts because my stomach aches, growling at me to focus on shoveling the food inside. I feel as though I could eat and never stop. I suppose it's the forced fasting that makes me feel this way, but God, it feels like I can never get enough to eat.

As the song ends, I follow the lead of my masters and politely applaud. Lorenzo applauds the loudest, his hands smacking together annoyingly just behind my head. Olivia stands and moves beside the piano, taking a simple bow and Lorenzo is beside her within moments. Renata pushes to stand from her chair, but Lorenzo holds up a palm.

"Wait," he begins.

I'm surprised he starts in English, though I assume it's for Olivia's benefit as she's American. Much of my life here is spent listening to other people speak in a language I don't understand, so this is a nice reprieve for my straining mind.

Renata looks surprised—and unsurprisingly annoyed—as she halts mid-rise and lowers back into her chair.

"I need to ask the family for permission," Lorenzo says.

Renata replies in Italian.

"English, please, so Olivia understands."

Renata tilts her head to the side. "Permission to do what?"

"To marry Olivia."

Vigo barks out a single laugh, leaning back on the couch and stretching his arms around me and Bianca on either side of him.

Renata sighs. "You wish to marry our talent slave?"

"Yes. I've fallen in love with her and I want to take care of her."

"Dearest Lorenzo, you're already taking care of her. You don't need to marry her to take care of her." Renata looks at them appraisingly.

"I wish for her to become a part of the family, to be treated as such. I wish for her to be my wife and bear my children."

Oh, God, I think I'm going to be sick.

Poor Olivia.

To think of being forced to marry and bring children into this nightmare. But when I look at her, I see this news doesn't come as a surprise, as if they've discussed this before. Her cheeks blush pink with hope, not fear—I can see it in her eyes.

"It's not unheard of for a family member to marry a talent slave," Vigo states. "Though I think it's only been done with a

Head of House. Perhaps *I* should marry her."

I glance surreptitiously at Vigo and see his smart-ass smirk and I have to force myself not to roll my eyes. I actually have to breathe through the nausea that rolls through my insides.

Renata lifts an annoyed eyebrow at her brother. "Do you *wish* to marry her, Vigo?"

"Of course not," he scoffs.

"I don't know why you insist on being so flippant. These are serious discussions, Vigo. In a year, you'll be forty and it will be time for you to select your own bride. I suggest you stop making light of marriage, knowing full-well that your own is on the horizon."

His smirk fades away as she speaks. "I have no desire for a bride."

"It's not a choice, Vigo. You need to continue the family line with the Vittori name."

"And why don't *you* just have the children?" Vigo says to Renata. "You never even had a chance to legally change your name before Giovanni died. You're still a Vittori."

Who is Giovanni, and what does he have to do with Renata's last name?

"I would never besmirch my husband—rest his soul—in such a manner as to marry again. And if I did marry, my name would no longer be Vittori, now would it? How do you propose the name should be passed along then?" she snaps at him.

Vigo shrugs and boredom washes down his features.

"You *will* select a bride next year," she says with a snap of finality before returning her attention to Lorenzo and Olivia. "As for the two of you…" She pauses. "What do you have to say about this, Olivia?"

Olivia swiftly lifts her head from its bowed position, looking first at Lorenzo beside her. He gives her a gentle nod and she looks at Renata.

"If the family wishes to have me, I would be grateful to marry Lorenzo."

"Do you love him?"

Olivia swallows. "Yes."

"Are you willing to give him children?"

"Yes."

"And you understand how your role will change with the family? You will no longer be a slave, but a wife. You will become Mrs. Fiore. Your duty to the Vittori family will come above all else and that may involve dealings which threaten your safety, your well-being, the very core of who you are as a person. Are you prepared to take on such a burden?"

Lorenzo places his hand on the small of her back and she must find strength in that. She lifts her chin a little higher.

No.

Tell them no.

"Yes, I'm prepared," Olivia says and it's clear that she means it.

Renata's eyes narrow as she takes in a deep breath, regarding the two of them with precise consideration. "We would need to find new talent and with only weeks until we host—"

Olivia boldly interrupts Renata, "I would still like to perform."

I turn my head to watch Renata, sure she won't be favorable to such an interruption. But I'm wrong. A slow smile lifts her cheeks.

"She's loyal to the family," Lorenzo says. "Please."

Renata nods as she looks at Vigo.

"Fine," Vigo says. "Of course, we'll have to put it to a vote with the board, but I don't see why any of our colleagues would deny it."

Lorenzo and Olivia let smiles light their faces as they both sigh in relief. Lorenzo hugs Olivia with such force, it nearly knocks her backward.

It breaks my heart.

What has made me so undeserving?

What have I done that's so miserably awful as to give me this lot in life?

To see anyone happy in love right now makes me sick. It makes my chest feel tight, my muscles feel weak, my belly roil with nausea, my head spin with dizziness.

It makes me sick.

Sick.

Actual bile rises in my throat.

Oh, God, I'm going to be sick.

I can't vomit here in the piano room, on Renata's precious carpet. Even when my stomach threatens to purge its contents, I have to consider the consequences of my body's involuntary reactions.

I jump up and run, heading for the bathroom that's just down the hall. The moment my ass lifts from the couch, Vigo yells for me, jumping to his feet and chasing after me. I make it to the bathroom before he catches up, shove the door open, and reach the toilet just in time to purge the only food I've eaten in twenty-four hours.

"Fuck." I hear him at the open door. "Are you sick?"

I want to give him my middle finger, roll my eyes, and tell him, *"Obviously,"* but I bite back the urge. Instead, I just nod, which only adds to the dizziness.

He leaves me.

I don't know if he's coming back to get me.

I don't know if he's just going to leave me here in the bathroom all night.

I don't know if I'm going to vomit again.

I just feel *off*.

All I know is that I'm a sad, sick, pathetically broken little doll, and I'm running out of time for Ezra to save me.

CHAPTER 22
NIKOLAI

I EMPHATICALLY DESPISE the quarterly meetings hosted by the Vittoris. Since it's hosted at their home in Italy, the entirety of their extended family—at least those associated with the work of the four families—are in attendance. It's a noisy, boisterous affair that only serves to remind me that my own family is gone.

The one singular thing I have to look forward to at this particular event is seeing the woman I've so precisely groomed to hate me over the years.

I had planned to bring Sasha as my escort for the evening, but that hadn't worked out. Suffice it to say, I'd lost control of myself, and in a moment of fury over Ezra's pathetic depression, my rage took hold. In my fury, I'd killed her.

I didn't feel badly about it. She wasn't the first person in my life that I'd murdered.

But I'd felt…something.

Not that I felt anything about murdering Sasha—the groveling little whore had it coming. The *something* I'd felt was for the reminder of what I'd given up, the understanding that I'd sold a girl I'd never genuinely wanted to die, and tried to replace her with someone like Sasha.

Anya made me hate her viciously sometimes, but she never bored me. I'd always enjoyed watching her internally struggle through the torment I handed her, especially watching her with her partners and the power struggle she endured. But Sasha never really seemed to have anything going on in her stupid little head.

The something I'd felt when I strangled the life out of Sasha was regret because I'd sent Anya away. I understood that my anger had reached its peak because I missed the bitch who betrayed me.

I missed Anya.

In that feeling came the furious realization that the regret I felt could not be rectified. The woman I regretted discarding could *not* be replaced, and so, the replacement had to go.

That is why I killed Sasha.

Because of Anya.

I brought Ezra with me to this reception for two reasons. The first was that he'd asked...begged, really. His ridiculous sniveling over her appealed to my regret because on some level, somewhere inside my heartless soul, I understood what he missed. He and I weren't so dissimilar after all. We were both reckless, impatient, impulsive—he even had a little violence in him, though he seemed to be able to tamper his. I recognized the innate goodness in him, the light inside of him—a light I'd once thought I might have possessed had I been born outside the world of the four families.

But I couldn't change my fate and the darkness was a part of me. Still, I had a disgusting fondness for Ezra, a soft spot I hadn't had with Anya's other partners, and I knew it was there because I saw so much of myself in him.

The second reason I brought Ezra with me is that I enjoy his companionship. He hates me and I love the spirited rivalry it elicits between us. I want more from him. I desire him. I *will* take from him.

Someday.

When the timing is right.

When my father's voice gets the fuck out of my head and lets me be who I am.

"Where the fuck is she?" Ezra says to me in a hushed tone.

He's surly about the fact that we've already witnessed the Vittori talent—the pianist who seems much brighter than I remembered her being in the past—and have been at the reception for an hour and still haven't seen Anya. I'm also on edge about the fact that she hasn't made an appearance, but I don't let on. This is a business event first and foremost, and I cannot allow that to be overshadowed by a personal interest.

"I don't know," I bite back at him as Delia and Murphy approach. "Be *quiet*."

I greet my colleagues from the O'Shea family in kind, though I find Ezra's continued agitation only seems to fuel my own. Murphy is telling me about the bride he's chosen for himself that we'll be voting for approval at the meeting later, but my attention is drawn away toward the top of the wide, curving staircase.

Vigo has appeared, dragging along a wisp of a girl at the top of the staircase. I start to turn my attention back to Murphy and Delia, but then I realize that it's no wisp of a girl ambling along behind him.

It's Anya.

So thin that I hardly recognize her.

Ezra lurches forward, brushing past me as he spots her, and I reach out to snatch his elbow, yanking hard to pull him back.

"Where do you think you're going?"

He looks at me with annoyance and nods his head toward

Vigo and Anya descending the steps.

"Stand behind me," I snap at him. "Do you think you can just leave my side and stroll over to a Head of House? Mind your place, *mal'chik*."

He settles into his place behind me, though his presence is anything but stable. His agitation is palpable, and though I normally enjoy putting him on edge, I feel my own instability at the sight of her. I can't focus on controlling him when I'm so bothered trying to control my own volatile reaction.

I manage to smile and nod in polite conversation with Murphy and Delia. I try to behave as though I'm paying attention, but the frailty of the girl I once considered strong enough to be mine continues to steal my attention.

What has he done to her?

"Bloody hell, what has he done to her?" Delia echoes my inner thought.

I follow her eyes to see that she's looking at Anya and Vigo, as well.

"Wanker," Murphy adds. "It's one thing to deny a meal or two when breaking-in your slave, but she looks as if her grave's already been dug."

I breathe in deeply through my nose, anger rising at the confirmation of my colleagues that my former talent slave, my beneficiary since her childhood, has been vastly mistreated. I storm forward, no thought to my steps, just a boiling, festering need within my chest to demand answers as to why *my* slave has been so poorly lacking.

As I push through the throng to meet them at the bottom of the staircase, I hear the rushed clicking of Delia's shoes as she rushes past me. Her hand touches the crease of my arm as she moves in front of me and I have half a mind to whip the back of my palm against her face for her interference.

But then Ezra passes me on the opposite side in a flurry and my attention must go to him. I grab him by the elbow and fling him back behind me as I step forward.

Delia has already closed in on Vigo, stepping swiftly and forcefully into his space as Anya curls in around her center, shrinking away from him, from *us*.

"I thought we had an understanding of the provisions in your contract with Nikolai." Delia's nostrils flare with indignation, her lips pull tight over her teeth as she speaks. "We spent an entire *night* at the last quarterly meeting going through it together."

She's as black-and-white about following the rules as any of us—perhaps more so.

Vigo's eyes graze across her regal form with a flicker of interest. "Perhaps you should spend another night going through it with me, Cordelia."

Delia taps his wrist. "Not here, Vigo." She turns away from the rest of us, taking a few steps and he follows her like a dog—she's the only woman Vigo has ever let lead him. I would say their pairing is unusual, but many pairings within the four families are on the side of unexpected.

I turn back to Anya, hovering there in a shapeless, blue, silk gown. It hangs from her body rather than clings to her curves, and I can't help but mourn the loss of those womanly imperfections.

In fact, I had hoped I'd see something more there at her waistline...

I reach for her, grabbing her right wrist at the exact moment Ezra grabs her left and she's suddenly a frozen deer in the forest having come face to face with two predators. I'm the only true predator here, so I take her by force.

She nearly falls into my arms from how weak she's become.

I wrap my arms around her waist and brush the hair across her forehead, studying with narrowed eyes as she sways in my hold, her back arching so she can look up at me with fierce, cold eyes. The blue is particularly glacial tonight, brought out by the matching color of her dress.

"What has he done to you, *rabynya?*"

She may not have the energy to stand, but she somehow finds enough to retort, "*Rabynya?* No. Not, *rabynya. Sono una bambola rotta.*" She gazes up at me with a disquieting sneer. "I am a broken doll now."

There are a million things I could say to that unnecessarily sarcastic comment, but not a single one of them finds its way past my lips. Looking down at her now—compared to all the ways I've looked down upon her before—I feel…guilt.

I should've known better than to think that Vigo would uphold his end of the contract. I'd carefully crafted the contract of sale to provide clauses that should have ensured Anya's well-being while she remained alive, though of course, the length of that time was his to choose.

I thought having it on paper would be enough.

Clearly, it's not.

Even Delia, whom I'd consider a friend under appropriate circumstances, doesn't seem capable of helping him understand. She had spent time with Vigo at the last quarterly meeting reviewing the contract of sale at the recommendation of the board. Undoubtedly, they had squandered their evening hours engaging in more interesting matters between the two of them. It was happening even now. Though Delia had pulled Vigo aside at the sight of Anya, one glance in their direction shows me that she's too easily taken under Vigo's spell.

Regardless, it's not her place or her problem, and I don't wish to make it so. I could let the board select a consequence for

Vigo's breach of contract, but that may result in an unfavorable outcome for Anya.

Apparently, I give a shit now.

I'll deal with this myself.

Anya shoves her weak palms against my chest, hardly even registering as a push against my bulk, but I release her and let her step back.

I turn away from her and go to Vigo as Ezra pulls her into his arms. I don't care that he does it, it *almost* seems reasonable at this point—given her state—that someone should hold her up so she doesn't crumple to the floor and break a hip on the way down.

She's fragile now.

She was never fragile in my care.

She was strong. She could take anything I did to her.

Now I fear she may tip over if I exhale too strongly.

I approach Vigo as he's leaning in to whisper something against Delia's ear. "I want to buy her back."

They both freeze, holding their intimate position except for Vigo's head that turns toward me. "Buy her back?"

"You heard me."

Vigo kisses Delia on the cheek before pulling away and turning to face me squarely. "No."

I sigh. "Name your price, Vigo."

"No. I'm not selling her back to you. We've had this discussion before, and it's done."

I step forward, gritting my teeth with frustration. "Name. Your. *Price.*"

"Four million," he says with a mocking smile.

I stifle a laugh. "I sold her to you for less than one and her value has depreciated in your care." My upper lip snarls and my nostrils flare as Vigo crosses his arms over his chest, casting a sideways glance. "Fuck. I'll give you two million."

Vigo throws his head back and laughs. "You can't be serious, Nikolai. Who in their right mind would pay that much for a talent slave who has lost her talent? For a woman who looks like *that*..." He nods his head toward her and I glance.

Ezra holds her sweetly, his arms wrapped around her tightly as if he's afraid to let her go.

He should be.

I observe her overly slender form, the brittleness of her body, and though I can't argue with the look of her, I can argue the reason that she looks that way.

"She looks like that because of *you*," I tell Vigo. "In my care, she was healthy. She had curves, desirable flesh. You've dissolved that flesh through starvation until nothing but bone is left."

"And that is my right as her owner."

I swipe a hand over my mouth, feeling the weight of my vengeance to have sold her to him in the first place sit down heavily across my shoulders.

"Three million," I offer.

Vigo laughs. "I wouldn't have sold her back to you for four million. I wouldn't do it for five. The agitation this causes you is worth far more than any sum you could offer me. Consider that my final say on the matter. Anya is mine, and she will remain mine until the day she dies."

My fists clench at my sides and I don't even have to turn and look to know how Ezra catches on fire from this conversation. His adrenaline spike is visceral, and I feel it at my back, fueling my own.

"I'll give you ten," I say and it's my final fucking offer, my final fucking *ridiculous* offer to end this matter.

"You're a real chancer, aren't ya?" Murphy says, coming up beside me and clapping me on the back. "Quite the risk offering up such a large sum for a slave in her condition. Take this to the board, Nikolai."

I shrug his hand off my back. "This is no game of chance. I understand the risks of her remaining in his care. And if I take this to the board, she'll be decommissioned."

"Why does it bother you, Nikolai?" Vigo asks, taunting me with a tilt of his head. "Does she matter to you now?"

I don't have to answer his questions.

"Ten million for Anya." I hear how pathetic and desperate the offer sounds.

Ten million for a slave?

"No," Vigo says, his face dropping swiftly into seriousness as he reaches out a hand toward Anya. "Come with me, my little Russian doll."

Anya looks up at Ezra and it's as if a million words are spoken between them with just a look. It's almost as though she's saying goodbye to him and it feels like someone has driven a knife into my hollow chest. I have no heart, so the knife only grates between my rib bones, slicing around, trying to find purchase on the beating pump that doesn't exist.

It reminds me just how empty I am.

Vigo takes Anya and they go, heading toward the grand staircase. She's hardly arrived at the reception, only to be gone again in a flash.

What was the point of bringing her down here in the first place?

I glance up at them as they climb the staircase, Vigo taking the steps at a near jog as Anya barely drags herself up by the railing. He reaches the balcony landing at the top and turns to watch her frail form amble to follow. Vigo's eyes meet mine and a dreadful smirk appears on his face.

I immediately understand why he left with haste—to

punish *her* for *my* offer. Except it's not a punishment if she hasn't done anything to deserve it. It's just torment for torment's sake—for Anya and for me.

My offer has been denied.

I may be empty now, but I remember the promise of Anya's warm body and penetrating eyes and the way that would fill me for the moments we were together. It was the only thing that kept me getting out of bed and continuing on when my family had been wiped out. That promise kept me from eating a bullet on several occasions.

Now I'm faced with a choice.

Accept that I can't buy her back and that I will be forced to live without her or do something about it.

I can do something about it tonight.

I look at Ezra, who looks as though his grief and rage might swallow him whole. The decision I've made is going to require reckless abandon.

I knew no one who was as recklessly impulsive as Ezra.

I have an idea of what I want to do, though I wish I didn't feel so compelled to do it.

It's risky.

Dangerous.

Yet I know it's time for me to play my trump card, take responsibility for what I've done, and ensure Anya's future.

I don't want to feel guilt or shame or responsibility. Those are feelings I'm not accustomed to and feelings I don't intend to have for much longer.

I must rectify my shame by taking back what's mine, the only family I have left. It will cost me my reputation and respect within the four families, but what can they do? There are no other Mikhailov men to replace me...and apparently none on the way.

Consequences with the board be damned.

I'm going to steal Anya back.

I'm taking her tonight.

CHAPTER 23

Anya

I SLUMP TO sit on the cold tile floor the instant Vigo brings me into his bathroom upstairs. I'm exhausted. The last dregs of my energy have been drained. I just want him to leave me for the night so I can rest.

I should be wary about the fact that he's brought me to his room, rather than return me to my translucent box in the basement. My tired brain doesn't have the capability of worry. Even seeing Ezra again, though it electrified me for the moments he held me, wasn't enough to jolt me from this overwhelming exhaustion.

Vigo leans over the sink, peering at his reflection in the mirror. He picks a comb through his hair, adjusting the style to perfection, and turns his head to one side, then the other to inspect his profile. He straightens and runs his hands over his lapels to smooth his jacket. "I'll be gone for several hours."

I nod feebly from my pathetic position on the floor, my back leans against the wall beside the clawfoot tub.

"I thought you might enjoy a change of scenery for your evening, so I'm keeping you here rather than returning you to your box."

Every word I speak in response is dripping with sarcasm,

though I find a way to hide the tone in my voice. "That's very kind of you, *Papà.*"

He pauses before he slowly spins to look at me. "I've had a lovely little idea rolling around in my head and this seems like the perfect time to try it out."

A quake bursts inside my chest, shooting warning vibrations throughout my entire body. I scoot back, straightening my spine against the wall behind me.

"I will gladly go back to my box tonight and save you the trouble."

I *want* to go back to my box.

He's got that look on his face that tells my heart to beat faster, to get the adrenaline pulsing through my veins so I can run.

He moves in front of me, holding out his hand. "Come here."

Somehow, I manage to lift my trembling hand to meet his and he pulls me to my feet. My body sways toward him, my head light and dizzy because all I've consumed today was some water early this morning. Vigo holds me steady with his hands on my waist.

He tilts his head toward the clawfoot tub and his teeth appear behind his lips as they part into an awful grin. "Get in the tub."

The word burns my lips as it bursts forth. "*No.*"

"Yes." His eyebrows lift with glee. "Look, it's not even filled. I just want you to sit in it, that's all."

That's not fucking all and we both know it.

He's a lying, tormenting, sick son of a bitch, and we both know that, too.

"Get in. Unless you'd like to suck my cock first and *then* get in. That would be fine, too."

The last goddamn thing I want is his dick in my mouth. Though my heart threatens to explode from my chest in panic over the tub, I turn to move toward it.

"Good girl," he tells me, letting go of me.

I take one step forward toward the porcelain bathtub and gradually lower my quivering hands to rest on the edge, gripping it tight. I pinch my eyes shut and search my soul for a bit of strength, just enough to get my leg over the edge. It takes every ounce of emotional strength I have left, but I do it. I lift my leg, swing it over the edge, and drop my foot slowly to the bottom.

I blow out all the air in my lungs as I steel myself against the rising panic, sucking it all back in to give myself the strength to bring my other leg over the edge, too. The stiletto of my shoe slips along the porcelain bottom as I shift my weight, but I right myself quickly. I cross my arms over my chest as I rise, shivering as I stand in the tub he's tortured me in over and over again.

Vigo comes forward, reaching out to touch my arms and rub them in a motion that mimics comfort. His touch is anything but comforting.

"No injection tonight, I promise."

I shake my head in disbelief; I don't trust his word.

"No injection. Just sit. All you have to do is sit."

His eyes implore me to submit, to do as I'm told. I lower because I'm tired, wary, and weak in every sense of the word. Tears well and begin to drip down my cheeks, but I lower. I tremble and cry on my way down, but still, I lower.

The porcelain tub is hard and unforgiving beneath my butt, and it's uncomfortable to sit here in the center of it. I couldn't relax my body enough to lean against the edge if I tried, so I remain upright, my knees bent in front of me.

Vigo's not happy with this though.

He places a hand on my chest and pushes hard. The fabric of the dress I'm wearing glides easily along the smooth surface and he pushes me until my back is resting against the far edge of the tub.

I'm rigid, my head shaking from side to side. Vigo grabs my cheeks and bends deep over the edge, touching his nose to mine. "All you have to do is sit here." He kisses my forehead before he releases me and steps away.

I'm frozen as he walks into his bedroom.

Is he leaving me here? Like this?

I shut my eyes, squeezing them to blink away the remainder of the tears that form pools there. I open them wide again when I hear him return.

My head snaps to look at him and I see he's come back with a cable tie. Instantly, my hands fly out to grip the edges of the tub, but it's no use. In a flash, he grabs both my wrists and squeezes them together.

"No, *no!*" I cry and thrash, trying to wiggle free from his grip.

He's quick, lassoing the tie around my wrists and securing it so tight that it digs into my skin painfully. It's as if I can feel the bones of my wrists touching, grating against each other.

"Don't leave me here." I quickly descend into hysterics, sobbing and shouting, "*Please*, don't leave me like this. *Please!*"

Vigo smiles, touching a finger to his lips as if to hush me, before darting out of the room again.

I'm getting out of this fucking tub.

I turn my body and stretch my fingers, doing my best to grip the edge with my crossed hands. I can't get purchase with my feet as my narrow heels easily slip over the smooth surface.

I stop abruptly when Vigo comes in carrying an oversized standing mirror and something dangling from his fist where he holds the wooden frame.

He doesn't pause, doesn't stop, doesn't even look at me. He just moves forward. He lifts the gigantic mirror, twisting it sideways, and flipping it toward me.

I shout and move back, releasing my grip from the tub's edge just in time to avoid having my fingers smashed. He sets the mirror, glass side down, over the rim of the tub, covering it completely across the shortest length, the frame hanging off the edges. My spine presses to the back of the tub as I scoot away, but he keeps moving.

As he starts to slide it back toward me, I realize what he's doing. He's trying to trap me with it. He's trying to cover the tub with a fucking oversized mirror.

The end of it shoves toward me until I can move no further. The top framed edge of the mirror crowds me, taps against my chin and I straighten to lift above it, but then he shoves it against my throat.

He grins at me above the top of the tomb he wishes to create for me. He yanks the mirror back a couple of inches and tilts his head down. "Duck your head."

Air jumps in and out of my lungs in quick, short bursts, my chest hopping with the panicked intake of oxygen.

"No," I tell him. "No!"

"Yes," he says. "This or the injection, your choice."

My face twists in pain at the impossible choice he's giving me. I don't think I can face the injection again, the inability to move while remaining awake. But I also don't want to be trapped inside this tub. I know that's his intention—I see the coarse rope he's brought in now along with the mirror.

I choose without any choice at all, the words falling from my lips freely. "No injection."

He nods. "Under you go, then."

My entire body shakes, the epicenter of a quake radiating out from the pit of my stomach. Somehow, *somehow*, I let myself slip. I let the smooth porcelain take me as my body slumps down the back edge. Vigo slides the mirror over my head. It's massive, large enough to cover the entire top of the tub, trapping me inside with my own dark reflection.

"Are you comfortable in there, *bambola Russa?*" he asks, then laughs.

The mirror shifts, sliding further over the edge by my head and light appears suddenly at the far end by my feet. He's left a gap there.

He's left a gap where the faucet runs.

He can't.

He won't.

He wouldn't.

Of course, he will.

I put my hands against the glass and push.

I expect the mirror to be heavy, but not to be immovable as it is. Maybe I just really am that weak now.

"Put your hands down, Anya. I haven't finished tying it in place yet."

Tying it in place?

I scream, "Let me out!"

"Hush, *la mia bambola Russa.*"

I scream.

I shout.

I squirm and thrash.

But there's no point. My muscles are weak. My body is exhausted. Vigo can't be persuaded once his mind is made up.

And I feel done.

I'm done.

I let my head fall back to rest against the tub and give myself up to the sobbing mess I've become.

The mirror shifts left and right, and I hear him loop the rope around, over the mirror, wrapping beneath the clawfoot tub to secure it. Over and over again the mirror shifts and he tugs the rope…shifts and tugs, shifts and tugs.

When the shifting finally stops, there's a beat of silence in the room. It's the strangest, most horrifying beat of silence I've ever experienced.

Is he gone?

Will this be it?

Spend a few hours in the tub and that's all?

No, that can't be.

Just as I'm about to take a breath to settle into the silence, he speaks. "I'm curious to know whether you have the strength to keep your head above water, *bambola Russa*. Has your brief encounter with the slave boy given you your fight back? I suppose we'll find out soon enough. I've been wanting to do this since you tried to kill yourself last quarter. Poetic, isn't it? To be trapped with your reflection considering you tried to kill yourself with the broken shards of it before."

I open my mouth to scream at him at the exact moment that I hear the familiar squeak of the faucet handles being turned, at the exact moment water begins to flow heavy and fast from the spout into the small gap he's left. Cold water pours onto my feet and I yank them back with a jerk, only to result in my body slipping farther down in the tub.

The water slowly warms to tepid as my panic overheats to boiling.

I scream.

I shout for help.

I beg for mercy.

The fabric of my dress saturates. A thin layer of water runs under my legs, spilling beneath my back and the pool starts to rise.

Slowly, *slowly*, the water rises.

I stare up at my shadowed reflection in the mirror and see

a dead girl staring back at me.

This is it.

This is how I will die.

And the only regret I have is not falling in love with Ezra sooner, faster, from the moment I saw him and felt that immediate spark of awareness that he and I were in some special way connected.

Soul mates.

Meant to be.

Made for each other.

I love him, even though he's failed me.

I hold no blame for the fact that he couldn't save me. It was an ill-fated promise he made, and I'd known it from the start.

And to think he's here tonight, perhaps with a plan, hoping for a chance to reveal itself to him so he can take me away from this place. But I think we both knew the only way I was leaving was by death.

I hope he knows that I tried my best to stay alive for him.

Vigo whistles a tune that would sound cheerful under normal circumstances but is haunting in its joviality now. The roar of the water as it spills into the tub mingles with the eerie tune, wrapping around my fear and choking it into panic.

I scream one last time, loud and long, with all the anger my soul possesses for what the universe has done to me.

But still, the water rises.

This is the end of everything.

Vigo waits until the tub is practically overflowing to turn off the faucet, and as soon as he does, he's gone.

I think I might try to wedge the heel of my stiletto beneath the drain stop, maybe lift it enough to get the water to drain out. But then I realize I can't. The drain is internal, activated by a small metal lever that I can't reach from inside the tub.

"Shit!"

Shifting my body, I unintentionally roll sideways. My muscles are weak, and I struggle to keep my face above the surface. As my cheek dips into the water, my body jerks, thrashing until I'm facing up again. A wave rolls through the tub, pulsing against the side and returning, though some of the water spills out at the gap near my feet.

Maybe I can splash out enough water to give myself some space to breathe without straining every muscle in my body to stay afloat. I thrash some more, trying to get as much water from my porcelain coffin as I can.

It takes less than a minute of battering my body against the water before I'm forced to stop.

My body is weak.

I feel truthfully and completely drained now.

I slip under the surface in my exhaustion, barely able to bring myself back up again. I can't stay afloat. And even when I can hold myself above the surface, the mirror reminds me of what's beneath, showing me a reflection of my watery grave.

Vigo knew my strength was gone.

He'd been preparing me for this particular torture, withholding nourishment, exercise, the basic things a human needs to stay alive, to survive. He knew I might not survive this.

I'm not going to survive this.

Oh, God…I'm not going to survive.

I quickly shift from a slow growing panic into outright madness. I flail in the water, fling my arms and legs, let myself drift beneath the surface to whip the water with my body, hoping to spill as much water over the edge as I can.

The barrier Vigo crafted is rudimentary, so of course, it isn't a water-tight seal. Still, it's proving to be effective enough because the water stays with me. The waves I create with my whipping body just hit my reflection in the mirror above me and crash back down to smother me again from above.

The fearful girl I see in my reflection taunts me and my madness shifts focus. Though I don't have the power to even nudge the barrier above me, I lash out at it all the same. I curl my fingers into fists and pound my knuckles against the glass, over and over and over. All I manage to do is splinter the surface, bloodying my hands for my effort.

I can't keep doing this.

I'm done now.

Done with all of it.

The fighting. The torment. The struggle.

I'm done.

I float, using what's left of my adrenaline to keep my face above the surface.

But I know I need to let go.

Giving in is what's best for me now. This was always my fate and fighting it only prolongs the suffering.

I can't do it anymore.

Then why am I still holding on?

I keep fighting because of him, because of Ezra, because of that dangerous fucking hope he brought into my life that somehow we could be together and happy.

I want that life with him.

I want it *so* fucking much.

Wanting something this much sets fire to the frozen shell around my heart and burns me with a blaze of angry fire, fire I can't let out because I'm trapped in this water-filled coffin. It's enough blazing energy to punch out his name in a piercing shout, a last-ditch effort to beg the universe to change my fate, to change *our* fate.

"Ezra!" I scream.

It's a declaration, a shout to no one and nothing that Ezra is the first thing on my mind, the last thing on my mind, the *only* thing on my mind as I prepare to let go of life.

I pound my fists at the splintered glass one last time. It sends a rippling crack in a diagonal line, cutting across the reflection of my face. I blink, the last of my tears falling as I watch how the sapphire color of my eyes deepens into a dark navy-blue in the mirror.

"Please," I mutter sadly at my reflection.

A plea to the girl in the mirror to fight, to find her strength, to hold on just a little longer.

You promised him…

You promised you'd hold on as long as you can.

I press my eyes shut, force my shallow breaths to lengthen in a long steady flow, and focus on floating. All I have to do is float. Float through one count of eight, then another, and another until this careful dance with death is over.

I bring forward the memory of our dance in Nobility Hall and focus on the routine. I run it through my head step by step, beat by beat, as if preparing for the performance—an encore of the dance that changed everything. Each eight count gets me closer to the end of this, closer to peace.

And so, I count.

One. Two. Three. Four. Five. Six. Seven. Eight.

CHAPTER 24
EZRA

I BLINK, STILL frozen in disbelief at the state of my blue-eyed girl as she disappears from sight. My entire being is still in shock from the sight of her, practically dragging herself up the staircase by the railing.

Fuck, she'd been so frail.

Skin and fucking bones.

I think my heart has stopped beating.

My lungs have forgotten how to take in air.

My body has forgotten how to move.

But then, everything explodes back to life all at once. My system is flooded with the incessant need to run to her, to save her, to do fucking anything at any cost to spare her future torment.

I move without thinking, ready to take off at a run. I make it one step before Kostya leaps in front of me and I nearly slam into his chest. Then Nikolai grabs the collar of my jacket, flinging me backward. He grabs my shoulders and physically turns me away from the staircase.

"Go. Move. *Move.*" Nikolai shoves at my back, pushing me through the throng of guests.

He pushes me until we make the clearing and turn down a hallway beneath the staircase.

I need to go after her.

I slam to a halt, spinning around to face Nikolai. He grabs the lapels of my suit jacket, fisting the fabric and shoving me until my back is against a wall.

"Shut up and listen to me, *mal'chik*," he tells me as Kostya catches up to us, standing at our side. "I'm stealing her back tonight. I need you to focus so you don't fuck it all up, do you understand me?"

Stealing her back?

He wants to steal her back?

My muscles twitch at the thought. I was ready to fight to the death to save her, but I didn't have a plan. The only strategy I had come up with was improvisation. That may work with my dancing, but I have no idea what the fuck I'm doing here on my own.

But I can't wrap my head around working with Nikolai. Helping him steal her back would only mean bringing her back into servitude to Nikolai.

But that's better, isn't it?

At least then she'd be with me—maybe we could plot a real escape together.

"Are you serious about this?" I ask him.

"Am I ever anything but serious?"

I don't even know how the fuck to respond to that.

"I'm listening. Tell me what to do and I'll do it."

His jaw ticks. "I wish all your concessions were given so easily."

I grit my teeth. "When it comes to Anya, you know I'll do anything."

"Be careful with your promises. Someday I might come collecting."

"Are we having a pissing contest or do you want to tell me your plan?"

He pulls me toward him by my jacket and then slams my back to the wall again. I hit with a *thud* and the air rushes from my lungs as the back of my head bounces off. He lets go of me and takes a small step back, glancing at Kostya before looking at me again.

"You're going to do exactly what your instincts tell you to. You're going after her," he says.

"What?" Frustration washes over me and I throw up my arms. "Why the fuck did you stop me then?"

"Because I need us on the same page. You're going to fight me off here and run after her. Back through the party, up the stairs."

"And that's your plan? I'm just supposed to run after her? Then what?"

"Then we take her back."

"Together? Or do you plan to off me once I deliver her back to you? Because I'll tell you what, I'm not letting that happen. She fucking needs me, especially with you."

"This isn't a negotiation," he hisses through his teeth.

"You can't do this without me. She's on the edge, Nikolai. If you kill me once you have her back, she'll find a way to kill herself—you and I both know she will. She'll have nothing left if you do that."

His eyes blink with offense, flickering with something resembling hurt. "She would have me."

It almost makes me feel sorry for him.

Almost.

I sigh. "I will help you. You know I will because I want her the fuck away from the Vittoris. But I will also protect her from you at the expense of my own goddamn life." I step forward into his space. "I will lay down my life for her and if you make it come to that, then you'll have *nothing* left because she will chase me into death. You *know* that."

He grinds his jaw. "Are you *done*? We're wasting time."

"Tell me that you hear me, Nikolai."

"I hear you." He plants his palm on my chest and shoves me, bouncing my back off the wall again. "Now hear me. I'm still your goddamn master and you will obey me, so listen closely. Anya is *mine*. She has always been *mine*. I made a mistake selling her to Vigo, but I'm ready to rectify that mistake. I'm bringing her home because she belongs to *me*. Help me get her back to Mikhailov Manor and we will discuss your status as her pet. And mine. Now. Do we have an understanding?"

My fist desperately wants to collide with his face, but I fucking hear him. I have to hear him and go with this because I want my girl back. I was going to chase after her anyway…at least this way, I'll have back-up.

I suppose when you're in hell, it's better to go with the devil who rules than the rogue demon. At least the devil can grant my wishes before taking another piece of my soul.

All that matters is Anya.

I feel her fading.

It's a snap that bursts right over my heart, the familiar vibration of her slipping away from life. I'd felt that snap before—when Nikolai had drowned her in the pool.

"Understood," I tell him. "Tell me what to do."

He lets out a breath. "You're going to run and Kostya and I will come after you. Simple. It won't seem suspect to anyone here. You *are* an unruly slave, one who just can't seem to control his goddamn emotions when it comes to that girl. You go after her and we go after you."

I shake my head, trying to make sense of this too-damn-easy-to-actually-work plan. "If I run, everyone will see. They'll just follow you to help you get me under control. We won't be able to help her then."

"No one will follow. There won't be a need with Kostya and I handling it, and we'll tell anyone who tries the same. You wouldn't be the first slave who tried to run impulsively at a meeting. We don't have much time. We need to take her before everyone starts leaving the reception. There will be enough people moving about then to cause a distraction so we can sneak out with her. I've always hated the excessive guest list when the Vittoris host, but I suppose large numbers play in our favor today."

I link my fingers together on top of my head. "But they'll know. They'll know what you did when you don't show up to the meeting, won't they? What happens then? Will she even be safe if you take her back? What will they do?"

"What happens then is my problem, not yours. But we need to take her back to Mikhailov Manor tonight. There's something she needs, something I need to tell her, something I need to give her."

"What?"

His nostrils flare and he grabs my shoulder, shoving me back in the direction of the reception. "We're wasting time. *Run.*"

Fuck.

This is really happening.

Not only is Nikolai letting me go after my girl, he's demanding it. When my heart unexpectedly drops into my gut, I don't give it another thought. That sinking feeling punches me with the instinct I've been waiting for and it's guiding me to do just what he said. *Run.*

So, I run.

I rush back into the reception and barrel my way into the throng of people milling about. My sights are set on getting back to the staircase. My shoulder bumps into someone on my right and as I veer left, I nearly slam into a pair of chatting women. I turn and sidestep between them as they jump back, spilling whatever was in their glasses.

As I reach the bottom step, I hear Nikolai's voice booming after me. "Ezra. Stop!"

I glance at him over my shoulder, seeing him and Kostya rushing after me, but I know he doesn't want me to stop. It's all part of the plan.

I take the steps two at a time, propelling myself up the staircase as quickly as I can. I reach the balcony landing and I hear footfalls on the steps behind me.

"It's fine, we've got him." I hear Nikolai say and hope that's enough to keep everyone else the fuck away.

It just seems too damn simple, though in my time with the four families, I've come to understand that nothing happens with an ounce of reason.

Left is right.

Up is down.

The moon is the goddamn sun.

I move through the open archway, looking left and right, unsure which way to go. But then my pulse starts pounding, adrenaline kicks in full force, and I feel like I just know where to go.

I turn right.

I take off on a run down the hallway. There's a row of doors, and though I feel a sense of urgency now, I don't even know where to start.

But then fate deals me the perfect hand.

A door opens and Vigo steps out. My heart stops but starts again with a fury as he closes the door behind him. He looks up and he sees me, and we lock in on each other with a heated stare. He cocks his head to the side and a slow smile twists his features.

Heat simmers beneath my skin, pulsing through my veins, boiling into desperation to punch and kick and hurt this man. I want to break his nose again. I want to break every bone in his body. I want to watch him bleed.

I take this matter into my own hands just as Nikolai and Kostya arrive behind me. I charge, sprinting down the hallway. Vigo is too cocky for his own damn good, opening his arms and widening his stance tauntingly, daring me to attack.

But I don't need a dare for this.

Something's wrong with Anya, I *feel* it, and I need to take him down fast.

I crash into Vigo at a run, and though he tries to hold his ground, I'm stronger. I charge him backward as I shove my body against his midsection. I don't stop pushing until he loses his footing and stumbles awkwardly to the ground, falling onto his ass.

I nearly roll over him on the impact, but I manage to land on top and stay in control. I punch him in the side, then again on his bony hip before he gets his bearings. With a grunt, he lands a jab to my jaw and the force knocks me off-balance. I topple sideways and he rolls on top of me, hitting me with a fury of fists.

Two to my cheek.

Three to my stomach.

One that lands on my shoulder.

Another on the side of my head.

Vigo disappears as I blink away the black spots across my vision, his weight suddenly lifted from where it sat hard on my middle. I scramble to my feet to see Nikolai slamming him face-first to the wall.

"Where is she?" Nikolai growls.

I go straight for the door Vigo came out of, jiggling the

handle, but it doesn't budge.

"She's in here. But it's locked. There's a keypad," I inform Nikolai.

"Tell us the code, Vigo."

Vigo laughs, his cheek pressed flush against the wallpaper. "No. Do you really think it will be that easy to take her from me?"

I watch as Nikolai reaches into his pocket and pulls out his switchblade, flicking it open with his wrist. He shifts to bring the knife around to Vigo's throat and his grip on him loosens. Vigo manages to whip around to face him, but Nikolai shoves his weight against him, jabbing the tip of the blade at the center of his throat. Vigo freezes, but the sinister smile doesn't fade from his face.

"You want to know what's funny?" He chuckles. "She might be dying in there right now and here we all stand, on the wrong side of the door. And I'm the only person who can let you in."

Nikolai presses the blade and a single drop of blood pools, rolling down Vigo's throat. "Tell me the code."

"Nikolai. *Nikolai*." Vigo clicks his tongue. "I'm so sad for you right now. You've let your slaves slither their way into your mind and rot your senses. What kind of threat is this?" His eyes flick down to the blade. "Are you going to kill me? What do you think the board will have to say about that, hmm?"

Nikolai holds steady in his ruthlessness. "Tell me the code."

"No."

"Tell. Me. The. Code."

A muffled scream comes from beyond the door that we can't open, and I swear to God it sounds like my name. We all turn to look and Vigo takes advantage of our distraction.

Just as I return my attention to Vigo, his hand slips inside his jacket. It all happens in a flash. Nikolai returns his gaze to

Vigo, Vigo whips out his gun, cocks it, and presses it to the side of Nikolai's head.

Vigo's smirk turns into a sneer. "Ask me again to tell you the code. I dare you."

The sound of her voice and the adrenaline pumping through me steers me away from reason and into pure, base instinct. I see an opportunity in their stance, in the way Vigo holds the gun at an awkward angle.

I attack.

I barrel into them, knocking them both to the ground sideways, and the gun goes flying. I'm lucky Vigo doesn't accidentally pull the trigger, luckier when it lands a yard away and doesn't go off, but I'm also fucking lucky that it worked. Vigo is disarmed.

Trying to get to it first, I clamber over them, but Vigo rises up, knocking me sideways over Nikolai. Vigo gets onto his knees and crawls toward it, reaches for it. Kostya leaps, snatching away the gun just in the nick of time. Stepping forward, he aims it at Vigo.

"Open the door," Kostya says.

We all look up at him and I'm surprised to see the worry in his eyes.

"What, are you going to kill me?" Vigo says, raising his palms like a trapped prisoner. "What then? If I'm dead, I can't give you the code."

Nikolai twists his body, reaching out. He stabs Vigo with a brutal thrust to the outside of his thigh.

Vigo screams, falling on his side as Nikolai leans over him. His hand is still on the knife that's jammed inside Vigo. He twists the blade and Vigo shouts even louder. Thankfully, there's enough noise from the guests downstairs to drown out the screaming, but Nikolai slaps his hand over Vigo's mouth all the same.

"Tell me the code or I will take your life, consequences be damned." Nikolai bends, leaning in close, their noses nearly touching. "Do you see how serious I am now, Vigo? Your life means *nothing* to me. But hers? I want her life back." He chuckles. "I'm willing to bet ten million sounds like a pretty good offer now, doesn't it?" He rotates the blade inside him again, eliciting another sound from Vigo that resembles a dying animal. "Too bad that's off the table now. But I'll give you this...If she's still alive and you ensure that we make it back to Mikhailov Manor unharmed, I'll refund what you paid for her in full. Good faith."

"The board," Vigo practically spits with fury. "The board will have your head for this."

Nikolai rips out the knife, pulling out a stream of blood that spurts across the hallway, splashing across my clothes. "The board can do whatever the fuck they want *after* I've taken her home."

Nikolai stands, holding the blade at his side, blood coating his hand and jacket sleeve. His hair has fallen from its perfectly styled, slicked back look into pieces, matted in places from blood spatter.

"The code," Nikolai says, and he truly looks like the devil himself.

I'm horrified by the sight of him.

Vigo groans, covering the wound with his hand. Contemplation wavers in his eyes, but then he swallows...a decision made. He proves his cowardice, conceding, showing in fact that he is but a lowly demon under Nikolai's devil reign.

"7-4-2-5."

With lightning quickness, I type in the code and nearly die from relief when it opens. Instantly, I forget about it all.

I forget about Vigo lying bloody in the hallway.

I forget about Nikolai hovering above him with a devilish glare in his eyes.

I forget about Kostya holding the gun.

I push the door open and run inside to save my blue-eyed girl.

CHAPTER 25

Anya

ONE. TWO. THREE. *Four. Five. Six. Seven. Eight*
One. Two. Three. Four—

My eyes snap open. I blink against the clear water. My dark hair forms a floating halo around my head and the reflection in the mirror above is distorted by the soft rippling effect of the water I've sunk beneath. I jolt, startled again as another thump reverberates against the side of the tub, echoing through the water as a dull roar.

Another thump, then another.

The splintered crack in the mirror turns and light peaks in just above me.

The mirror has moved.

I watch, almost peacefully in my breathless delirium, as it shifts, as it jolts with force from one side to the other. Then suddenly, it jerks back and I can see light above me. Though it's not just light there.

It's life.

Pulsing, vivid green life.

I knew the last vision I would see was of Ezra's green eyes before drifting into unconsciousness. I *hoped* for it. But I'm surprised by the overwhelming vibrancy of this oxygen-deprived hallucination.

I'm pulled from my reverie with a whoosh, waves rippling into whirring droplets as my body rushes backward with a jerk. Sound returns full force as my head breaks through the surface and suddenly, I'm alive again. I feel hands grip beneath my arms as I'm dragged toward the back of the tub. Up and over the edge I go before my body falls to the floor.

My mouth drops open wide on instinct, gasping, sucking in as much air as I can gather now that I'm free from my watery prison.

"I've got you," the voice behind me huffs, pulling me backward, nestling me between strong legs.

Is this real?

Am I alive?

I pant for air as I blink rapidly, taking in the sight of the white tiled floors beneath me. I see my silk blue gown clinging to my legs, the silver sparkle of the stilettos strapped to my feet and a man's legs on either side of me. His hands grab the hair that's stuck to my cheeks and pulls it aside as my eyes follow the line of his leg, back and back. I turn my head and lean to the side so I can see my savior, but of course, I already know who it is.

"Ezra," I say. "Ezra?"

I feel the air leave his lungs as his chest sinks, my body slumping back against his. "It's me. It's me, baby. I'm here. I've got you."

We breathe together.

My eyes meet his in utter disbelief.

I watch him as I wait for the dream to end, for the illusion to shatter. But this is real.

It's real and he's saved me.

A whole new sense of urgency washes over me because I

can feel it pounding from his chest. He's come to save me and there's no time for the reverie.

"I'm gonna get you out of here, okay?" he tells me.

My brow furrows as I look at him. "Are you really here?"

He grabs my shoulders and turns me, drags me backward, lifts my fragile body and sets me on his lap. My love cradles me in his warm arms and suddenly, everything in the world feels right again.

"You're really here," I admit to myself. "Oh, God, you're really here."

I shiver in his arms but I am, in fact, in his arms and that's all that matters.

He squeezes me tighter and bends to capture my lips as I look up at him. It's a quick, soft kiss to my lips followed by harder, more insistent kisses to my cheeks, forehead, and hair. I realize then that he's trembling, too, though his must be from the rush of chemicals in his veins as he came upon this horrifying scene and worked to save me.

"You saved me." I blink at him in awe.

His chest still heaves with the heavy breaths of exertion from freeing me, from seeing me nearly drown in the tub. But a slow, charismatic, and undeniably characteristic smile spreads across his face, lighting up his eyes, and the world has never looked brighter.

"I don't think you've ever looked so happy to see me."

He makes me smile. I was just knocking on death's door and still, Ezra makes me smile.

Though I want to remain in his arms forever—with his warmth enveloping me and his smile brightening me—I'm quickly coming back to life. With that returns the realization that time is not on our side in this life.

"What now?" I ask.

"Can you stand? Walk?"

I'm still breathless, but I manage a nod. "I can. I can run if you need me to."

His eyebrows knit together. "I might need you to. Hang on, stay right here. Don't move."

I don't question him.

My faith in him is so strong right now that I'll do whatever he says, because he found me, he *saved* me. I nod my understanding as fervently as I can, which is to say, barely at all.

Carefully, he lifts me from his lap and sets me down on the tile. He slips out from beneath me and slowly stands, his hands never leaving my body, not for a second, as he turns and bends to face me. He makes sure I've got enough balance not to topple over as he props my back against the wall. I watch him the entire time, trying to understand when I became so helpless and needy, when I gave over my trust to him so completely.

When he brought you back from the dead.

He gives me a hurried grin and I smile back.

"I love you," I tell him, because the words just have to come out.

"I love you," he says quickly with a bright flicker of flame behind his eyes.

He dashes past the bathroom doorway and rushes into Vigo's bedroom. "She needs dry clothes." I hear Ezra say to someone.

Moments later, there's a response. "Here. This is best we can do. Hurry."

Kostya?

Ezra returns almost immediately, clothing laid over his arm. He crosses the room and sets them on the countertop before he turns toward me. His eyes dart around the room until he sees the towels resting on the bar on the wall across the room. He hurries to grab one and adds it to the pile on the countertop. He comes to me and crouches to his haunches and dear God, I can't stop looking at him.

"We need to get that dress off you and into these dry clothes, okay? We have to hurry."

"We're really leaving? You really found a way for us to escape? Did Kostya help?" I'm so hopeful with the urgent way he speaks, the way his body rushes through the movements.

He puts his arms around me and lifts me from the floor until I'm standing upright before him, drenched and trembling in his hold. I sway a little from the quick transition from sitting to standing, but he keeps me steady.

"It's not…This isn't a real escape, Anya. But I am getting you the fuck away from the Vittoris."

I shake my head as his eyes skim over my dress, trying to figure out the best way to remove it when my arms are still bound in front of me with a cable tie around my wrists. He finally decides upon tearing the straps, slipping his fingers beneath the one on my right shoulder, and giving a sharp tug to break the thin piece of fabric.

"I don't understand."

He reaches for the other strap and rips that one, too. "Nikolai. He sent me for you."

"Nikolai." My face contorts in confusion. "Nikolai Mikhailov? The man who called me a slut and a whore and sold me to Vigo?"

Ezra puts a finger to his lips to hush me, lowering his voice. "He's in the hall. We need to hurry."

Ezra's hands skim my curves as he slips the broken dress down, peeling it from my body. His gentle touch ignites my soul and wakes me up, bringing me back fully from the dead into screaming, urgent life.

But as he quickly dries me with a white towel, I feel…confused.

Ezra has come to save me, but this is no rescue if I'm returned to my former master. Though, the alternative was to have died in the clawfoot tub on my right. I glance over at it as Ezra helps me remove my shoes.

He wraps one of Vigo's plain, white dress shirts around my back, bringing the sides together in front of me. I let my arms fall so he can button the shirt over the top of them. It's not perfect, but it's dry clothing that will cover me until he can cut the cable ties.

"Shoes. Fuck, how do I get you shoes?"

"I don't need shoes. I'll go barefoot."

"We're going outside, Anya."

"I'm a ballerina. My feet are already destroyed from dance. I really don't care, just forget about the shoes and get me out of here."

Get me out of here…and take me back to my former master?

How on Earth has Nikolai become the master I prefer?

What is wrong with me that I feel relief?

He nods. "Then just stay with me, okay?"

"I'm always with you, E."

He freezes, locks in on me.

"Say it again, A."

His strong hands grip my cheeks and he presses in close. I snatch my bottom lip between my teeth as he lowers his face to mine.

"I'm *always* with you," I tell him again.

His tongue sweeps out to lick his lips and then he kisses me, a slow gradual press that turns into a possessive bruising. I part my lips to seek his tongue and he gives it easily.

I could be under the water right now and still be able to

breathe with the way he kisses me. His kiss breathes life back into me, and I only wish I could put my arms around him right now. But the kiss ends far sooner than I want it to, because it *has* to, because we need to leave.

He leads me out of the bathroom, out through Vigo's bedroom, but I freeze in the doorway, taking a step back in fear.

Blood.

Everywhere.

It pours from Vigo's leg.

It drips down Nikolai's outstretched arm.

One master holding the other at gunpoint.

"Her hands are bound," Ezra says.

Nikolai dares a single glance back at me. He double-takes as he sees me with my wet, tangled hair, dressed only in an oversized dress shirt, barefoot.

"Bring her here," Nikolai commands.

Ezra grips my elbow, pulling me forward beside him. I follow his lead, glad to have it when I feel so overwhelmed, so exhausted, so weary.

We come up beside Nikolai and he hands the gun to Kostya. Then he turns to me, giving me a once over as I do the same. I feel like cowering in front of him. He's covered in blood, disheveled, his eyes wild and unhinged. I can't believe he's kept his temper so controlled—it's so unbelievable that I'm certain he'll unleash it upon me any second now.

"Give me your hands," he tells me.

Ezra helps pull the hem of the shirt up as I push my hands forward. Nikolai wipes the blood off the flat edge of his switchblade on his slacks and brings it to my wrists. I flinch as he slips the tip between my wrists and the plastic cable tie, remembering the scars he gave me on my thigh with this very knife. He slices the tie free and folds his blade, returning it to his pocket.

I snatch my hands away as Nikolai turns. I wiggle my arms through the sleeves of the buttoned shirt and work to roll them up over my forearms. Ezra takes my hands in his, caressing his thumb gently over the red indentations made by the cable ties digging into my flesh.

I jump when Vigo screams, turning to watch as Nikolai jabs his finger into a wound on his thigh.

"I guess we'll be leaving the party a little early tonight. Give my best to the board. I'm sure they'll be interested in scheduling a follow-up with me soon," Nikolai says.

Wait. What is happening?

Why is Nikolai doing this?

Why does he want me back?

Vigo laughs as Nikolai stands, ushering us past Kostya toward the staircase. "Go on. Take your leave. I'll let you go. But Nikolai…I'm coming after you. I'm coming for all of you. First," he pants through his pain, "I'll kill your slave boy. I'll string him up and gut him like a fish and make her watch. Then I'll do the same to her. And I'll kill you last, Nikolai."

I don't hear anything after he threatens Ezra.

Gut him like a fish?

Over my dead goddamn body.

I don't take Vigo's threats lightly.

He's sick, twisted, and abhorrently vile.

And I've had enough.

He nearly killed me tonight. He's put me through a hell worse than I ever could have imagined, even after belonging to Nikolai for all these years. Now he's lying here on the floor, weak, bleeding, pathetic…

And threatening to gut my man?

Fuck no.

I see red.

I see his blood and I want more of it.

Something twists inside me, a desperate, nagging need that demands to be fulfilled—a need that *must* be filled before another second of my tragic life ticks by.

It's anger.

It's rage.

It's a fury of brutality.

It's an urgent need to prevent his violence with violence of my own.

My feet move me, march me forward, and I'm at Kostya's side in moments. I hear Ezra shout at me as my hand slips down Kostya's arm. Nikolai reaches for me as my fingers cover Kostya's grip, but he doesn't get to me in time. With my index finger over Kostya's on the trigger, I aim and squeeze.

CHAPTER 26
EZRA

BLOOD EXPLODES FROM Vigo, coating my skin in the viscous, crimson life force.

Anya is red.

Red from her forehead all the way to her bare feet.

Her arms slowly fall to her sides and her fingertips slip from their grip over Kostya's. Her sapphire eyes blink, a blue light shining out from the crimson coating that frames them.

Fuck.

She just killed Vigo.

"Anya!" Nikolai snaps, but she just stares. "We have to go. *Now.*"

I take her by the hand and drag her away.

Together, we run.

I grip her elbow as we reach the staircase, worried she might fall in her tortured state. But her adrenaline must be furious inside her because she keeps the pace with ease. The party is still going on downstairs, but people are moving. We're not the only ones on the staircase and there's talk of a gunshot.

They'd heard, but Nikolai's status ensures we aren't questioned by the passing guests who don't serve on the board. He moves in front of Anya as Kostya and I flank her sides.

She's the bloodiest of all of us, and only wearing a man's dress shirt, so we all silently agree she needs to be hidden. We slow our pace to descend the steps but people are looking, taking notice.

I focus my rampant burst of energy on protecting Anya, following Nikolai, and getting the fuck out of here. Somehow, we make it to the front door and because we're with Nikolai, the guards let us pass. But as we pick up our pace again outside, we hear the chaos erupt inside.

"Which car?" I ask Nikolai quickly.

We rush along the row of parked black SUVs that all look the same to me. He points at a vehicle, only two car-lengths away now, as we pass the fountain in the center of the paved square.

Kostya jogs ahead, the SUV flashes its lights as he unlocks it with the key fob in his hand. I catch Anya by the elbow as she stumbles with our fast pace, weak and weary. I stop and bend with her as she doubles over, my arm across her back. She cringes and makes a face as she presses her hand to her belly.

"Are you okay?"

"Just a stomach pain, I'm fine," she rushes her words.

The moment before we straighten together, just before we rise to our heights, a gunshot rings out, a bullet whizzing by and striking the car in front of us. I wrap both arms around Anya, pulling her in front of me to cover her from the gunfire as it rings out again and again.

Nikolai turns back, coming after us. He grabs Anya's arm and pulls but I don't want to let go of her. Still, I won't let my pride get in the way of her safety, so I relinquish my hold and I push my hand against the small of her back, shoving her forward as Nikolai pulls.

As we run away, Kostya turns and runs back toward the house, pointing Vigo's gun at the person firing at us. It's one of the guards we passed at the front door—he must have been alerted about the discovery of Vigo's body upstairs.

"Go!" Kostya yells, tossing the car keys in our general direction as he shoots.

"Get the keys!" Nikolai demands.

I let go of Anya and turn back, taking two quick steps and bend to pick them up from where they landed on the ground. As I rise, Kostya falls, his shoulder jerking back, nearly spinning him all the way around before he lands.

He screams out his agony on a single syllable, "Go!"

"Shit!" I chase after Anya, positioning myself behind her to protect her as multiple guns crackle the air with violence.

We have to leave Kostya—he's too far from us now to help him and he's not the one we need for survival. I shove down the twinge of guilt that arises, knowing that he tried to help us. I'll let it grip me later when we're not in immediate danger.

We make it to the car and just as I reach for the handle, Nikolai and Anya go down—he falls and she's dragged down on top of him. Blood sprays and Anya screams. My pulse pounds, my ears ring, there's a terrified moment where I just stand and look in horror, not sure who's been hit or where.

Then Anya stands, unharmed.

She only fell because Nikolai dragged her down with his grip.

Nikolai gasps, blood spilling from somewhere in his midsection. The part of me that's wanted him dead for so long cheers, but then fear grips me. If he dies, there is no escaping the Vittoris. He's the only person who can get us off these grounds and I *have* to take Anya away from here. If we don't escape now, we'll both die here.

"Get in the car," I tell her as I pull open the back door and grab Nikolai beneath his arms.

I use the strength that only adrenaline could grant me to hoist him from the ground. Anya runs around the car, climbing into the back seat and reaches across. My beautiful, exhausted, malnourished blue-eyed girl finds some strength left to help me do what needs to be done. Our eyes catch for a single moment as I shove and she pulls. We feed each other in our gaze—fortify our collaboration, solidify our connected determination to survive this.

Nikolai falls limp, lying across the bench seat, and Anya catches his head in her hands, guiding him to rest upon her legs. I slam the door shut and run to the driver's side, just in time to avoid another onslaught of gunfire as more people run from the house.

We're off and driving in no time, heading toward the end of the driveway and the gate that locks us in.

The gate.

The fucking gate.

"How the fuck do we get past it?"

"Nikolai," Anya says. "What do we do?"

"My cell phone," he gasps.

I watch impatiently in the rearview mirror as Anya frantically checks his pockets. She finds his phone inside his jacket pocket. She holds it above him with trembling hands and he reaches to unlock it with his fingerprint. He instructs Anya to tap through several screens and he unlocks pages twice more with his fingerprint scan before entering an eight-digit passcode.

Anya's eyes narrow and she quietly says, "That's my birthday."

"Easy to remember," Nikolai replies on a breath.

She taps once more and like a fucking miracle, the gate mechanism whirs. It slowly swings open, too slowly for my preference. I back the car up and come forward again, angling around the gradual opening to drive through as it's still swinging. The tail of the car bumps the iron bars on the way through, but it's just a tap.

"Follow…the drive," Nikolai says. "Then left."

I do as he tells me, going far faster than I probably should on these dark, curving roads. I need to move quickly, but I also need to avoid getting into an accident. If we wreck the car, we're fucked.

We follow the winding gravel through twists and turns, hills and dips. When we reach the end, I nearly sigh in relief to be moving onto a paved road. I turn left at Nikolai's direction and speed off into the darkness.

Silence falls over us.

We travel into the night in tense quiet.

We haven't seen anyone following us, no car lights from behind.

We're all startled when Nikolai's phone begins to ring.

"Who the hell is calling?" I peek at Anya in the rearview mirror.

She meets my eyes before looking down at Nikolai. He must have tapped the screen to answer because next, I hear him mumble the name of the caller.

"Renata."

Her voice is on speakerphone and we all hear her clear as day, her voice is low in a calm sort of fury. It's unsettling.

"Nikolai. What have you done?"

"What I had to," Nikolai replies, though the words come out on a whisper.

Is he dying?

How much time does he have left?

I punch the accelerator. We don't have time to waste because I have no clue how to get off this island. As much as I hate to admit it, we need Nikolai alive.

"You *murdered* my brother. He's dead, Nikolai!" Renata's voice wavers almost imperceptibly.

I glance in the mirror again and expect to hear Nikolai's voice in response, but instead, I see Anya with the phone, pulling it closer to her lips. Her voice comes out raw, strong, indignant, *furious*.

"*I* murdered him," she tells Renata. "I shot him with his own fucking gun, and he deserved it."

Half of me is in awe of her bravery, admitting that it was her, knowing that she needs to take that power back for herself. The other half wants to stop the car, rip the phone from her hand, and scream at her for confessing. I'd rather have Renata believe it was Nikolai, or Kostya...or *me*. I don't know what our future holds, but it terrifies me to think that anyone from the four families might have a reason to seek vengeance against her.

"Anya?" Renata sounds surprised to hear her speak.

"Yes," Anya replies.

"How are you with him?"

Nikolai forces out his words and manages to put some strength behind them. "I took back what's mine."

"Anya doesn't belong to you," Renata bites back.

"She's mine. I'll prove it."

Prove it?

Anya's eyes catch mine in the mirror and she looks as confused as I am.

"We're coming after you." Renata's voice sounds calm and collected, dangerous and deadly.

"Always welcome in my home," Nikolai lets out on a single breath of sarcasm.

He pants and my pulse ticks up a notch, fearful he'll pass out before we get off this island.

Renata chuckles and the sound of it is eerie as fuck. "Good. Because I'm coming after you and I'm bringing the entire board with me. We'll deal with you, Nikolai, and your precious ballerina."

Fuck.

A long, haunting silence settles around us again, only punctuated by the sounds of Nikolai's heavy, labored breaths. I look once more in the mirror to see Anya looking right back at me. Her eyes tell me of a million different thoughts and emotions rushing around inside her mind.

I'm feeling them all, too.

But I force all of them from my supportive gaze except for one.

Love.

I give her every ounce of love I feel for her through that brief, single glance in the mirror, reminding her that she's not alone in this nightmare. We're in this together, all the way, until the very end.

It softens her.

Just a little.

Just for a moment.

Because all the fear and dread comes rushing back to the surface for both of us as Renata lets out a satisfied sigh and says something that chills my bones.

It scares me because Anya has admitted that she was the one who ended Vigo's life. It shakes me with a radiating panic that springs from the center of my stomach and radiates outward through my entire body.

The horrifying thing that Renata says presents with resigned commitment in her tone.

"Blood taken requires blood given."

The phone beeps.

The call ends.

And I drive faster.

To be continued…

Pas de TROIS

THE FOUR FAMILIES | BOOK THREE

BRYNN FORD

Release Date

January 12, 2021

PLAYLIST

Devil Devil by MILCK

Walk Through the Fire by Zayde Wølf ft. Ruelle

Consequences by Camila Cabello

The Night We Met by Lord Huron ft. Phoebe Bridgers

We Must Be Killers by Mikky Ekko

Wolves by Selena Gomez & Marshmello

Falling by Harry Styles

Someone You Loved by Lewis Capaldi

lovely by Billie Eilish w/Khalid

Can You Hold Me by NF ft. Britt Nicole

Secret Love Song by Little Mix

Bruises by Lewis Capaldi

I Wanna Dance with Somebody by Rachel Brown

Hold On by Chord Overstreet

The Ruler and the Killer by Kid Cudi

ACKNOWLEDGMENTS

Writing this book kicked my ass...and I loved it. I couldn't have done it without the help of some truly awesome people.

First, I have to thank my readers, especially since I'm still floored that I have any! I'm so grateful you picked up this series and came along on this dark little journey with me. I appreciate you more than I could ever express!

To my beta readers—Rachel, Danielle, and Ashlee—you are awesome! Your insights and notes were so valuable. You gave me confidence that it wasn't a complete hot mess, and helped me to see a few wacky details I needed to sort out. Rachel, thank you for also creating a Story Bible for my series to help me keep track of all the details. Danielle and Ashlee, you make the best teaser pics and edits—they make me feel like a "real writer" and remind me that (holy crap) my books actually make readers feel some kind of way.

Silvia, your editing work is brilliant. Down to the simplest details, and restructuring my overly-worded sentences, you clean the hell out of my manuscript. You're the best!

To all the folks at Najla Qamber Designs, your team is amazing! Najla, the cover you made is nothing less than spectacularly gorgeous and exactly what I had dreamed of! Nada, I'm floored by your book interior design expertise. You bring that extra something special to the reader's experience (and make my books look gorgeous!).

To my husband for corralling the kids away when I just needed to focus, *thank you*. I don't know what I'd do if I didn't have the time and space to write, and you always make sure that I do.

I'll end this by thanking dark romance authors everywhere. Your stories gave me the courage I needed to boldly write, bravely publish, and fearlessly chase a dream. You inspire me!

ABOUT THE AUTHOR

Brynn Ford is an author of romance in all its beautiful and sensually taboo forms. She is a lover of the dark, twisted, and playful, and strives to bring the unmentionable aspects of passionate romance into her stories.

Brynn resides in the Midwest with her husband and sons, whom she expects will someday be embarrassed by their mom's books. When she isn't obsessively writing, you may find her binge-watching favorite shows while eating far too much junk food or fanatically reading, always seeking to lose herself in the emotional roller coaster of a damn good story.

She is quite the idealist, despite her fascination with the wicked and warped aspects of humanity. Some of her stories may run out of words before a happily ever after, but she's a firm believer that her characters continue to live on outside the pages in the minds of her readers. Stories don't end just because there aren't any more pages to turn.